# THE SUMMIT SOCIETY

Lisa M. Miller

Brother Mockingbird Publishing

Other Books by Lisa M. Miller

The Running Path
My Skull Possession



Library of Congress Control Number: 2024947930

Cover Design by: Alesios Saskalidis
www.facebook.com/187designz



For more information please contact:
Brother Mockingbird, LLC
www.brothermockingbird.net

ISBN: 978-1-960226-24-2 Paperback
ISBN: 978-1-960226-25-9 EBook

To my family and friends for their unwavering support
and love. You are my true secret society.

# Chapter One

Orientation day arrived, and the freshman class buzzed with excitement, desperate for information on the mysterious and life-changing secret society. Conversations escalated from hushed whispers to a crescendo of fast-paced comments, a collective energy bubbling over like a shaken soda can.

One student whispered, "I heard Wyval undergrads are favored for the Northeast chapter. And did you hear it's ranked as one of the top societies in the world?" This comment ignited a symphony of eager questions and statements.

"My mom said if you are a member, your future is golden, despite the high stakes. It's worth it," another wide-eyed teen confidently announced. The words carried the weight of a coveted secret, tethering the students to an unspoken code of curiosity and anticipation.

As a student ambassador, Tressa Litton couldn't help but empathize with the cluster of nervous teens. Memories of her bewilderment and excitement during her early days at Wyval University flooded her mind, stirring a mix of understanding and nostalgia. As for the topic she was about to discuss with the freshman, Tressa wished it appeared in the frequently asked question section of the orientation booklet. She paused and looked beyond the incoming students, letting her gaze settle on one of the reasons she came to Wyval University. Besides the solid academic programs, the picturesque campus, nestled within the embrace of the Appalachian Mountains, made it an easy decision for Tressa when considering various colleges. She soaked in the breathtaking tapestry of emerald green streaked with the first hints of autumn's fiery russet and burnished gold.

"Is it true Wyval students have the best chance over other universities? And, like, I heard you are basically set for life if you get in," said the platinum blonde seated near the front of the group, her high-pitched voice piercing the air. "That's my goal by graduation," she said, her hair illuminated by the sun as she tossed it over her shoulders. She lowered designer tortoise shell frames, persistence and impatience seeping from behind long, dramatic lashes. Her laugh was contagious as she nodded to clone-like girls huddled nearby, hanging on her every word.

Tressa recalled her first day at Wyval, sitting on the lawn in front of Flood Hall, listening to her orientation leader. Unlike the instant in-crowd making themselves front and center, Tressa remembers resting against the huge maple tree, enjoying shade and anonymity—plus, her pale skin always fared better out of the direct sun. In the early days of her freshman year, Tressa had more questions about the availability of art history courses than the details of joining a secret society.

"Set for life? I don't know what you mean. I'm sorry, what is your name again?" Tressa asked.

"It's Candi. Candi Milton."

"Candi. Right," Tressa acknowledged, realizing that she had read the name on the registration roster earlier. The girl's gleaming hair nearly skimmed the ground as she reclined, hands stretched behind her. Tressa's hair didn't gleam, and the ends barely reached the top of her shoulders. She tugged on one of the strawberry blonde curls as she stared at Candi, thinking of the appropriate response. She went with the school's suggested answer. "So, thank you, Candi, for mentioning extracurricular activities. We highly encourage all students to get involved in expanded campus life. Sports, writing groups, language clubs. I think we have everyone covered."

Candi rose to her feet, her tiny denim shorts accentuating her long, slender legs. Her friends followed suit, gathering behind her as she took charge of the conversation. "We all know about the activities from the student welcome guide. I hoped to hear about the Summit Society. *That* is the track I need to be on."

Tressa's face flushed as she spoke, her rounded cheeks now matching the color of her hair. "I'm happy to share any information I have on the various clubs and activities here at Wyval. I'm confident we can find a match for everyone," she said, keeping to the narrative. " Do you have any other questions?"

Candi's long, shiny nails sparkled like amethysts as her slim hand shielded her whispered conversation. Despite spending three years on campus, Tressa knew she was never part of Candi's type of crowd. This first day of senior year was a stark reminder of that fact.

Tressa sifted through her folder, double-checking that she wasn't assigned to any additional orientation groups. There was some time before the freshman mixer, so she decided to take a stroll back to her apartment. The smell of freshly cut grass mingled with a cool breeze, reminding her of the last days of summer and the beginning of fall. The familiar stone path snaked through the campus, and the towering trees gave her a natural canopy that filtered the warm sunlight. The buildings and dorms dotted the landscape, and their brick and glass facades gleamed in the afternoon sun. The path was convenient, leading her to the off-campus apartments that bordered the university property. As she walked, the orientation session consumed her thoughts. The university advised school ambassadors to promote involvement in organizations and activities while ignoring the existence of a secret society. Tressa found irony in the university's denial of the Summit Society, even though the intrigue and curiosity surrounding it drove yearly enrollment. Allegedly, the invitation to the society occurred in senior year and came with a sworn oath of secrecy, bizarre initiation rituals, and intense demands to prove loyalty. Every Wyval alum claimed to know someone invited to join the society, and the select few who received the golden opportunity were said to have gained access to valuable connections for post-graduation paths and beyond. Tressa knew the stories but needed to be convinced that the clandestine club's origins were anything more than a clever marketing tactic. Regardless of the truth, the Summit Society attracted students who hoped for exclusive membership status rather than working hard to determine their future.

# Chapter Two

"Sorry. Late for a meeting!" a voice yelled, followed by hurried footsteps echoing like thunder in the stairwell.

As Tressa tried to paste herself against the corridor wall, her shoulder collided with the rough concrete, and she winced while clutching her books as they wobbled in her arms. She allowed the impatient senior to continue his rapid descent—the scent of sweat hiding behind woodsy cologne trailing behind him.

Tressa sighed, but at least her classmate had the decency to apologize for the lack of consideration. As she fumbled with her keys, the door to the apartment swung open, with her roommate Alex standing in the doorway. His tousled hair fell over his eyes as he leaned into the hallway to investigate the noise, scanning the corridor to see what he missed.

"What's going on out here?" Alex asked. Tressa's roommate put on a good show of looking out for her, but she also knew he never wanted to miss out on anything fun.

"The blur shooting down the steps? I'm pretty sure it was Jake from the fourth floor. He almost took me out," Tressa said, rubbing her sore shoulder.

"Unbelievable. Classes haven't even started, and everyone is in such a hurry. Anyway, how did orientation go?" Alex inquired.

"It was the usual—many questions about schedules, bookstore hours, and off-campus activities. And, of course, there were a few girls who obviously belonged to the instant in-crowd and were only interested in one thing," Tressa said, continuing into the apartment.

"How do they know about me already?"Alex asked.

Tressa plopped onto the threadbare couch. Dust particles danced in front of her as she massaged her shoulder. "You know what I mean. Everyone wants to know how to get in and what's involved."

"Speaking of getting in, maybe it will be you this year," Alex said with a smile.

"I wouldn't count on any invitations showing up in the mail. Not for me, at least, but maybe it will be you," Tressa quipped.

"Speaking of mail," Alex said, ignoring the suggestion. "I thought rent included utilities," he said, throwing a utility bill onto the table.

Tressa nonchalantly tossed the bill aside. When their former roommate, Jess, decided not to return senior year and would no longer share expenses, they knew rent and bills would be higher. Tressa and Alex agreed to keep the apartment and find another roommate, but they only upheld the first part of the deal. Regardless, the apartment's charm and proximity to campus outweighed the extra expense. The lofty ceilings added a touch of luxurious roominess to the space, compensating for the worn wall paint. Even the cabinets, with their outdated terracotta hue, were overshadowed by the allure of a small patio offering a breathtaking view, a trade-off that Tressa couldn't resist.

"Anyway, what are the rumors about receiving an invite?" Alex asked. " I believe I heard it's September or October."

"Stop," Tressa said, throwing a sequined pillow across the room. "I'm not discussing something that I have no interest in, especially since I'm not the type."

"Well, that's wrong. You are the smartest girl I know, and you are the type for many reasons. Especially because we know redheads are awesome," he said, running his hand through his hair, deep cinnamon strands falling across his brow as he shook it back into place.

Tressa loved when people asked Alex why they were such close friends. He always replied, 'It's a ginger thing.'

"I'm heading out—soccer practice. Coaches have us doing doubles for the next few weeks, plus some games. I'm sorry, my dear, but you won't see me much this semester. Although, are you going out tonight?" Alex asked, raising his eyebrows.

"Can you bring someone back to the apartment later? Is that what you are asking?" Tressa said. "Sorry, I'll probably be here all night. But I'll stay in my room."

The sequined pillow almost toppled the floor lamp as Alex launched it back in her direction. "Give me some credit. I haven't even met all the new students yet," Alex said, picking up a soccer ball and bag. "Later."

Tressa rolled her eyes. While only a few days passed, she knew it would be different living with Alex. An extra roommate made it easier to juggle the dating scene. When someone brought home a date, the other two headed out for drinks or a movie. Tressa's availability was usually the most flexible. And there was the time when Alex and Jess were a thing, but that didn't last long. The three were more like brothers and sisters, so Tressa never even thought twice when he suggested keeping the apartment after Jess backed out. She hoped it was the right decision.

•••

September barely unfolded, and summer seemed to linger. Tressa felt her hair frizzing by the second. She searched for an elastic tie from an unpacked bag, feeling immediate relief with her curls pulled back from her face. The apartment usually didn't feel this humid. Tressa grabbed a book and disappeared into her favorite hideaway, or as Alex named it, the egg chair. Her fingers laced in

the woven wicker, and her folded legs vanished into the marshmal-
low cushion as the seat slowly undulated from its perch. The warm
afternoon sun poured into her room as there was little to block
the expanse of glass, making the wall feel open to the field below.
On move-in day, Tressa's mother was ready to explode when her
daughter told her not to worry about decorating her space. She
could see her planned visions of wall hangings and window treat-
ments slipping from her grasp like sand through a sieve. However,
Tressa did agree to let her mother order the egg chair. Tressa grew
to love the cocoon retreat, appreciating the comfortable seat as a
soothing place to unwind at the end of the day, enabling her to
block out the outside world. The pricey furniture piece was a good
choice—only the best for a Litton.

# Chapter Three

Tressa's academic interests set her apart from her peers at Wyval. Instead of heading to happy hour with her classmates, she preferred to stay after class and discuss the Italian Renaissance with her professor. This dedication didn't necessarily translate into social success; three weeks into the semester, this year was no different.

"Meet you at The Loft in a few?" the tall blonde asked, her golden complexion still echoing the remnants of a summer spent poolside.

Tressa spun around, surprised that the fellow senior had spoken to her, let alone invited her to happy hour. She tried to spit out a feeble excuse when an equally bronzed guy jaunted up the auditorium's steps.

"The Loft? Sweet. I'll head over now," he said, almost barreling into Tressa. "Sorry!"

With a swoosh of the door and the combination of floral and spice scents, the duo disappeared.

A raspy voice pierced the uncomfortable silence. "I guess she wasn't asking you."

"I'm sorry?" Tressa said in the direction of the remark from the darkness.

"The girl making plans for happy hour. You seem a little disappointed she didn't ask you to meet her," the voice continued.

Tressa clutched her books tightly while her suede cross-body bag hung at her hip. As she drew near, Tressa's gaze fixated on a color palette most commonly reflected in oil dancing on top of the water, vibrant pomegranate hues, deep indigo, and subtle teal tones woven into a tangle of maple brown hair.

"What are you staring at?" the girl said, arms tightly crossed.

"Nothing, I didn't know anyone else was here," Tressa stammered.

"Yeah, well, I try to lay low and hang out in the back of the class. People tend to ignore me or, like you, stare," she said before turning and walking out.

Tressa scampered up the remaining steps and braced her arm against the door. The girl looked down at Tressa, her chunky heeled boots adding at least four inches to her towering height.

"You are pretty short," she snickered, looking down at Tressa.

"Okay, look. I only wanted to say I think your hair looks cool," she said before slinking past the edgy classmate. Though words echoed behind her, Tressa kept her focus straight ahead. She had heard more than her share of comments about her height or lack of popularity. The invigorating walk back home helped clear her head, and the stress dissipated into the cool night air until she walked through the door.

The lights were out in her apartment, but that didn't mean Alex wasn't there. She hoped he wasn't entertaining a guest. Netflix was auto-playing through suggested previews as she stepped on the remote.

"Tressa?" croaked Alex. "You're home? What time is it?" he asked, reaching for his phone.

"I just got back from class. Sorry if I woke you," Tressa said.

Tressa didn't wait for a response and withdrew to her bedroom, slamming the door behind her. The curtains fluttered in the breeze, failing to provide any actual cover from the moonlight. She watched as the silver beads on the smoky gray drapes danced and shimmered in the soft glow, their light casting shadows on the walls.

"Are you just going to sit in your cocoon all night?" Alex asked. She never heard him come in but knew slammed doors in warped wooden frames rarely stayed shut. "What happened, Tressa?"

"It's just one of those nights. Right after my late class, I thought I'd go to happy hour, and then I was reminded how my weekend would remain uneventful," Tressa said.

"By who?" Alex asked.

Tressa sunk into the oversized cushions, barricading herself with pillows. "It doesn't matter," she said, trying to hide her disappointment. "I guess it was the sequence of events. This girl made a few snide remarks as we were leaving class when my only comment was on her crazy hair, and I just wanted to say that I thought it looked cool. On top of that, she gently reminded me how short I am."

Alex removed the pillow barricade, grabbed Tressa's hands, and pulled her to her feet. He rested his hands on her shoulders. "Well, you aren't a giant, my little five-foot firecracker," he said.

"Five foot two inches, to be exact," she said with a quick eye roll.

"Hold on. You said this new girl had crazy hair?" Alex asked.

"Yeah, a crazy combo of colors, like a vibrant kaleidoscope. She was super tall, so who knows, maybe she was jealous of my view of the world."

"Oh wait, I think you met Mauri Pierce. You haven't heard about her?" Alex asked.

"Let me guess. You have your eye on this freshman, too," Tressa commented.

"No. Mauri is a senior but transferred to Wyval this year. I can't say if she was jealous of your stature, but I guarantee she wished she *could* join you for happy hour," Alex explained.

"She didn't say anything about happy hour," Tressa said, un-clear where this conversation was going.

"I mean, she can't go to happy hour. She's not even 21 yet."

Tressa was confused. "But she's a senior?"

"An accelerated senior. Haven't you heard of the prodigy from Belmoor? I'm sure she feels much more out of place than you. Come on, let's end this pity party. We can have our own happy hour," Alex said, pulling her toward the living room.

"I miss Jess. I wish she finished her senior year with us," Tressa said. She watched as Alex grabbed a bottle of wine from the fridge. It felt wrong starting the year without Jess.

"Here, drink this. You'll feel better," Alex said, pouring from the ten-dollar bottle of fruit wine.

Tressa sipped the overly sweet rosé blend. She knew she would have a headache in the morning since it was a change of pace from the usual selections her mother collected in the renowned Litton wine cellar.

"So, if you run into Mauri again, be nice. You two would get along famously. Imagine being the smartest girl on cam-pus, besides you of course, and you can't even go to the bar if you want to. Imagine that, a prodigy and an heiress," Alex said. Tressa furrowed her brow as her friend put up a hand in defense.

She poured another glass and forgot all about future head-aches. She hated that Alex was right.

# Chapter Four

Tressa found it challenging to concentrate on Professor Dawson's lecture about the upcoming assignment. Her eyes drifted to the ticking clock above him, and she nervously tapped her phone, trying to hasten time. As the end of class approached, her anticipation grew, and she became determined to confront the edgy new girl.

"I hope everyone has a restful extended weekend. I suggest you start working on your papers immediately and get them out of the way. Remember to choose a fresco that reflects either civic life or class structure. Okay, enjoy the extended weekend, and I will see everyone next week," said Professor Dawson, concluding the lecture.

As Tressa twisted in her seat to get her bag, the edge of her sweater got caught in the corner of the chair. A shadow loomed over her as she pulled the fabric from the hinge.

"Ms. Litton. Do you have a second?" her professor asked.

After scanning the auditorium and watching the last students, including Mauri Pierce, file out the door, Tressa slunk back into the hard wooden seat. "Yeah, sure," she sighed.

"I won't keep you, Tressa, but I want to ensure everything is okay," Professor Dawson said, tilting his head. He raked his hand through his messy, chocolate-brown hair, and Tressa was struck by the intense gaze of his vivid blue eyes. Despite her best efforts, Tressa found it difficult to determine his age. Due to his impressive knowledge and youthful look, she assumed he must have fast-tracked his doctorate immediately following undergrad.

"Oh, I'm working on the paper. I'll be focusing on Ambrogio Lorenzetti." Tressa shuffled through her folder, glossy reproductions fluttering to the floor. She relaxed when the conversation turned to the intricacies of Italian Renaissance art and not why she stared at the clock the entire class.

"Ah, I see you chose the darker side of Lorenzetti," he said, holding the image at arm's length. "I am sure you know it is the worst condition," he said before returning the picture.

Tressa looked at the image before her. The sad, mournful faces, a fire-ravaged town, and apparent acts of violence matched the drab taupe and burnished gray color scheme. "I suppose I could have chosen one of the other two frescoes. Something a little more uplifting, right?" she questioned, tilting her head. Tressa felt drawn to the fresco that reflected people's darker side.

"I didn't mean the theme. It is ambitious to take this on due to the poor condition of the work. The exterior wall where *The Effects of Bad Government* hung suffered much moisture damage in the past. It is the least studied, but I agree with your direction to understand both promise and threat. Good choice, Tressa," the professor said with a nod. "I wish all my students shared your enthusiasm."

Warmth crept into Tressa's cheeks as if she had just downed a glass of wine. She was drawn to the beauty and complexity of the art world, but only a few people appreciated or noticed her passion. She couldn't help but feel inspired by someone like Professor Dawson. That was until he continued the conversation.

"You've seemed distant or distracted the last few weeks, constantly scanning the classroom. Is there anything bothering you? Are there any pressures with your other classes? I can imagine your schedule is the most challenging this year."

Tressa experienced a twinge of unease when she met her teacher's eyes but couldn't bring herself to look away. The faint lines near his temple and the exaggerated pout accentuated his handsome features, but Tressa wasn't seeking pity. She was sure he saw her before each class, her head buried in her laptop while others discussed evening plans. For weeks, she tried to meet Mauri after their professor's lecture. Tressa thought they might have more in common as two outsiders looking to fit in. Now, she realized not only did she look lonely, but she also looked paranoid.

"Professor Dawson. I'm fine. I'm looking forward to the break and catching up on work and sleep," she said, standing and gathering her things.

"Well, spend some time with Lorenzetti, but allow some downtime. Everyone needs a break," he said, letting her out of the aisle.

"Will do," Tressa said. "Enjoy the long weekend." She could feel his sympathetic look following her as she headed up the steps. Walking outside, she realized how this evening had taken such a detour.

As Tressa reached the entrance to her apartment building, the door almost hit her as she reached for the handle. Alex appeared, struggling with bags hanging from his arms while balancing a laundry basket.

"Do you need help?" Tressa laughed. "Are you moving out and leaving me for good?"

Alex's belongings created a small barricade between him and Tressa as he placed everything on the ground, surveying the heap. "Laundry and some things I won't need for the rest of the year. Yeah, it's probably too much. How about you? Are you going to be okay by yourself?"

"I'll be fine—I want to catch up on some movies, not to mention my art history project. You better get on the road. I'll see you next week," Tressa said. She watched Alex hoist his bags, the super-fitted hoodie riding up over his waistband, revealing his toned abs. His green eyes flickered in surprise as she tugged the jacket back into place.

"Hey now!" he said, blowing an air kiss. "Try to have fun this weekend, my dear. You do have the apartment to yourself."

Tressa chuckled as she watched Alex disappear into the parking lot, grateful for how much brighter he made her life on campus.

# Chapter Five

Tressa jolted out of twilight sleep just in time to watch the duo walk through the abandoned house. Handprints covered the walls, and the shrill pitch of Heather's screams was more annoying than terrifying. The basement was another story. That ending scene shook Tressa to the core every time. Josh faces the crumbling brick wall and the unseen force knocking Heather to the ground. Cut to sideways footage at the end, and done. Tressa was curious to know how often she had watched the original *Blair Witch Project* movie, but it was one of her favorites. She read an article about how the indie film shattered box office records while casting doubt that it was a true story. A limited budget with huge success proved that throwing money at something isn't always the answer. Tressa knew that all too well.

Her phone tumbled to the floor with a clunk as she untangled her legs from the blanket. Bleary-eyed, she searched through the cabinet, hoping to find something to help reverse the effects of her cheap wine overindulgence from earlier. With a rattle of the plastic bottle, two small green capsules rolled onto her hand before falling onto the floor. She dropped to her knees, feeling around for the medicine. That is when she saw it.

The cracked plastic strip at the bottom of the door allowed light from the hallway to seep in. Tressa found a letter-sized envelope, instantly forgetting about the pills. They could do nothing for what she felt right now. Every breath seemed exaggerated, every movement in slow motion. It could have been mail she or

Alex had dropped, but she didn't recall seeing it when she arrived home. The timeworn floor answered her every step with a creak, and the pristine white of the paper stood out against the dingy maple floorboards. Tressa gripped the textured envelope as she peered out of the small hole in the door but didn't spot anyone in the hallway.

Tressa traced the elegant letters that spelled out her name on the envelope. Her heart fluttered as she ran her finger over the waxy crimson seal, the only thing separating her from the contents inside. Tressa's hands quivered like a leaf struggling to stay connected to its branch's safety, but she peeled back the flap. The brilliant white card matched the fabric-like texture of its enclosure, but with it came a wave of disappointment. Nothing was on the card except a small trademark symbol on the bottom, most likely belonging to the stationary company.

"Ugh," Tressa yelled into the empty apartment, throwing the envelope onto the table. She couldn't help but feel a pang of longing hidden beneath her irritation, like a child who pretends not to care about a toy they secretly covet.

She sank into the couch cushions, staring at the envelope beckoning to be picked up. Tressa never denied that the Summit Society existed and knew organizations like it traced back for centuries, but she never dreamed of being a candidate. Or did she? Reaching over, Tressa grabbed the mysterious blank letter. The textured print felt luxurious as she touched her name on the envelope as if it would reveal information. She thought about Alex's words earlier, how she was the society's *type*, and a wave of nausea overcame her. What if this was one of his jokes? She and Alex behaved more like brothers and sisters than anything, with some sibling rivalry revealing itself over the years, but why would he do something like this? As she picked up her phone to text Alex that she didn't find the joke funny, a new thought flashed like an annoying pop-up window on a computer browser: was it Candi and a group of girls waiting nearby to see her reaction? The smug and confident beauty from orientation seemed more than annoyed when Tressa refused to play into her prying questions about a secret society, and she could be waiting in the hall right now to see Tressa's response to the retaliatory prank. Whether it was Alex or Candi, Tressa wasn't amused. She noticed something as she let the heavy cardstock float onto the table. Upon closer inspection, the trademark symbol consisted of black and white squares. It was a QR code.

Tressa assumed the small blocks would lead her to a website promoting the distributor of the high-end stationery, but a flicker of hope remained, thinking it might be something more. Without giving it additional thought, she focused on the tiny box with her phone, and immediately, the screen turned smoky gray. She furiously tapped at the glass and pressed the volume buttons, worried she had downloaded a virus instead of an app. Suddenly, the screen returned to normal and took her to what looked like the app store page. A small icon with a mountain peak looked like a new app to download, supporting her marketing ploy theory. There was no information below it, no recommendations, and no reviews. Her finger hovered over the 'get' button, wondering if proceeding would corrupt her phone. Staring at the small picture, it finally clicked, and so did Tressa. As she selected the button to download the app, the smoky gray screen returned, slowly dissolving to reveal a message.

Congratulations, Tressa Litton.
Welcome to the first step of your journey.
Your unique QR access code is no longer valid, and you will not find proof of this unlisted app.
If you decide to delete it, there will be no more invitations.
As you navigate your candidacy program, you are not permitted to discuss any information except with those associated with the organization.
You must complete three tests to prove your problem-solving ability and loyalty.
All communication will be received through this app.
Good luck

**ACCEPT**

**EXIT**

Tressa had a choice to make. As she weighed her options, thoughts raged within like a hurricane. One choice would be to hit 'exit' and return to her evening of watching Netflix, expecting a call from Alex explaining how it was all a joke. She may return after the break to face the likes of Candi Milton and friends snickering when they see her on campus. An envelope slipped under her door could be the work of anyone trying to make Tressa the brunt of a joke, but to go to the trouble to create an app? That was too much work. But what if it did mean something? Tressa knew that some students applied to Wyval, the school where the Summit Society allegedly originated, simply for the opportunity to be a part of something significant. Rumors claimed that Wyval admitted more members than any other school hosting chapters of the prestigious organization. Throughout history, it was believed that famous people such as world leaders, celebrities, and those from great fortune had connections to organizations that ensured their success, power, and opportunities. The thought of having a way to guarantee a successful life seemed tempting. Still, Tressa knew that with her stellar academic career and the fact that she already made some connections in the art community, she was already paving her path. Not many people knew Tressa's background, and the start of her freshman year also gave her anonymity. She got to where she is now without being propped up by the Litton legacy.

She hovered over the exit button while a few more thoughts danced in her mind. The sinking feeling about the happy hour invite, Alex's busy social calendar, and the instant in-crowd. Tressa never craved acceptance into elite circles but was more annoyed when her family thought they could help buy her way in. She couldn't deny the intense feeling of curiosity, but a wave of guilt tugged just as hard, knowing an acceptance meant she caved to the need to belong to something bigger. This belonging could be the ultimate step in carving out who she was.

The phone felt like a cinder block in her hand, perfectly matching the pressure on her shoulders. She placed her phone on the table next to the invitation, resting her lips against folded hands. She stared blankly at the TV stand, her gaze skimming over the Halloween decorations below. Halloween. That is where her answer seemed to lie. Tressa remembered the excitement of visiting haunted attractions in high school. She recalled zoning out and not hearing the screams and howls from friends as they approached the entrance. The whooshing sound of blood pounding in her ears, the wave of nausea as every step brought them closer to the experience, and the final fear-driven euphoria as she crossed the threshold, knowing there was no turning back. The allure always won out over the aversion to walking into the unknown. At this moment, she felt the same emotions coursing through her body, and she knew she was at the threshold. She was going in.

**ACCEPT**

# Chapter Six

Sunny yellow swirls danced in a sea of blended blues, interrupted by a reminder of the early morning hour and lack of messages. Tressa chose one of Van Gogh's most famous and serene works as her phone wallpaper, but even Starry Night couldn't calm her now. It must have been a joke. No response and no direction. Magical chimes echoed through the room, piercing the silence with the clamor of church bells. Tressa's hand shook as she looked down for the preview of the message alert. It was Alex.

**A: Yo, checking in on my girl. I know it's early, but how are you doing?**

**T: Why are you up so late? Partying all night, I guess?**

**A: Late? Tress, I can't stay this beautiful if I don't keep in shape. Not stopping my usual running routine because of the break. Why are you up? Thought you'd see this later.**

Tressa paused before responding. She knew it wasn't uncommon for Alex to be up early to go for a run. Was it a sign she should tell him about the invitation? Not that it mattered, as his message was the only thing incoming on her phone.

**T: Fell asleep early, woke up early.**

She waited as he typed and also decided not to say anything. She didn't want to look like an idiot if it was a cruel joke.

**A: Go back to sleep. That's what break is about. TTYS.**

Tressa didn't ask any more questions. Alex was right. She should take advantage of sleeping in, but 'what if' scenarios loomed over her. What if the Summit Society got in touch with her again? What if there was something she was missing? She knew every inch of the invitation, studied the script letters comprising her name, plied the tacky wax seal with her nail, and even held the weighty cardstock up to the light but came up with nothing. Hours had passed since Tressa scanned the code and hit accept, but no additional messages appeared. The screen transformed into a gray mix of swirling smoke.

As she retreated to her bedroom, the slow revolutions of the ceiling fan mirrored her energy level, and she fought to stay awake. She watched the dusty paddles turn as if motivated by a slight breeze. Her eyes, heavy with sleep, fluttered while her mind wandered to the looming presence on the kitchen table, her thoughts foggy with exhaustion. She could have sworn she had rested for only a few minutes when a noise caused her to bolt out of bed. Grasping for her phone, she realized she must have left it in the other room. How long had she been sleeping? As Tressa entered the kitchen, the sound of a message alert competed with the blood pounding in her ears. Swiping up, she also found the newest app on her phone, which had a small number one in the corner. The gray screen faded to reveal a string of text.

Work together, don't compete
Evidence will be concrete
Checking, checking row by row
Answer will be found below
Test One
Salt Lake Road 10 am

Tressa had no time to contemplate what she would find when she arrived at the address. She thought about letting Alex or her mom know where she was going, but she didn't want to test the app's ability to monitor her texts and calls. She could delete it, but it would also mean losing what could be a huge opportunity. Tressa shrugged into her favorite pair of faded jeans that fit like a glove and grabbed her Wyval sweatshirt and weathered baseball cap. Looking down at her well-worn cross trainers, she prayed whatever the morning held depended on functionality rather than fashion.

Rushing across the parking lot, Tressa was glad she also brought a warm jacket. A northeast morning in October often gave a preview of what the winter had in store. A small metal heart jangled against the container of pepper spray as she jammed her key into the ignition. Before pulling away, she did a quick mental checklist but still felt unprepared. Phone, license, cash, card. What else could she bring to an initiation?

Wyval's location blended both remoteness and convenience. To the north of the campus, thick forests of oak and hickory trees interrupted by an occasional grassy field created a peaceful but secluded environment. When heading south of Wyval, you are pulled away from the rural scenery, offering numerous dining and shopping options in a suburban setting. Tressa drove along the state route, not expecting to see more than a few grazing cows. As she settled into the drive, the enveloping warmth from the heated seats and the soft crooning of the 80s ballad station did nothing to alleviate the knot in her stomach. The more miles she put behind her, the more her mind raced. Tressa had no idea what to expect when she arrived at her destination, but as she turned at the yellow NO OUTLET sign, she knew people only came here for one reason.

The gravel sounded like kernels in a popcorn machine as they snapped under the tires of the SUV. The dead end was fast approaching, and she glanced around for other signs of life. Seeing a white four-door sedan parked at the end of the road replaced the warmth of the leather seat with an icy chill that made her clutch the keychain dangling near her hand. Tressa pulled up behind the car and watched as the door opened. Caution shifted to confusion as the female driver exited the car, her hand shielding her eyes from the sun, highlighting the bright hues framing her face. The girl's stature stretched skyward like the trees surrounding her. It was unmistakable and unbelievable, but it was her.

As Tressa slid out of the driver's seat and hopped to the ground, she watched Mauri's hand slowly drop to her side as if it was pushing through molasses, continuing to fumble in her pocket without taking her eyes off Tressa.

"Hi," Tressa said, shoving her hands into her pockets.

"You? You are behind this?" Mauri asked, the sarcasm reminiscent of their first meeting.

"Behind this? Listen, I got this message a few hours ago. I wasn't even sure if it was real, and well, here I am," Tressa said, trying to disguise the quiver in her voice. "I'm Tressa from art history."

"I know, I know all about you," Mauri said. She focused on her phone, jabbing at the screen, pausing several times to look up at Tressa. "Any idea why we are here, Tressa from art history?" Mauri asked.

Tressa pulled out her phone and opened the app, hesitant to discuss it with Mauri but assuming she was here by the same means of communication and for the same reason. Growing up nearby, most kids frequented the surrounding woods, and Tressa knew what lay hidden not far from where they were standing. If you understood the area, there was only one reason you would venture past the no outlet sign in front of them. She returned to her car and shoved her wallet into the glove box. She attached the keys to the lanyard around her neck and watched Mauri, her gaze transfixed behind Tressa.

"Nice Land Rover," she said.

"It's a few years old," Tressa said. " Listen, if you want to do this, we better get moving. It will take some time to walk through everything," Tressa said, heading to the narrow dirt path.

"Wait, you know what we are supposed to do? Where are we going?" Mauri asked, catching up with Tressa with two long strides.

"We are headed to Miner Town," Tressa said, continuing to walk.

"Miner Town? What are you talking about?" Mauri asked, her voice a mix of aggravation and confusion. "I didn't see signs for anything but Salt Lake Road, and now we are at a dead end. The message mentioned concrete. I figured it referenced something near an overpass or a bridge," she said.

Tressa ignored Mauri's suggestion and moved farther along the path toward the tree line, confident enough since she knew the area, suspicious enough since she didn't know what or who could be hiding inside. Her footsteps were the only interruption to the isolated silence until the slam of a car door echoed around her, and the crunch of gravel indicated Mauri decided to follow.

# Chapter Seven

Tressa carefully maneuvered through the deep ruts, mindful that a twisted ankle would only hinder their progress on this task. The uneven terrain and crumbling structures required visitors to watch and calculate every step. Even though Mauri seemed unfamiliar with this destination, she strode ahead as if she did.

"Do you want to wait for me? I've been here before, you know," Tressa called out.

Mauri stopped, her backpack sliding off her shoulders as she turned. "I'm assuming we just keep walking forward unless you don't think I'm capable," she said.

As they pressed on, Tressa found herself intrigued by Mauri's appearance. The tall girl struggled to secure her hair at the nape of her neck, causing a few strands to fall around her face like the remnants of a rainbow after a storm. Tressa couldn't recall if Mauri wore glasses the first day they met, but her chunky frames complemented her angular features. Her lips were stained with a deep shade of burgundy, interrupting an otherwise natural-looking complexion. As they continued the journey, their silence measured as deep as the crevasses below their feet.

"I don't think we got off to a great start," Tressa confessed. "I'm not sure what I did or didn't do, but I'm feeling incredibly anxious right now, questioning the reality of our situation. To be honest, I'm half expecting someone to capture this and turn me into the next internet meme," she gestured with her arms. "I can already envision it—'The look you get when you think you're cool, but you're really just a dork.'"

Mauri remained silent, her gaze shifting between the ground and the path ahead. She offered no response to Tressa's rant, figuring Mauri thought she was crazy or felt the same apprehensions.

Dirt and rocks sprayed across the path as Mauri dug the heel of her Doc Martin's into a mound of earth. "So what's back here anyway?" she asked, maintaining a neutral tone.

Tressa seized the opportunity to engage in conversation as if everything was normal. She gestured ahead, and Mauri slowed her pace to walk beside her. "Anyone from the area knows about Miner Town. You need to see it to understand. By the way, where are you from?"

"I'm from South Jersey. I'm sure you heard, but I graduated early, and Wyval had the best art program without being too urban or crowded. I grew up near Cape Wood, and while the beach scene is nice, the crowds are not," Mauri replied.

Tressa sensed a growing connection, like an invisible cord slowly pulling them closer. She understood better than anyone about needing some space. Her mother would say otherwise, but she chose Wyval for similar reasons. "Yeah, I get it. My mom would have preferred me to be Ivy League status, but when she heard about some of the other options available at Wyval, it seemed to keep her interested."

"The Summit Society, right?" Mauri asked.

"Yeah. My mom is more impressed by the idea than I am," Tressa said.

"But you are, too. You're here, aren't you?"

Twigs crunched under Tressa's sneaker, and something scurried in the bushes nearby. She stared straight ahead, unsure how to answer, but knew Mauri was correct. Tressa signed up for this—a chance to discover new opportunities out of her comfort zone that might have a huge return.

"I don't know. I'm not committing to anything," Tressa shrugged while Mauri smirked. "But, hey, we are almost there," she added, glad to change the subject. The familiar site came into view as they cleared an overgrown section of the path. Black, gaping window openings reached above the treetops like watchful eyes guarding the entrance to the wooded clearing while the lines of the flat-topped roofs cut the horizon in two. Tressa turned to see Mauri frozen in place, her expression changing from smug to amazed. She gripped the straps of her backpack like she was ready to parachute out of a plane.

"Come on. Let's take a look around. And hopefully, we don't become a meme," Tressa said, her comment as serious as it was sarcastic.

"Tressa, what *is* this place?" Mauri asked, looking mesmerized by the ghost town. Rectangular, boxy buildings rose from the ground, creating a monotonous landscape of sand-colored exteriors marred with a colorful splash of graffiti. Tressa moved closer to one of the crumbling two-story buildings. She disappeared inside, feeling a wave of nostalgia wash over her, having explored these buildings countless times as a kid. "As I mentioned earlier, it's an abandoned city constructed out of concrete," her voice echoed in the empty room. The smell of earth and smoke filled her nostrils, and the dampness surrounded her like her mom's wine cellar, minus expensive bottles of Cabernet Sauvignon. She navigated through broken amber glass strewn like puzzle pieces and carefully stepped over cigarette butts and crushed beer cans. Sadly, nothing had changed.

"Did people live here? It looks primitive," Mauri said. Without taking her eye off the spray-painted lavender iris masterfully outlined on a far wall, she slid her bag to the crook of her arm. She pulled out a professional-looking camera to document her discovery. "Wow, look at some of this artwork."

"Artwork with a splash of profanity," Tressa said as she focused on creative phrases drawn on the wall. Each display tried to outdo the previous with a more profane expression or word, peppered in with some creative but graphic images. She remembers exploring the rubble with her cousins years ago, giggling at the gritty graffiti.

Mauri leaned out one of the windows, creeping vines overtaking the frame. "Did you hear that? It sounds like someone walking outside."

Tressa stood still, her heart racing, waiting for someone to appear in the window. Besides the sound of her rapid breaths, she didn't hear anything.

"Maybe it was an animal or something," Mauri said, trying not to act too rattled.

"Anyway, as far as the history of this place, the town was built in 1911, a project to house workers and their families employed by local coal mines," Tressa added. "The community popped up overnight, with prefabricated slabs of concrete slapped together—materials inexpensive and the process quick. Families moved in, but trips to the outhouse behind the structures made them less desirable. Add in the constant battle with moisture, mold, and frost, and this concrete city was a bust," Tressa explained. She paused momentarily and tried envisioning what it was like living here over a century ago, at least from what she saw in photos. Old newspaper clippings showed rooms lit by candlelight, families retiring at night after workers returned from a trying day in the mines, sprawling flower beds, and awnings desperately trying to give each cookie-cutter structure some individuality.

"It had to be freezing in here," Mauri said. Late autumn sunlight splashed onto the floor through the crumbling hole in the ceiling as she explored the room. "Maybe pipes are stripped out, but where did the plumbing thread through? I don't get it." She placed the thick black camera strap around her neck and jutted her hands into her coat pockets.

"Nope. No plumbing," Tressa said.

"Yeah, you lost me there. No thanks," Mauri said.

"I've read that the walls dripped with condensation, and people would find their clothes frozen in closets by morning," Tressa said. "It's no surprise it was abandoned in 1924."

"Crazy that it is still standing. Well, sort of," Mauri said, kicking a chunk of concrete.

"Oh, the colliery that owned it tried to get it demolished. After loads of dynamite failed to implode the first building, they gave up altogether," Tressa said. "So here we are today. A hidden town in the middle of the woods made of concrete." She turned to find Mauri missing.

A small shower of dust and gravel sprinkled like a rainstorm above her head. She winced as she noticed the tips of enormous black boots peeking from the edge of a floor defined only with a gridwork of rebar sparsely filled with chunks of concrete.

"Mauri, be careful. You should probably come back down here," she pleaded, knowing several kids had suffered injuries in the unstable structure. She was relieved to hear footsteps descend the narrow castle-like steps and pulled out her phone to see if there were any new messages or instructions. "So, did you get the same message as me?" Tressa asked, hoping Mauri had something different to add to their search.

"Search row by row; answer found below. Something like that? I'm glad the concrete part made sense, and you knew where we were headed. What do you think about the rest? What exactly are we looking for?" Mauri asked.

Tressa shook her head, staring at the message on her phone.

Her heart fluttered as she re-read the last line, a feeling of hope replacing the despair surrounding them. She knew what they needed to check next.

While exploring years ago, Tressa remembered her grandmother telling her not to investigate the building's basements. The underground spaces, filled with water and debris, make knowing who or what you could encounter impossible. Most weren't even passable due to the sinking foundation, fallen walls, or water levels creeping to the top of the basement steps. But they needed the answer below.

# Chapter Eight

Navigating the first few abandoned dwellings was exciting, but as Mauri and Tressa expanded their exploration, the novelty wore off, and the search became futile. Not every building had an accessible basement, and the ones they searched turned up empty, including their current location.

The flashlight was of little help in their investigation. The narrow beam did little to reveal anything, let alone clues, to help them during this challenge. Frustrated, Mauri ran her hand over the crumbling texture of the walls, her fingers investigating the ledges for anything besides dirt and rocks. "How do we know what we need to find? Do you think someone will meet us here?"

Tressa strained her eyes, trying to spot anything in the darkness, but the lack of discernible shapes made her uneasy. "I have no idea. I don't know what we should be looking for," she said. "And honestly, I'm not sure I want to meet anyone in one of these basements."

Tressa's hand trembled as she steadied herself against the wall, eyes scanning the uneven steps ahead. The smooth, cold stone gave way to uneven patches. Despite the abandoned city being a hub for fire department drills and paintball warriors' colorful splatters, Tressa couldn't shake her grandmother's warnings over the years about the 'unsavory characters' lurking in the dilapidated buildings. They needed to finish their search before encountering anyone not associated with the Summit Society.

As they returned to the first floor, Tressa leaned out the window, scanning the perimeter of the old town. "I know we can skip those houses across the way," she said, pointing to the listing structures parallel to where they stood. "The first floor has just about sunk into the basement. You can't even get in."

Tressa watched from the window as Mauri exited and approached the next vacant house. She barely disappeared through the doorframe when Tressa heard her yell.

"What is this?" she exclaimed, her voice bouncing off the wall.

Tressa knew Mauri had found one of the most intriguing buildings, the place urban explorers searched for. She joined Mauri as she stood studying the opposite wall, trying to take in every detail of the decaying architecture.

A detailed painting adorned the wall, similar to the troubling Italian Renaissance artwork they had studied. Tressa looked upon the grotesque horned creature holding a small figure in each hand, suspended from their feet with blood dripping below. It looked just as she remembered, but she couldn't believe no one had painted over it by now. Flanked with pentagrams and telltale numbers, it was a deviation from the walls of gang signs, obscene symbols, and other graffiti expressions.

Tressa chuckled as she addressed the unsettling image. "Well, you found the most popular attraction here—Devil House." The symphony of rattling aluminum bounced off the walls as Tressa pushed trash aside to reveal another masterpiece. Silver spray paint outlined a pentagram on the floor, but it wasn't as ornate and detailed as the drawings surrounding it. "Looks like some of the drawings from our class, right?" she asked, breaking Mauri's horrified stare.

"What makes this building so different?" Mauri asked.

"Besides the isolation serving as a discreet backdrop for some other activities, there were rumors about ritualistic activity. In the late 1990s, parents warned their teens to steer clear of this area, which, of course, made it more attractive. Rumors circulated about people finding animal carcasses and candles, and even stories of kidnappings. It turns out it was a bunch of kids with a lot of idle time and spray paint," Tressa said.

Mauri turned her gaze away from the circle and spun around. She wrapped her long arms around herself, returning her gaze to the mural.

"Nothing ever became of it, but the name Devil House stuck and made for great campfire stories." Tressa paused for a moment, her eyes distant as she remembered the past. "But enough about that. This is the last building with a semi-accessible basement. As long as I can get down there, we need to check it out," Tressa said, her toes curled tightly in her sneakers.

Mauri aimed her light into the abyss below. The vibration from her arm rippled against Tressa.

"Nervous?" Tressa asked. Maybe it was familiarity with her surroundings, but her curiosity overpowered her fear, not to mention the excitement of finding whatever they were here for.

"No," Mauri grumbled. "It's just so damp here," she said, pulling her jacket tight, struggling to restore confidence to her voice.

Tressa faced a dark, gaping hole that seemed to lead nowhere. She knew Mauri, who was almost a foot taller than her, couldn't navigate the confined space as easily as Tressa. Crouching down, she balanced on her toes and fingertips, searching for the steps that used to be there.

"What are you doing? That does not look safe. Where are the steps to get into the basement?" Mauri asked.

Tressa's leg swung freely, not making contact with anything as she reached for the steps that used to be there. "Trust me, the steps are here, but they broke away from the foundation years ago. Hold my arms so I can get farther down."

"Tressa, I don't know if this is a good idea. What if it's filled with water or whatever?" she asked.

The few extra inches allowed her to get deeper into the space, but her muscles felt like they would snap as she pointed her toe and extended her leg. The tip of her sneaker scuffed against something hard.

"A few more inches," she said. Tressa heard Mauri huff and puff in protest but felt her body lower. "Okay, it's still here. And my foot's not wet, so I'm fine. You can let go now," Tressa said, her arms on fire as she dangled above the remnants of the steps. Her hand released Mauri's grasp, and she landed on a crumbling step.

Tressa dusted herself off and reached for her phone. After illuminating the small rectangular room, piles of rocks, a crumpled blanket, and other remnants of past parties became visible. In the far corner, she saw something that appeared out of place. Tressa carefully navigated the uneven surface and avoided standing water. She made her way over to the other side of the room and reached for the object. Tucking it under her arm, she scampered back to the opening and thrust the small envelope through the hole for Mauri to grab.

"Here, take this first," she said, holding the white envelope. Mauri quickly grabbed it out of her hand. At that moment, Tressa realized the level of trust she had assumed with her fellow candidate. The skeptical part of her scanned the area to see if anything could boost her up in case Mauri decided to disappear, but before she could find something, a wiggling hand appeared above her head.

"Hey, Tiny Tressa, grab my hands," Mauri said, leaning into the hole. Tressa pushed off the broken step as Mauri yanked her arms. Both girls tumbled to the floor, sending debris scattering.

Tressa's eyes fell on the envelope with the familiar wax seal. Mauri tore open the envelope and concealed the contents in her hand.

"What is it?" Tressa asked. She could see her friend holding something tightly between her fingertips.

"It's a small stone," Mauri said, cradling the blue, half-moon piece in her hand. "What are we supposed to do with this?

"Let's get out of this building so we can see it in a better light," Tressa said, brushing off her jeans.

Mauri carefully replaced the piece, folded the envelope in half, and slid it into her pocket. As they were about to leave, she paused.

"That's weird. My phone just buzzed," Mauri said, touching her pocket.

"Mine, too."

They both pulled out their phones to notice the app indicating a message. Familiar gray smoke swirled on the screen, but no instruction or message appeared. This time, an image appeared.

Tressa watched as a circle materialized in the center of the screen. The outline of a tall mountain slowly took shape at the center of the circle, dividing it into three slightly outlined sections, creating a segmented medallion shape. But what caught her attention was the bottom of the screen—pulsating with a bright, sapphire light, mirroring the color and shape of the mysterious stone they discovered.

"This is like an interactive game. I think we press it," Tressa said, her finger hovering over the screen.

Mauri nodded in agreement, and both girls watched as the glimmering blue shape filled in one-third of the circle, the shape reminding Tressa of a pirate medallion. The screen emitted a soft, ethereal glow, and a message appeared beneath.

**Test one completed.**

# Chapter Nine

The Land Rover roared down the highway as a 90's boy band blared from the speakers. Tressa tapped her fingers on the steering wheel, her mind buzzing with a million thoughts. Glancing in the mirror, she saw Mauri following close behind. She was glad she had agreed to meet her for a bite to eat so they could unpack everything that had just happened. Tressa considered calling Alex to share the events of the past few hours but thought better of it and stowed her phone back in the console. She wanted to share her excitement with someone, but at the same time, she felt like she had crossed a line and couldn't turn back without jeopardizing her chance of being initiated into the Summit Society.

Tressa pulled into the parking lot, and a few cars were parked outside Stan's Pub. A few neon signs gave the otherwise worn exterior a small sign of life. She hoped they still had a decent menu since it was her idea to meet here before heading back to school. Tossing her hat onto the seat, she ran her fingers through her hair, trying to make it look presentable. Fast food napkins and receipts fluttered to the floor as she rummaged through the glove box. Tressa looked in the mirror, wiped away dirt smudges, and applied lip gloss.

Once inside, it took Tressa a moment to adjust to the dim interior. The faux wood paneling was barely visible, with warm amber light struggling to reveal much besides a row of booths and a long bar along the wall. Despite the tired atmosphere, Tressa felt a nostalgic sense of welcome. Mauri had already found a seat, her face obscured by a menu.

"Hey, looks like it's just us," she said, sliding into the booth.

Mauri flipped the menu a few times, peering over her glasses. "I don't imagine there is a vegan section on this menu," she said without looking up.

"Oh, cool. Are you a vegan? I've always considered switching, but I can't give up my favorite buffalo chicken sandwich. If it bothers you, I won't order it," Tressa stammered.

"Relax—severe dairy allergy. If I stick with a vegan menu, I'm usually safe. And it's not just us," Mauri said.

"Oh, right. I know many people with dairy allergies," Tressa said, rhythmically tapping her menu on the table.

Mauri leaned against the torn vinyl backrest, staring quizzically at Tressa after her erratic outbursts. "Are you okay?"

"I am. I'm sorry, I just," Tressa paused. "I need a drink. Do you mind if I order something?" she asked, feeling her face flush.

"Don't apologize," Mauri said, shifting her focus to the cracked plastic at the corner of the menu. "And I meant *we* are not alone."

Tressa turned to see an older man hunched over at the bar, talking to himself or possibly the bartender. "I doubt they can hear us," she whispered.

"Anything for you, miss?" the server asked, causing Tressa to nearly fall out of her seat. She did a double take and noticed the bar unattended, wondering if this guy would be cooking their food, too.

"Anything white and dry is fine," Tressa said, wanting to retract her words as she stared at the man.

The server's squinting eyes looked like coin slots framed by angry eyebrows. His black hair was slicked back, pen behind his ear.

"We have bottles in the cooler and two beers on tap," he said with a sigh, pointing over his hulking shoulder, but he failed to mention specific offerings.

"Whatever is on tap is fine. How about the Lager?" Tressa asked, hoping it was one of the choices. "And the chicken sandwich and fries, hot, please," she added.

He turned to Mauri without any other questions.

"Water and fries for me," Mauri said, her eyes on her phone.

Tressa waited until their drinks were in front of them before bringing up the topic at hand. "Any response? More directions?" she asked, her voice low.

"No, nothing yet," Mauri said. "Do you think there are others?"

"It's possible," Tressa said, her mind racing. "I mean, up until this point, I wasn't even sure what was true and what was just hype. But, it seems like we are candidates." As she spoke the word, the gravity of the situation finally sunk in. From the minute Tressa received the letter, she didn't have much time to process everything. It was way out of her comfort zone, and she had difficulty believing it was her and, apparently, Mauri.

"Maybe it's just us? Wouldn't others have shown up if they received the same directions? Unless they had different tasks," Mauri added. "It's also possible they didn't believe it or thought it was fake. The app, though, seems legit. Did you try searching for it? It's definitely unlisted, and I'm sure those QR codes have already expired."

Tressa felt a growing uneasiness now that she had a chance to think about others rejecting the invitation, assuming it was fake. Her mind kept returning to the idea of someone following them to record their journey and make them the brunt of a cruel joke as if they would be considered for a secret society. However, the idea of the exclusive app made it seem unlikely someone would go to such lengths to play a prank.

"Well, aren't you lucky we were paired to work together? You would never have made it out of the basement," Mauri quipped, more akin to her snarkiness.

Tressa took a long sip of her beer, centering it on the coaster, before responding. "Aren't *you* lucky I knew all about the area in the first place?"

Mauri pursed her lips and nodded in agreement, unable to deny Tressa's familiarity with Miner Town, making their assignment easier. They both had something to offer.

"I'm not sure of the timeline on this. Rumor is you must pass a few tests before being considered for initiation. Isn't it killing you not to tell anyone?" Tressa asked.

"Not especially. There was no one really to tell. I hesitated to graduate early from high school but was bored. Not to mention, it was a full ride, and I couldn't let my grandmother down," Mauri said.

"Your grandmother?" Tressa asked.

"Yeah, that's who I lived with for years. My parents aren't in the picture."

"I hear you. It's tough. Divorced?" Tressa asked. She knew the feeling all too well. Her mother's divorce guilt and overcompensation were getting old. Sometimes, she wished her grandmother was still around so she could live with her.

"No. Dead," Mauri said.

"Oh. I'm sorry," Tressa said. "I had no idea." It was easier to climb out of the concrete basement than get out of this conversation.

"Anything else I can get ya?" the server mumbled as he placed the red plastic baskets on the table. It was perfect timing.

"No, I'm good," Tressa lied while Mauri shook her head.

The corners of her mouth were on fire after biting into the sandwich, and she wished she had ordered another beer. It would help everything go down a little easier right about now. The server turned his attention to the small tube television propped up in the corner of the room. Tressa focused on the argument unfolding on Court TV, hoping it could shift the conversation.

The chirping sound caught the attention of the ornery server seated at the bar, and Tressa wiped the hot sauce with the wilted napkin before fumbling with her phone. That's when she heard it again.

"That's me," Mauri said, holding up her phone.

Warmth crept into Tressa's face like the rising level of a hot spring. She hesitated before touching the new message as if she were deciding on the correct wire to diffuse a bomb. The picture of the puzzle piece disappeared to load a new message.

Congratulations to you all<br>
Learn to reach high, but do not fall.<br>
You'll get a hand on the second.<br>
More to come when we beckon<br>
Test Two

Mauri cradled her phone, and Tressa leaned over to see the replicated message.

"Can we have our check, please," Tressa said, yelling over to the server.

# Chapter Ten

Tressa stopped at The Gallery, the campus dining area, for lunch. She didn't have much to eat at her apartment and didn't want to drive anywhere.

"Do you have a meal plan?" the cashier asked.

"I'm sorry, no. Actually, I meant to get this to go," Tressa said, looking back over her shoulder. The lunchtime crowd of students and faculty created a long line, and she didn't want to get out of place to grab a to-go container. "Never mind, I'll eat it here," she said.

Tressa scanned the room, the noise and chatter of conversations reminding her of high school rather than college. She didn't recognize anyone but spotted an empty round table in the corner. To avoid the crowds of students pouring into the school cafe, she bee-lined to the back of the room before her chance to sit in solitude disappeared.

She swirled a shoestring fry in the small paper container of ketchup. She liked the food at The Gallery, but the lack of company wasn't always appealing. She looked up when a trio sat at the table beside her. She gulped her iced tea and shoveled the last few bites of lunch into her mouth.

"Oh, I heard they picked three guys this year. You know *they'll* go through lots of crazy initiation rites," one of the guys at the table said.

"Really? Someone told me it was only one since they have more candidates from other schools, but I heard the same thing.

I think they had to steal something from Allan Hall. I just hope I have a chance in a few years. How great would that be? Financially and socially secure for life," another student exclaimed.

Tressa stopped shoving fries into her mouth and decided to stay at her table longer. She smirked, wishing to spin around and tell the freshman group they were wrong.

"Can you imagine having an awesome job handed to you after graduation?" the student continued.

"Just for being part of the Summit Society. It's so cool. My cousin knows someone in it and said they meet yearly at one of the members' mansions. Expensive cars pulling up, fancy ceremonies and initiations, all Skull and Bones stuff," one of the freshmen quipped.

The mention of fancy ceremonies made Tressa chuckle. She wasn't sure what would come, but she longed to share the fancy details of crawling around crumbling concrete and avoiding broken glass. As she crumpled her napkin, she paused and let doubt creep in. What if they were right? What if the real initiates are anyone other than Tressa and Mauri?

Pushing her plate away, Tressa took out her notebook and studied the scribbles on lined pages. A selection of words, grouped alphabetically, haphazardly floated beneath the written-out message from her text. A column of the exact phrases vertically lined the side of the paper, random letters circled and crossed out. The bottom of the page looked like a game of hangman minus a figure suspended from a bracket. Tressa always thought she was good at solving puzzles, but if this next clue was something cryptic, she wasn't getting it.

"They probably have the initiation now, right around Halloween. I'd love to be part of it," the girl behind her said in the most annoying, whiny voice.

The conversation reminded Tressa about tonight's plans to visit the Steele Hotel, one of the area's most famous haunted attractions. She already had her version of wandering around a dilapidated building, waiting for something to jump out. She didn't see the need to replicate the experience, but she made a promise to Mauri. Besides, she needed to get her mind off of things. It had been almost ten days since their first test, but no follow-up from the last message.

# Chapter Eleven

Tressa had been putting off going home to get her winter gear for as long as she could. On campus, the fashion was shifting from hoodies to knit hats and puffy coats. While she knew her mother would gladly ship her an entirely new wardrobe if she asked, Tressa preferred to avoid the hassle. She pulled on her long-sleeved shirt, her fingertips barely peeking out of the thermal fabric. With a backward flop onto her bed and a struggle to get her foot into her boots, Tressa heard a conversation drifting into her room.

"Hey Alex!" she yelled from her bedroom. As she moved to the doorway, she saw Alex at the kitchen table and realized why he hadn't answered.

"I've been there before. It is awesome," Alex said, enunciating every word and adding an exclamation with his hands.

Mauri sat across from him, her long legs crossed, making it hard to figure out where the tights ended, and the hem of her short skirt started. The inky black color trended from boots to lipstick, but her nails looked like rubies glittering through the strands of hair wrapped around her long, slender fingers.

"Oh hey. I didn't hear you come in. I'm just about ready, and I can drive," Tressa said.

"Perfect! I told Mauri you wouldn't mind driving us, and she can have a quick drink with me first," Alex said, grabbing two glasses.

"Wait. Us? Hold on, and Mauri doesn't drink," Tressa said, her face feeling like someone had just turned on a space heater.

"I told Alex about the Steele Hotel, and since he doesn't have any plans, he's coming with us," Mauri said. Tressa couldn't believe what a difference a couple of weeks made. It just proved Alex could break down anyone's protective barrier.

"I thought you did have plans. Weren't you going with Trixie or Toffee or something?" Tressa said, glaring across the table.

"Tracey is her name, and yes, we did have plans to go to a party, but no, I'm not going," he said, head tilted in the air. "I'd rather hang out with the coolest girls on campus," he said, squeezing Mauri's shoulder.

"She canceled, didn't she?" Tressa asked.

"Well, maybe. But going to a haunted house on Halloween sounds like much more fun. Thanks for driving, Tress," he said, holding up a glass, scarlet liquid splashing over the rim. "We should probably head out." He left little room for negotiation.

As they got in the car, Tressa's gloves rested on her lap while her fingers lingered near the vent. The warm circulating air smelled of wood, cinnamon, and winter. She couldn't remember Halloween feeling so much like Christmas.

"So, Steele Hotel. Abandoned for the longest time, they resurrected it as a haunted house. Local colleges put it together, and all the money goes to Habitat for Humanity. They do a great job," Alex said, leaning in from the backseat.

"You need to fasten your seatbelt," Tressa said. She tried to make eye contact in the mirror, but he popped back, clicking in as told.

"Yes, ma'am," he chuckled.

Tressa wished her two friend universes could remain separate, not merge. She didn't want to feel like a third wheel again, reminiscent of the short stint of Alex dating Jess. Tressa missed Jess, and the dynamic her friend brought to their apartment. She treasured the moments they shared at The Gallery, their Friday night hangouts, and their mischievous delight in teasing Alex. For weeks, Tressa felt that comfort return with Mauri, but she was afraid to let her guard down. Glancing over at Mauri, her midnight-stained lips still spoke in youthful bursts. Her heavy kohl-lined eyes accented with moody purple shadow fluttered when Alex teased her about high school. Beneath the looming dark, steely exterior seeped a softness of naivety and inexperience, picked up by Alex like a bloodhound. Mauri was no Jess, but she contrasted Tressa's lightness and complimented her interests. As she watched Mauri ball up her scarf and throw it at Alex, Tress knew their sense of belonging wasn't the only thing they shared.

"Can I park here?" she asked. Tressa's gloves fell to the floor as they bumped through the field, navigating the sea of cars. Alex and Mauri scrambled out of the vehicle before Tressa could look for a closer spot. She watched Alex help fasten the glowing necklace around Mauri's neck, the blend of colors matching her hair.

"Necklace?" he asked, extending the unattached glow stick without offering the same accommodation. "They say if you wear this, no one will bother you."

"I'll pass," Tressa said. "I heard it means the opposite." She wanted to get this over with; the last thing she wanted was more attention.

The trio headed to the old hotel, the queue of cautiously excited ticket holders snaking a line into the parking lot.

"Bang!"

Shrieks came from the second floor, followed by laughter. Whatever made the cannon-like sound repeated every few minutes, followed by screams pierced with cackling hysterics. While Alex and Mauri argued over the best horror movie of all time, Tressa's heart thudded in her chest with every step closer to the entrance.

"Tress," he hissed. "What's wrong? You're not afraid, are you?"

She watched some cast members walk around from the back of the dilapidated building, cigarettes in one hand and scanning through their phones with the other. Tressa felt paranoid but could have sworn they were looking her way.

"Alex, you know how I feel about this. I thought I would be okay, but I want to get it over with," she said.

"Tressa, come on, it's Halloween," Mauri said, hopping up and down and digging her hands into her pockets.

As they moved onto the porch, Tressa made eye contact with everyone around them. They probably thought she was the crazy one. She jumped when something skimmed across her head. A gloved hand rested on her shoulder.

"Checking in? How many in your party?" the figure grumbled.

"What? Oh, three," she said as she turned around to ensure she still had Alex and Mauri.

"The hotel is ready for you, Tressa, but are you ready for the hotel?" the robed figure whispered.

Tressa stared at the cloaked figure, wondering how he knew her name. "I'm sorry, what was that?"

The ticket taker smirked and raised one eyebrow. "Enjoy your stay," he said while greeting the next guest.

Walking into the first room, the space filled with an overpowering smell, an earthiness mixed with chemicals. Tressa grimaced and walked through the threshold. Alex grabbed her hand, and Mauri attached to her like a barnacle. They trudged through a fabricated cemetery as a single entity, colliding with each other at every scare. Token zombies emerged from behind the tombstones, and something wispy tangled in Tressa's fingers as she pressed onward. A tunnel with strobe lights, a laboratory strewn with mangled body parts, and a wandering clown who seemed magnetized to Mauri's necklace greeted them along the way. Tressa wasn't sure if Mauri's blood-curdling screams every few seconds were organic or theatrical. A reassuring hug from Alex every time made her think the latter.

Tressa pulled up the rear, trailing the group, but latched onto Alex's hand. She couldn't shake off the feeling that someone was watching her every move, not just the regular creepy actors. As they reached the top of the steps, she lost her grip.

"Alex," she whimpered. She felt a hand abruptly thrust in front of her and the need to steady herself by grasping the railing. "Alex?" she yelled, trying to look past the hooded figure. She felt sweat beading at the small of her back, knowing she was now alone.

"Sorry, little girl, no more than two on the bridge," the figure scowled.

"But we only had three in our group," she pleaded, standing on tiptoes to make out what was ahead, shrouded by a burst of mist from a fog machine.

"You may pass now," he said, unaffected.

She paused, staring at the cloaked person, awaiting any indication that he singled her out. Was everyone testing her? Was she the only one forced to walk alone? As she tried to anticipate the next scare in the narrow, pitch-black corridor, she hopped from foot to foot as something hit her ankle. She barreled forward, grasping onto ropes guiding her over wobbly wooden slats. Swirls of white smoke encircled her legs like creeping ivy. Her heart now pounding like a freight train, she made it out of the makeshift swamp.

"Alex? Mauri?" she yelled, waiting to be reunited.

The passageway took her into a small closet-like enclosure. Before she realized there was no exit, a door slammed shut with a bang. Her shoulder pounded against the wall, finally giving way, dumping her into a spacious area that looked like a funeral parlor. Alex and Mauri stood near a casket.

"I hope this is the end," Tressa said, wiping cobwebs off her shoulder.

"Oh, Tress, I'm sorry," Alex said, pulling her head against his chest. He exaggeratedly kissed her curls before holding her shoulders, trying to erase her anger.

Mauri mouthed the words "*sorry*" as they moved toward a tour guide leading them to the end of the haunted attraction. Tressa trotted down the steps and headed for the Land Rover. Alex slipped next to her, threading his arm in hers and pulling her close as they walked.

"Hey, you're not mad, are you? Mauri was never here, so she needed to figure out what to expect. They only let two of us at a time, and I thought you'd be okay."

Tressa ripped her arm from his grasp, fumbling for her keys. When Mauri suggested they do something on Halloween, Tressa was thrilled to make plans. The haunted house would be her last choice, but she thought they would have some laughs tonight and figured she'd push through. Two people shared some laughs tonight, but she wasn't one of them.

# Chapter Twelve

"To understand and accurately depict the human body in their drawings and sculptures, many artists turned to anatomists to inform their artistic work. In keeping with the season, we will delve into the effect of decapitation and dissection in paintings," Professor Dawson said, dimming the lights in the auditorium.

Tressa leaned forward in her seat, ignoring her classmates' utterances of disgust and surprise. She knew about da Vinci's deep study of the human body, but she was unaware of how many corpses he dissected to help compile his drawings. The intricate network of ligaments, muscles, and bones wove together in a delicate but raw glimpse into something other than The Mona Lisa.

"Keep in mind, unless performed by a physician, the Catholic Church deemed dissection illegal. Many artists became fast friends with doctors, hospitals, and yes, grave robbers," Professor Dawson explained, his playful gaze scanning the audience, anticipating their reactions.

Leaning back, Tressa tapped her foot, waiting for the presentation to continue. Glancing down the row, she realized that Mauri hadn't shown up for class.

"Ms. Litton, can you give us an example?" her professor questioned.

She glanced at the large screen and saw he had moved on to the next slide: death and decapitation. "Um, Caravaggio? He seemed to be obsessed with the grotesque, especially decapitation."

Nearby classmates met her response with inaudible whispers and snickers.

As Professor Dawson walked to the center aisle, he crossed his arms, and his sleeves clung to his biceps, the fabric straining against his muscular build. "Good observation, Ms. Litton, but I asked about the event that shaped many artists' works in the 15th and 16th centuries. Please try to stay with us and keep your focus," he said, eliciting a few laughs. "The Black Death is the answer I was looking for."

Hushed laughter settled on the auditorium like a creeping fog, and Tressa knew it wasn't because of Professor Dawson's humor. She tried to stay focused on the image of Saint John the Baptist filling the white space, blood dripping below. Instead, she counted down each remaining minute of class.

Tressa did not want a further lecture about her mental absence, so she was out the door before Professor Dawson could even make eye contact. Dim lamp posts guarded the winding path, the amber glow intensifying as dusk rushed in, marking the end of a long day's schedule. The brisk walk helped her to release some of her tension. Before she tried her keys in the door, Alex's laugh echoed from behind.

"Oh, I didn't know you had company," Tressa said.

Alex straddled a kitchen chair, his face resting on the sleeve of his soccer hoodie. Mauri sat in Tressa's favorite seat, her black flats resting on the other chair.

"Don't get up," Tressa said, trying to keep her breath slow and steady.

"Tress! I was leaving, and Mauri dropped by to wait for you," Alex explained, holding his hands up defensively.

"Mm-hmm," Tressa murmured, noticing that Alex seemed to mouth something to Mauri before quickly leaving the room.

"Since you missed class, you'll have to get your notes after he posts them. I wasn't feeling it today, so I don't think I'm the best resource." Tressa mindlessly straightened the small kitchen and mopped the countertop silently, avoiding eye contact with Mauri.

"Like Alex said, I stopped in to talk to you. I'd rather discuss this when he's not around anyway," Mauri said.

Tressa could see the writing on the wall and expected this to happen. "Okay, so what's up?" she asked, figuring Mauri would ask her advice about Alex.

"I've been thinking about this for days, and it's been killing me. I'm usually pretty good at this, but no matter what I do, I can't interpret its meaning," Mauri said.

"He's a great guy, Mauri, really he is. But I hate to say it, Alex loves a good game, and you might be his latest challenge," Tressa said, hoping Mauri wouldn't mistake her advice for jealousy.

"Alex? Challenge? What are you talking about?" Mauri asked. "Maybe some other girls fall for your charming friend, but do I look that gullible? I may be young, but I'm pretty good at reading people," she laughed, her usual edge creeping back. "So, are you okay?" Mauri continued, pulling her phone out of her pocket. "Because if not, I won't show you what I found."

Tressa decided not to make herself sound even more foolish than she felt. "You found something?" she asked, not addressing any accusations.

Mauri scrolled through her phone, "Here, take a look," she said. All Tressa could see was the most recent message.

"I know, I got the same thing. Did you get another message?" Tressa asked.

"No, I didn't. But, like I said, puzzles, math, and riddles are my thing. I couldn't help but think that since we hadn't heard anything else, we must have missed something," Mauri said. "I knew there must have been some meaning about where or when we would en- counter our next test. It was driving me crazy—that's why I skipped class."

"Yeah, me too. I gave up, though, thinking maybe we got played," Tressa agreed.

"Look again. The answer is right in front of you," Mauri said.

Tressa reread the message, but nothing changed.

"It's not a clue about what; it's a clue about when. Read it again," Mauri pointed out.

Congratulations to you all
Learn to reach high, but do not fall.
You'll get a hand on the second.
More to come when we beckon
Test Two

It was like one of those pixel eye charts. When you finally see it, you can't believe you missed it before.

You'll get a hand on the second.

She looked at her calendar, fully aware of tomorrow's date—November 2nd.

# Chapter Thirteen

A built-in weekend alarm clock wasn't a huge selling point for the apartment. Still, the cozy steam heat was worth the racket, and Tressa became immune to the early morning cacophony of clanging metal. She fumbled with the coffee filter and measured water through sleep-blurred eyes. Her phone would stay glued to her hand since there had been no new messages. If Mauri was correct, something might happen today.

"Good morning, you ray of strawberry sunshine," Alex said, followed by a yawn. He nodded when Tressa held up two coffee mugs.

She waited near the toaster, holding back a snarky comment about Mauri being his rainbow sunshine. Droplets of coffee sizzled as she hastily grabbed the pot, unable to wait for the morning caffeine jolt.

"Do you want a bagel?" she asked.

"Just a coffee and Advil, please," Alex muttered. "I should have stayed here with you girls last night."

Tressa couldn't resist being impressed by his ruggedly handsome appearance despite the dark circles under his eyes. His ivory, freckle-dusted complexion was illuminated by natural copper highlights in his hair that caught the overhead light. As he raked his fingers through the wayward strands, it created an even more disheveled charm. Tressa had noticed how his high school lacrosse invitational shirt hugged his wiry, chiseled torso. Despite his post-party morning bedhead, Alex's look seemed effortless.

"Thank God the season is almost over. I'm not sure I can handle any more Saturday morning matches," he said, giving Tressa a painful look as if someone was stabbing him with a needle.

"You'll be fine. You always are," Tressa said.

"Right now, I would say I'm staying home tonight, but you never know, I might get a second wind," Alex said as he drained the last bit of coffee from his mug. "If not, do you want to go for pizza?" he asked.

"Sure, I'll see what's going on," she stammered. Tressa wondered if she would be hunkered down on the couch, engrossed in binge-watching old episodes of The X-Files, working on essays, or if she would be crawling around an abandoned building. "And good luck today," Tressa yelled as Alex shuffled to his bedroom. Tressa knew the pizza option would be his last resort for weekend plans.

Before the afternoon escaped her, Tressa knew she needed to sift through pages of notes, try to organize her thoughts, and finish her English paper. The stanzas of Edgar Allan Poe's "The Bells" floated in her head, rattling together, making it challenging to analyze. She rarely let any assignments linger through the weekend, but her sharp focus fleeted in recent days.

> *"How the danger ebbs and flows;*
> *Yet, the ear distinctly tells,*
> *In the jangling."*

Tressa woke up with a start as her hand slipped from her temple, disorienting her for a moment. She took a deep breath and tried to focus on the words before her, pushing the sudden jolt out of her mind.

> *"And the wrangling,*
> *How the danger ebbs and flows."*

She must have read the passages ten times, struggling as much with interpretations as she did with fluttering eyelids. She grabbed the throw blanket and realized the steam pipe's clamor competed with the bells' clamor. She barely surrendered to the softness of the feather-filled pillow when she heard a familiar sound. Her heart palpitated, and she looked at the little text bubble with Mauri's simple message.

**M: Get ready. It seems like test two is tomorrow.**

Tressa checked her app, but there were no indicators of new messages. Her shaking fingers selected the call button next to Mauri's name.

"What does it say?" Tressa blurted.

"Not much. Wait, let me put you on speaker," she said, her voice becoming more distant. "It's a series of numbers. Here, let me read them. 110222, 1700, 619"

Tressa tried to digest everything Mauri shared while refreshing her app.

"I still didn't get anything," Tressa said with panic.

"Relax, I'm sure it's meant for us both," Mauri reassured.

"Right," Tressa commented. She wouldn't bet her inheritance on it. "Okay, from what you read, I'm sure you know what the numbers mean."

"Yeah. The date and, I'm assuming, military time. I'm not sure about the last part," Mauri said.

"Can you send me the message? I want to look at it with my own eyes. Maybe it will make sense. Will it let you take a screenshot?" Tressa asked, but there was no response. "Mauri?" she said, breaking the silence.

"I'd rather not send or share messages," Mauri said in a hushed tone.

"Okay. I guess we will wait. Or maybe you wait." Tressa couldn't imagine she would be trusted this far, pulled into the tangled web and then excluded. She scrambled, thinking if she had said anything about the society besides speaking to Mauri. Tressa felt the opportunity slowly sliding from her grasp.

Mauri sighed. "Relax, I just feel it's best not to circulate anything. Let me read through it again," Mauri said, breaking the uncomfortable silence.

Tressa let the sound of Mauri's words sink in, scribbling down the string of numbers, staring at them as if they were jumping off the page.

"Oh my God. Mauri! It's the mailbox!" Tressa screamed.

"Your mailbox? Did you get an actual letter this time?" Mauri asked.

"No, my school mailbox. That's my number. In the student commons. 619!"

It made sense. The school mailbox was a small, old-fashioned post-office-type grid, filled with small combination controlled openings. Tressa often stood in front of the daunting row of tiny glass windows, petrified to retrieve the contents. Not all papers and tests were returned digitally, and the snail mail method was exciting and terrifying.

"I guess we know where we will be tomorrow at 5 p.m.," Tressa said, hoping the "we" part was accurate.

# Chapter Fourteen

With only five hours of sleep, Tressa had a lot to do before the 5 p.m. revelation, but at that moment, getting out of bed wasn't one of them. The bright sun cast bold lines across her ceiling, highlighting the crack in the plaster that looked like a piece of art. Tressa often wondered if she would wake up to find white paint flakes scattered across her bed. Today, she realized that the crack resembled a graph line, dividing her life into two segments–before and after the invitation. Before the invite, Tressa's life was just fine. The four-year journey at Wyval will end, and she has the potential to get a job that fits her mother's standards. After the invite, her life has similar components, but she has the chance to be part of something elite and start her career because of *her* accomplishments and who *she* knew, not because of what money could buy. As she contemplated her life plan as a geometry graph, Tressa heard the familiar creak of her door.

"Still sleeping? Just checking on ya," Alex whispered, popping his head into her room.

"I'm awake. Just trying to get a game plan for the day. I have a ton of stuff to finish and a lot going on," she said, slipping her feet into thick woolen socks. I probably won't be home tonight."

"Oh, well, who is the lucky guy," Alex said, eyes wide as saucers. "Or, hiking partner," he said quizzically, watching her tuck away boots and extra socks into her bag.

"Funny. Anyway, I have to stop at my mom's house for a quick visit and take some extra things home. I should be back by early morning," she said, trying to keep her doubt from coming through.

"Everything okay with your mom?" he asked.

"She's fine. I need to get more winter clothes and return some things, so I plan on staying overnight. You know how she gets if I don't spend some quality time at home," Tressa explained.

Alex stared at her cold weather gear and shrugged. "Well, give her my love," he said, blowing an air kiss before walking away.

Focusing on preparing for this next adventure, Tressa debated on a set of thermals and extra gloves. Her bag looked like it would burst at the seams, so she nixed any additional items. However, as she glanced at the picture on her nightstand, a slight pang of guilt tugged at her. The image showed a tiny girl with a strawberry-blonde ponytail standing beside an elegant woman who sparkled with grace and confidence. She promised herself that, eventually, she would make time to stop by home for an actual visit.

Laundry, clanging through *The Bells* essay, and wrapping up a few other assignments chipped away at some of the time, each hour feeling like a day. By 4 p.m., she felt drained and needed a break. She toyed with going for a run or having a glass of wine but decided against both and headed to the commons to meet Mauri. The campus was quiet, allowing her to appreciate the beauty of the buildings she had rushed past countless times. The Victorian-style administration buildings, including Wyval Hall, originally built as a residence for the Lenhein family, now served as classrooms. As she got closer to the student center, she stared at the transition from ornate trim and sprawling porches to a more modern building with clean lines and plenty of glass—a testament to the progressive timeline of Wyval.

"Couldn't wait either?" she heard a voice from behind the rack of Fritos and MilkyWays.

Mauri walked over to the counter, her thoughts in line with Tressa's as she paid for Gatorade and sunflower seeds.

Walking toward the row of mailboxes, Tressa wanted to rip off the Band-Aid. She couldn't imagine being excluded in this next step, but she still hadn't received a guarantee she wouldn't. Pale yellow light barely made the small copper boxes visible. Tressa's fingers trembled as she worked the dial slowly as if diffusing a bomb. Her eyes locked with Mauri's as she reached in and retrieved a stack of flyers, postcards, and a distinct square envelope.

"Guess I don't check my mailbox enough," Tressa said, rifling through colorful notices of mixers, food drives, and other events neither girl planned on attending. Her hand casually deposited everything but the heavyweight letter in the nearby trash. The gentle sound of wax tearing from linen-like paper interrupted the buzzing of overhead lights. If looks could burn holes through paper, the letter might have already been reduced to ashes.

"What's in it?" Mauri whispered.

Tressa pulled out two small rectangular slips of paper. "There are two tickets," she said.

The word *two* made Tressa feel like someone had just lifted a weighted blanket from her chest. From the look of confusion on Mauri's face, Tressa realized why her mailbox played a role in this puzzle. A girl from South Jersey wouldn't be familiar with two admission tickets to this local attraction.

"It looks like we are doing a tour tonight," Tressa said, holding the passes to the old jail. She heard the chirp almost on cue as if someone was listening or watching.

Enjoy your overnight stay.

# Chapter Fifteen

As Tressa drove down the familiar route, her Land Rover hugged every curve. She was grateful for two things: first, that the apartment was empty when she went to grab her bag, and second, that she hadn't spent her teenage summers like the rest of Summit Peak, allowing her to be familiar with their destination. The comforting sound of the engine and the beauty of the scenery passing by made her feel at ease.

"I'm not going to lie. I was a little nervous and jealous because you got the message," Tressa said.

Mauri fidgeted with her small silver stud earring. She gazed at the monotonous line of trees as they drove higher into the mountains, revealing less and less of civilization. She shifted in the comfortable leather seat as the darkness deepened with every mile.

"And I'm not going to lie, but it's a little strange you are more familiar with the communication we receive, like it's tailored to your surroundings," Mauri retorted.

Tressa gripped the steering wheel, unable to respond. She had been questioning the link the two shared and why they were chosen since day one, but she knew they were there to compliment and not contradict each other.

"But whatever reason we are here, it's pretty cool that I'm not doing it alone," Mauri added.

Tressa smiled and felt the wall between them crumble into smaller bits.

"So give me the scoop on Coal County Jail," Mauri said.

"There's not much to tell, but I worked there for two summers as a guide. While most high school kids spent summers at the beach, I volunteered as a guide and greeter at the jail and museum. I'm pretty familiar with the location," Tressa said, proud of her accomplishments.

Mauri uncrossed her legs and sat forward in her seat. "No way. Same thing. I spent my summers at the gallery for local artists and the maritime museum back home. After my parents died, my grandmother told me I needed to keep busy."

Tressa waited for Mauri to continue. She didn't want to pry but wondered about Mauri's childhood.

Mauri flicked on the overhead light, staring at the tickets as if secret information would jump off the small rectangular cards. "9 p.m. tour. Doesn't that seem late?"

"No, it's normal. The jail closes to the public during winter, so they try to cram as many tours in before the holidays," Tressa explained.

The chirping alert sounded from both girl's phones simultaneously. Mauri immediately checked her phone, taking a second to read the new message.

"What does it say?" Tressa asked.

"It's similar to the last message, *enjoy your overnight stay*, but with more details," Mauri said, pausing to continue reading to herself. "Oh wow, I guess we will be there all night. Listen to this," she said before sharing the message out loud.

> While at the jail, you will scour,
> send your proof every hour.
> Showing date and time will be
> best to fulfill this second test.

As they pulled up to the fortress-like structure, towering windows loomed, reinforced by a harsh grid of iron bars. Tressa's mind raced. She knew it would be possible to get back into the jail after hours, but she didn't like the idea. She was relieved to see a few other cars in the parking lot. This meant tours were still happening, and Tressa knew it would make things more manageable. She also knew it would be better to park down the road on a side street. "I hope you don't mind, but we will need to take a bit of a hike," Tressa said.

As they found a place to park and returned to the historic landmark, Tressa watched Mauri gaze at the foreboding structure.

"It's cool that you worked here, but I thought the haunted house vibe wasn't your scene," Mauri said as they walked up the wide, stone steps, the looming building tall and intimidating.

The iron handles on the weathered oak door felt cold as Tressa struggled with the door's weight. "Real haunted places don't scare me. Real people do," she whispered as they waited in the lobby.

"Wait, this place is haunted?" Mauri exclaimed.

Tressa smiled as a remarkably petite woman approached.

"Tressa Litton. Is that you? I told Gerry the girl walking up the steps looked like an older version of Tressa. And here you are!" she said, pointing at the cameras. "Haven't you had enough of this place to last a lifetime?" the woman said.

"I think so, Mrs. Swithers, but my friend Mauri has never been here, so we wanted to visit before you close for the season. Here are our tickets," she said, handing the passes to her former co-worker. Throughout the tourist season, whether it was the sweltering heat of summer or the frigid cold of winter, Mrs. Swithers always dressed impeccably. She wore glasses perched in her up-swept silver hair, and another set dangled precariously from a delicate chain resting against her navy blazer. As Tressa looked at the sign above her head, she felt a flutter in her stomach. She knew she would have to break most of the rules that everyone working at the Coal County Jail tried to enforce.

"Mauri, welcome. I'm sure you'll enjoy the tour. Come in this way; it's almost a full house tonight. We will be getting started soon," said the cheerful woman as she disappeared, giving the usual spiel to the couple behind them. The scent of roses and powder trailed behind her.

As they waited for the tour to begin, the girls walked around the small gift shop. A table in the corner was adorned with colorful postcards, pieces of shiny black coal, and other souvenirs. Rows of books organized neatly on wire racks featuring everything from coal mining in Pennsylvania to ghost stories and legends rested against the far wall.

As Tressa spotted Gerry, another former co-worker, a warm feeling of familiarity and guilt washed over her. "Hi, Gerry. It's so good to see you after all this time," Tressa said as she leaned in for a hug. Gerry rarely led tours but could be found selling photos and souvenirs as visitors exited the jail.

"Tressa. What a nice surprise. I hear you are finishing college soon," she said. Before you dive into the real world and work at some big-time art gallery, why don't you spend one more summer with us? We've been swamped after being featured in the local ghost-hunting television series, especially with the late-night ghost tours. We need someone like you to keep them in check, though. Some visitors try to bring their equipment in and stay after hours. You know how it can get, " Gerry said.

Her voice was soft and gentle, and Gerry's kind and trusting demeanor usually put Tressa at ease. She shifted her weight and, clearing her throat, said, "We'll see, Gerry. I'm hoping to land something right after graduation."

"That's our Tressa, never sitting still. Well, enjoy the tour. I may miss you on the way out. It's all Mrs. Swithers locking up tonight. Maybe you can stick around later to help for old times' sake," Gerry said with a wink and a smile.

Nervous laughter echoed in the high-ceiling room, and Tressa realized it was her own. At least the sticking around part wouldn't be a lie.

# Chapter Sixteen

The tour is always a captivating experience. Navigating the narrow cells offers visitors a stark glimpse into the suffocating, claustrophobic conditions once endured by prisoners. The peeling paint on the walls reveals decaying layers beneath, and the gray stone creates an atmosphere of profound despair. A peek into the bleak living quarters effectively silences tour groups as they contemplate the extreme loneliness and deprivation the prisoners suffered. A narrow, mail slot-like window allowed only a sliver of light to filter through, serving as a soul-crushing reminder of the outside world. As a tour guide, Tressa never grew tired of witnessing the reactions of both new and returning visitors.

"Imagine accommodations remained the same for over 125 years in these thick, massive walls," Mrs. Swithers said as the group searched for vacant folding chairs.

At this point in the presentation, no matter what the guide discussed, all eyes were on nooses, slowly undulating from the hefty rafters and hanging through the open trap door.

Mauri's slender neck extended upwards, her eyes transfixed as if studying constellations in the sky. "Were people really hanged here? Right here?" she whispered.

"Four famous ones," Tressa responded.

The creaking hinges echoed in the cavernous space as Mauri shifted in her folding chair.

"I'm not sure how well-versed you are in Irish immigrant history, but a secret society existed responsible for vigilante justice on behalf of Irish-American workers," she said, leaning close to

Mauri.

"Oh, believe me. I know all about the Molly Maguires. My Grandma O'Sullivan made sure of it. She still hates that I changed my name," Mauri whispered.

Mrs. Swithers gave her best grandmotherly shushing look, and Tressa immediately straightened against the hard seat back. She knew how annoying chatty groups could be when trying to lead a tour.

They ended the tour where they started, and Tressa mindlessly clicked water-filled souvenir pens while waiting for Mrs. Swithers to escort the last group to the front entrance.

"Well, it's nice seeing you again, Tressa, dear. It's nice meeting you," she said, nodding to Mauri. "Do you need more jail souvenirs?" she laughed while jangling her circular keychain.

Night fell as fast as the temperature, and Tressa was happy she packed an extra sweatshirt and blanket in her provisions. She watched the bouffant profile disappear down the rocky driveway, knowing it meant the jail was now vacant and locked. Sort of.

"Okay, now what?" Mauri asked, peering at the ominous building looming over the parking lot.

"We go back in," Tressa said, digging through her bag. "I hope you brought something warm."

"Yeah, um, and there's this," Mauri said, the light from the screen piercing the darkness. Tressa didn't even look at her phone for an update in the app.

Proof every hour.
Different areas.
Time served ends at 0500.

"Cute," Tressa said. "I guess my idea of taking tons of pictures and sending them from a warmer locale won't cut it. We will be roaming around taking pictures for the next few hours." Tressa stared at the light perched on the guard tower turret just above the entrance, looming like a night watchman, daring entry and exit. Suddenly, an uneasiness crept over her like those imprisoned here must have felt day in and day out. Someone was watching.

Gravel crunching underfoot echoed in the silence as they made their way to the back of the prison. Tressa thought about the attempted escapes over the years and doubted anyone tried to sneak in. Happy to end her shift early, Gerry left in a hurry and thankfully didn't notice that Tressa propped open the emergency entrance. While everyone else focused on stories of prisoner kitchen duty, Tressa shoved a makeshift wedge at the bottom of the door. Now, she felt relief when her fingers plied the edge of the door, and she felt it give. The range of the security system only monitored the front of the property, and Tressa was happy to see the disengaged exit alarm in the same state it was years ago. Ducking inside, Tressa realized while she strived to gain the trust of a new influential society, she needed to violate the trust of old friends. They went through the storage room and settled into the most welcoming place in the building. Mauri already had her beam frantically scanning the hall.

Trying not to have a constant reminder of their hangout for the next five hours, Tressa sat behind the glass case of t-shirts and coffee mugs. The surroundings looked different when illuminated only by the faint red glow of the exit signs. She shielded her eyes from a blinding fluorescent beam.

"Now tell me, after all your tours, did you see any ghosts?" Mauri asked, lowering her industrial flashlight.

"I don't know about seeing them as much as feeling them," she said. Closing up the jail alone was never a coveted aspect of the job. Several high school kids usually worked in tandem during the busy season under the guidance of Mrs. Swithers or Gerry. Always taking a partner to check the lower level was one of the rules. Ghost hunters and paranormal investigators were notorious for trying to stay after hours for their tour. "Just taking a few more pictures" was the response she'd get when stragglers holed up in the recesses of the dirt floor basement. Tressa couldn't shake the feeling that while they were the stragglers tonight, someone would closely watch their every move.

"Creepy," Mauri said, disappearing around the corner.

"Try not to swivel your light around. All we need is someone driving by and wondering why lights are moving around in the jail after hours."

She heard a click, followed by the clip-clop of Mauri's boots, as she headed to the central prison cell area. "Every hour, every room. Let's get our first picture," Mauri said. Gaping openings lined each side of the never-ending corridor, and black metal steps served as the centerpiece of the imposing hallway. Above, cells mirrored their counterparts below, unassuming until visitors entered each deteriorating enclosure of mind-numbing captivity.

Tressa dragged the heavy black gate behind her, slamming it shut, metal grating on metal.

"Yo, why did you do that?" Mauri asked, steadying herself with the wooden hand railing.

"Habit, I guess. Alright, let's get this one done," Tressa said, holding out her phone to document their location.

Wide-eyed stares and flash-lit hair peeked at the bottom of the image while wrought iron rails served as the backdrop for their selfies.

"Done. Only four more to go," Tressa said.

"Can I see it?" Mauri asked, bringing the phone close to her face while zooming in on the photo. "Did you see this? Are those orbs?"

Tressa pulled this from the FAQ file in her brain. "While many visitors capture orb-like objects during the tour, please remember that the building is over 150 years old, and many specks of dust will look like something else when illuminated with a camera flash. If you encounter any spirits or ghosts, please invite them home," she recited from memory in her best tour guide voice. Despite her attempts to explain away unusual images, she couldn't deny many visitors shared stories of similar experiences, such as a frigid blast of air in the same part of the prison, a light shove while ascending the steps from the basement, and orbs with definitive features not passable as only a speck of dust. Even though the recurring phenomenon was interesting, Tressa worried more about entering the dimly lit basement with groups whose pre-tour activities consisted of stops at some of the bars in town.

"Oh, God. You do sound like a legit tour guide. Is it safe up here?" Mauri asked, heading to the second level.

Mauri walked along the narrow catwalk, her steps reverberating like a rain gutter slamming against a house in a windstorm. Rows of cells continued to stretch into dark recesses, holding captive a variety of metal bed frames and crates like wooden tables in various states of deterioration. Years of despair and abandonment poured from each enclosure. A loud bang followed by scampering feet, and Mauri seemed to materialize next to Tressa.

"Okay, that was neat, but maybe we can hang back at the gift shop for a while," Mauri said, breathless. "Hey, wait," she stopped mid-sentence as she struggled with the closed gate keeping her from exiting the prisoner quarters.

"Wondering if it's locked?" Tressa asked, smiling as she whisked open the imposing iron bars.

# Chapter Seventeen

The warden's living quarters seemed like the best place to rest. The faded, peeling walls retained some semblance of everyday life, but Tressa couldn't shake the eerie feeling, given the proximity to the prison cells. She tapped the glass screen, 2:30 a.m. glaring back at her. The wind whistled mournfully through the rafters. In the past, the sound of a radio or television pierced the deafening silence of the old jail when Tressa was the last one to close up for the night, but now she tuned in to every creak, scamper, and groaning echo, amplified by the solitude. Mauri was fast asleep underneath a colorful palette of crocheted yarn draped over her shoulders—an afghan they had found in Mrs. Swithers's stash of things. Tressa was grateful for Mauri's occasional snoring as it interrupted the silence. She still couldn't believe Mauri had dozed off, but Tressa relished the break before their photo documentation continued.

She pulled up the app, looking for further guidance, but only a green checkmark appeared above their uploaded photos, complete with one of their phones displaying the date and time to prove they were still there. Tressa assumed they'd get another piece to add to the virtual puzzle in the app, but so far, they hadn't encountered anything.

She shivered as her palms pushed against the icy concrete, every muscle straining in her feet and neck as she tried to catch a glimpse from the lookout window. Years ago, the warden used it to oversee everything, accessed from his living quarters. Dim light filtered through the skylights, casting a faint glow, revealing narrow passages but little detail.

"Where would I hide something?" Tressa whispered.

"Hide what?" Mauri asked, still robed in a layer of crimson, pumpkin, and saffron yarn.

"A piece of that coin, or whatever it is. It has to be here somewhere, right? Maybe after we complete our stay?" Tressa suggested. She swiped through all the messages they received.

"Well, we didn't check all the cells. What about the one with the hand? The first message did mention a hand," Mauri said.

Tressa pulled up her phone and studied the messages for the hundredth time. She wondered if it could be as easy as it looked.

Congratulations to you all<br>
Learn to reach high, but do not fall.<br>
You'll get a hand on the second.<br>
More to come when we beckon<br>
Test Two

"You're right. What if it meant more than just the date?" Tressa couldn't believe she had missed the double-edged message.

Mauri was a few steps ahead as they headed to cell 17. The famous and unforgettable image brought ghost hunters in droves to the prison. The legend explains how one of the prisoners placed a muddy handprint on his jail cell wall, saying it would forever be etched to prove his innocence before he was led to the gallows. Everyone always wanted to glimpse the ghostly mark, debating whether it was a handprint or an area marred by dirt. Besides the unquestionable outline of a hand, little else existed in the empty cell.

"Reach high," Tressa said, recounting the message. "Mauri, can you run your hand near the ledge by that window?"

Mauri scrunched her face before extending her hand near the

narrow window, which was only inches high but meant to allow natural light into the cell. "Ew. How many years of dirt and dead bugs are up there?" she asked, her hand recoiling from the small window.

"Well, you know it won't be me reaching high, so can you check it, please?" Tressa pleaded. She watched as Mauri, eyes shut, stretched her arm and quickly ran her hand back and forth.

"There's nothing here," Mauri said, shaking her hand and wiping it on her coat. "I thought for sure we'd find something in this cell, though."

Disappointed, they did a sweep of a few other areas of the prison, collecting enough photos as their overnight proof. Knowing there was still one place to investigate, Tressa left her least favorite place for last. Daytime or the wee hours of the night, it didn't matter. The basement represented everything dreadful, cruel, and bone-chilling one would associate with being thrown into archaic solitary confinement. The missing piece of the coin had to be there.

The warm glow from the caged light bulb bathed the landing with a false sense of security before proceeding to the underworld. During this part of the tour, everyone huddled a little closer.

"I was hoping we weren't coming back down here. Seeing it on the guided tour was enough for me," Mauri said, almost cutting off the blood supply to Tressa's arm with her grip.

Shaking away her friend's grasp, Tressa ran her fingers over the cobweb-strewn wall. Wall sconces mimicked torches, adding to the atmosphere so many visitors referred to as the 'dungeon'.

"Imagine coming down here leading haunted tours around Halloween," Tressa said.

"Haunted ghost tours? It seems like you do like that stuff after all," Mauri said, ducking her head as they walked deeper into the damp corridor.

Tressa shrugged. "It wasn't an issue when I was leading the group. I knew what to expect." She failed to mention getting locked in one of the cells for nearly 20 minutes by some unsavory characters hired to work during the Halloween season. That is where her chain of trust with her peers broke down.

The thick stone foundation led to arched openings that revealed a cell with a dirt floor. An iron door secured the cell, and a small opening was used to pass food to prisoners.

"What you see is what you get," Tressa said, jumping back into her tour guide role. "The only things that need to be added are a straw mat and a bucket. Those were the only luxuries in solitary confinement. This form of punishment was used through 1980."

Tressa watched Mauri duck in and out of each opening, her flashlight's beam fiercely scanning the condensation-laden walls. Mrs. Swithers always said how Tressa's low clearance made her perfect for this part of the tour.

"I can't imagine staying in one of these for a few minutes, let alone weeks. 1980? How is that possible?" Mauri's voice echoed from the recess of the last cell. "Alright, nothing here. Let's get a picture and get the hell back upstairs," she said, pausing to catch her breath like she just ran a marathon.

The rust-colored backdrop flanked by flickering sconces could pass as a photo op at one of those Medieval Times dining experiences. The expressions on the girl's faces reflected less enthusiasm and more exhaustion compared to their first proof of location hours ago. Before they ascended the staircase, Tressa looked at the yawning space again to ensure they got everything. There was nothing.

After returning to the warden's quarters, they busied themselves by picking up wrappers and water bottles to destroy all evidence of their overnight visit. Tressa neatly folded Mrs. Swithers's afghan to return to the gift shop.

"So, no ghost, no additional puzzle piece, and no other messages," Mauri said, plopping herself on the corner of the old bed and scrolling through her phone. The old frame creaked, submitted to rust and time.

Tressa struggled to peer into the prison corridor, the unsettling feeling that they were not alone in the prison washing over her again. Her nose crushed against the flaking metal edge of the viewing slot, the smell of rust and dirt filling her nostrils. She stared out at the jail, thinking if the walls could talk, the stories of sadness, hopelessness, and anguish would pour out, not only from the prisoners but also from the victims of the crimes that led to their incarceration. Just as the muscles in her calf felt like they would snap as she rocked on tiptoe, she saw it. Her heart raced as she focused and made out what it was.

"Mauri, come here," she said. "Look through here. Focus on the beams."

"The beams? Okay," Mauri said, stooping to align her gaze with the opening. "What should I be seeing?"

"Look below the beams, right above the trap door," Tressa said.

"Oh yes! I see it. Tressa?" Mauri spun around to find her friend missing and heard the scamper of footsteps echoing beyond.

Tressa's relaxed curls bounced with every step as she bounded to the second level of the prison. Running the last stretch of the catwalk like a gymnast about to launch into a routine, she left the floor as she leaned over the rail.

"Tress, what are you doing?" Mauri yelled, pressing her face against the cold metal of the viewing slot.

"Hold on, I'm not sure I can reach it," she said, her fingers quite a few inches short of grabbing the stark white envelope. She knew Mauri could try, but the excitement surged through her veins, and she insisted on completing the task. Tressa hoisted herself over the rail and teetered on the platform's edge. Once she reached the wooden beam, she steadied herself with the noose that hung from the rafter and jumped to the platform below. Reaching high, Tressa grabbed the white envelope out of the awkward spot. She wondered if their puzzle piece sat on the recreation of the gallows the entire time–or if someone just placed it there.

"Got it," Tressa yelled in a high-pitched voice like a kid in a candy store.

The metallic echo of Tressa's footsteps clattered as she made her way back to Mauri. "Reach high, but do not fall," she said, shaking the envelope in front of her friend. "Something clicked when I saw it—you don't get much higher than that in this place. I knew it had to be what we needed," Tressa said confidently.

"Well, thankfully, you didn't fall. Here, hold it near the phones," Mauri said, fishing the familiar blue stone out of the envelope.

After the first test, they realized the stone piece must hold an RFID chip triggering the app. As Mauri held the small crescent near both phones, they immediately buzzed. The light from the screen reflected off their faces as the second piece of the puzzle filled in. Their second test was completed on the second floor of an old jail. Elation rather than exhaustion now reflected on their faces in their final photo. Tressa's heart still raced, and for a moment, the overwhelming sense of accomplishment made her think she could handle anything thrown their way, and maybe she was a perfect fit for the Summit Society after all. As the excitement and rush subsided, a twinge of fear crept in, wondering if she was prepared for whatever was next. Despite her fears, she knew she couldn't back down now.

"Mauri, can you do one last check to ensure we have everything? And if you wouldn't mind returning Mrs. Swithers's blanket. That would be the first thing she notices," Tressa said.

After making a final sweep to confirm no signs of their overnight stay, they exited the prison through the back door. The gentle click of the lock gave a sense of closure, marking the end of one adventure and the beginning of another. Since the institution went unused for many years, the barbed wire fence served more for aesthetics than security. Fortunately, the barrier around the back of the prison had its extra layer of protection removed years ago. Tressa scaled the barrier like a squirrel scurrying from a predator, vaulted over the top, and waited for Mauri to follow. She watched her friend navigate the tips of her boots in the awkwardly small openings. Her leg swung over the top like a tree limb crashing down, and Mauri clung to the top post as if suspended over a gaping cavern. After landing on the ground with a thud, she adjusted her backpack and looked at the incline before them.

"Are you sure they only check the cameras in the front?" Mauri asked, staring at the back of the prison.

"Just be quiet and follow me," Tressa whispered. She knew there were no cameras to worry about, but echoing voices against the stone could gain the attention of nosey neighbors. The waning moonlight did little to reveal much around them, and Tressa knew if they stayed along the tree line, they would be fine. The swooshing rustle of leaves and cracking twigs were the only sounds as they navigated through the wooded perimeter. Above them, tree branches intertwined like a protective net, keeping a vigilant guard to prevent anyone from leaving the prison or providing shelter for those who sought refuge. The promise of hot coffee pushed the pace, leading them to a small, winding dirt road and directing their escape closer to the side street where they were parked.

Tressa plucked a few traces of their early morning woodsy adventure from her hair and removed a hitchhiking branch from Mauri's backpack.

"Outdoor activities are the norm around here—early morning hikers and cyclists, so it won't be too weird walking in with this," Tressa said, holding up the wide nylon strap from her bag. "But I don't want to be remembered as the girls who walked in at 6 a.m. like they just ran through the woods."

The tinkling bells sounded similar to Tressa's message alert as they walked through the door. Immediately, she was met with a blast of heat, bringing feeling back through her fingers, still needing defrosting despite heavy wool gloves. The heady aroma of pipe tobacco bathed in burnt chocolate smelled precisely like the type of coffee they needed after the long night, not to mention keeping Tressa's eyes open for the ride home. After dressing up the sharp, bitter brew with a splash of flavored creamer, they started their trek back to the car. Like two tourists grabbing an early morning coffee, they strolled through the town like it was a typical fall morning. But there was nothing typical about it.

# Chapter Eighteen

Adjusting back to her everyday routine after the overnight adventure took some effort. When Tressa arrived home, she incessantly refreshed the app, hoping to receive an update or new task. She wanted the momentum to continue, the rush and thrill with each message and clue. As she walked to her bed, she peeled off her layers of clothing, changed into pajamas, and melted into her comforter like butter on toast. However, visions of barbed wire, metal cots, and swinging nooses prevented her from falling asleep. Finding Alex's room empty when she arrived home was a bonus, alleviating the need to provide an imaginary play-by-play of her overnight trip to her mother's house. She could do that later if necessary. Tressa planned on attending her 11 a.m. civics class, but a few more minutes enveloped by her comforter couldn't hurt anything. She tried to unpack the thoughts of where this journey was headed and the ultimate goal. For now, she closed her eyes, satisfied that she ultimately investigated a dungeon, found the missing puzzle piece, and escaped a fortress. It was far better than throwing back drinks at The Loft.

A loud bang woke her from a deep sleep. Tressa bolted out of bed and stood near her bedroom door, trying to listen for more noises from the living room. Shivers ran down her spine when she realized someone was in the apartment. She grabbed a handheld weight from the floor and slowly opened the door. Tressa knew Alex wasn't due back at the apartment until later that night, and Mauri didn't have a key. She noticed a dark shadow lurking near the refrigerator as she entered the kitchen.

"Whoa! Tress! You scared the hell out of me. What are you doing creeping around the kitchen? And what's in your hand?" Alex asked, taking the small dumbbell from her and placing it on the counter.

"What are you doing back already? I thought you wouldn't be home until tonight?" she asked.

Alex looked at her quizzically. "I was going to ask why you were asleep so early. Do you feel okay?"

She looked at her phone and realized she had slept through her classes, and it was nine hours later. "Oh, I, uh, I lost track of time. I must have dozed off, and you startled me. Sorry," she said, trying to give the impression she had only slept for a few minutes.

"Well, I'm glad I didn't get destroyed by that," Alex said, pointing to the hand weight. "Anyway, how is your mom?" he asked, disregarding everything that happened.

"My mom? She's good. I got in early this morning and then went right to class. I needed a rest, but I slept longer than I wanted to. Dealing with the family took a little more out of me."

"What did you do? Help bury bodies while there?" he asked, pointing to the floor.

Tressa was stunned by Alex's question and unsure how to respond. "What?" she asked before noticing the evidence of her hilly trek strewn across the floor in a mud-caked mess. "Oh, I don't know. I must have walked through something on the way back to the apartment."

"You think?" he laughed. "So mom is good. How about Ryan?" Alex asked.

When he entered the apartment, Tressa felt relieved that Alex hadn't asked any more questions about the mud and confusion, nor did she want to discuss anything about Ryan. If she did stop at her house in Summit Peak, it wouldn't be to listen to her step-dad brag about sales numbers. Even though he managed three real estate offices in the area, Tressa loved reminding her mother she married a shady salesman with more than love in his eyes.

"Nothing to report. Everyone is good. Mom sends her love," she replied while rummaging through the refrigerator. "No good leftovers? How old is this? I need something before I head out to Dawson's class," she said, balancing a small pizza box in one hand.

"You can have it. Leftovers from last night," he said. At least she'd have some sustenance before her class tonight. Exhaustion and hunger prevented her from engaging in any more conversations about leftovers, her stepdad, or muddy shoes.

As she headed out of the apartment building, the jarring blast of cold air gave her a reset, and sprinting the last few hundred yards to class was what she needed to bring herself to being somewhat functional. Slinking into a seat near the front, Professor Dawson ignored her late arrival, save for a glance, as she dropped her bag to the floor with a slam. Calming her breathing, she tried running her fingers through her mess of hair and fumbled for a hair tie when he called on her.

"Ms. Litton, what do you make of the conspiracies? They have been studied and contemplated for years, but since you've been exposed to them in the last few weeks, I'm curious about your subjective view."

Tressa couldn't believe her ears. How could he know? Her body felt like it would combust. If she spoke, her trembling voice wouldn't allow her to respond with anything remotely intelligent. Air expanded her lungs as she tried deep breathing to calm herself while she stared at the screen as if the answer would materialize. Out of sympathy or impatience, Professor Dawson moved on.

"Can anyone familiar with *The Madonna with Saint Giovan-*

*nino* tell me about the conspiracy?" he asked.

A voice piped up from a girl at the end of the row. Her hand waved with game-show-winning confidence, a TV-ready smirk to match. Tressa swore the girl stared at her before answering. "Painted in the Early Renaissance, the Madonna is featured with the infant Christ and St. John the Baptist. At first glance, the small spot in the sky above Mary's shoulder looks like a star, but a closer look shows a flying saucer-like object, with a man and his dog staring at the object from below. While some argue it is a shepherd gazing at a star, many insist a deeper meaning exists, giving it the nickname 'Our Lady of the Flying Saucer.'"

"Very good. For centuries, it has been argued that the blurry circle aligns with UFO conspiracy theories, making it a much-visited work at Palazzo Vecchio in Florence."

The muffled footsteps were followed by dimming lights as a picture came into focus, combining the heavenly with the extraterrestrial. Tressa knew the painting inside and out. She chose it as a topic with Professor Dawson's approval. As he continued his lecture, her fence climbing, gallows hopping, and prison-investigating activities caused her energy level to plummet along with her concentration.

Darting out of the auditorium as soon as class ended, she waited for Mauri outside. "Why do you think he brought it up? As soon as I heard the words *conspiracy* and *last few weeks*, I thought he was referring to the Summit Society," Tressa said to Mauri as they walked away. "I know it's stupid, but it's all I'm thinking about."

"I hear you. I felt like all the air was sucked out of the room when Professor Dawson said that, and it looked like you were about to pass out. It's hard not to discuss this with anyone, but we've come this far; we can't blow it now. I must admit, I was dying to let Ms. Know-it-all know that we aren't worried about earning brownie points for correct answers. If they only knew—I would love to flaunt it in their arrogant faces. "

# Chapter Nineteen

As the semester entered the final two months, Tressa sought solace in her work. She threw herself into her studies, spent late hours at the library, and conducted endless research on cults and secret societies. Lines blurred between legitimate and legend, irrefutable and imagined, the supernatural and scientific. One theme remained constant. People loved the idea of mysterious, highly sought-after inclusion for a chosen few. From the Skull and Bones to the Rosicrucians, clandestine meetings and symbols lured those looking for power, social status, or financial gain. Tressa didn't care about any of those benefits. Exclusivity, a sense of belonging, and deep, lifelong bonds of friendship enticed her more than anything.

Alex's busy sports schedule and nights of partying left him struggling as due dates approached. This gave Tressa more time to research without being questioned about her sudden interest in religious and political groups, a topic she always told him she preferred to avoid. It had been over three weeks without communication from the Summit Society, and Tressa was ready for more.

The northeast is known to experience winter-like conditions long before the December solstice makes it official. The white dusting on Wyval's campus teased stormy months ahead, and Tressa wasn't thrilled with the prospect. Anytime she mentioned her hometown, people gushed about her luck and proximity to some of the best ski resorts on the East Coast. She found it lucky when she scored a seat in front of a stone fireplace while her mom and stepdad flashed their downhill skills and their latest designer coats and pricey equipment.

Two alerts sounded on her phone.

The first message preview reminded her to claim her Amazon gift card—a total scam. The second message required Tressa to sit on the bench between Flood Hall and the path to her apartment. She tilted her phone to her chest, covering it like she was protecting answers on a test. She tugged at the oversized woolen mitten with her teeth, geometric patterns converting to magnifying water droplets on glass.

Congratulations on completing Test 2
Nightfall at the break
An overnight stay prepare to take
The devils turn, and a ramp 190 ride
for more instructions, choose a guide

When she arrived back at her apartment, she kicked off her sneakers as a small puddle of melted snow gathered beneath her feet. Tressa curled as deep into the couch cushion as her mind did around the message, but still no contact from Mauri. Tressa tried various combinations to unravel this latest clue until they could connect. Nothing jumped out at her, except it seemed like someone else would be introduced into the game—and the fact the message seemed to reference something a bit darker. During her research, the crazy initiation rituals and juvenile acts of debauchery left her neither surprised nor shocked. Some other depraved displays of allegiance were not just cult-like but occult-associated, flirting with legal and moral boundaries. It was that direction Tressa had no desire to travel, but she wondered if this message would lead down this dark path. She jumped at another phone alert.

*Chime.*

MP: I'm at your door.

Tressa assumed Mauri also got the message.

"So, how does this make sense?" Mauri asked, holding her phone next to Tressa's. More scribbles on crumpled paper covered the table than deciphered messages. It was clear the next adventure would again take place overnight, and they wouldn't be alone this time. Both girls agreed the guide referred to taking someone on the journey.

"Do we pick someone and let them in on the secret?" Mauri asked, gnawing at the pen cap. "I can't imagine we'd get this far and randomly bring someone in. How do we know it's the right person? We could blow this whole thing," she said.

Devil's turn. Devil's turn. Tressa's stomach turned, thinking of blood-soaked rituals and sacrifices. Hooded figures gathered around willing or unwilling participants, all for the sake of belonging. She could bow out. She should bow out.

"Maybe we pick Alex," Mauri said.

"What? Why?" Tressa asked.

"I think he's our perfect guide. You and I don't have a wide-reaching circle of friends, and he seems like the best choice for us both," Mauri said, looking at their scribbled notes.

Tressa knew she was right, but she wasn't sold. She zoomed in on Google Maps, trying to find an exit labeled 190, but nothing looked familiar. She looked at the intersecting circles and their contents. Number lines and scattered letters floated around the diagram like noodles in alphabet soup, but none created cohesive words.

"I think it would have to be within an hour's travel." Mauri asked, "Are there no roads, interstates, or exits labeled as 190 around here?"

Tressa shook her head. "I'm not seeing anything that makes sense. But what else do we have?" she said, tapping her pen. "We agree we are staying overnight, but when?"

Mauri tipped forward in her chair, the legs hitting the floor with a slam. "Nightfall at the break has to be the first day of Thanksgiving break. And I'm telling you, Tress, the guide has to be someone new. I'd say we ask Alex."

"Ask Alex what?" As their guide contender walked through the door, Tressa gathered the papers as calmly as possible.

Mauri lit up like a string of Christmas lights. Tressa wondered what happened to not falling for him or being gullible. She watched his every move as his head disappeared in the refrigerator and turned to the table with three Coronas and an opener.

"Beer before the break, I insist. Is that what you wanted to ask me?" he asked.

Tressa stared at Mauri, hoping to win a few seconds of her attention. If someone posted a picture of her right now on social media, they would not have to use a starry-eyed filter. Tipping back her bottle, the dazzling starbursts framing her head dissolved, replaced with an aura of annoyance. Tressa needed more time to unravel the meaning behind the message, but asking Alex to join their next adventure didn't seem smart. Keeping their journey a secret was not the only reason, as she wasn't sure she could handle Mauri melting like a snowman in a greenhouse whenever Alex looked her way.

"We were talking about hanging out before heading home for the break, and here you are," Tressa said, trying not to sound suspicious.

"Here I am," he said, splashing beer with an exaggerated outstretch of his arm. "One drink with my two favorite people, and I must start packing. I'm leaving tonight. No classes for me tomorrow," he said. After twenty minutes of light banter and detailed holiday plans, Alex finally retreated to his room to start his travel preparations.

"I still think we could have asked him," Mauri hissed, her silver bangles like wind chimes in a storm as she let her hands fall to the table.

Tressa was thankful Alex didn't pry into their discussion, and luck was on their side again, with test number three falling when Alex had other plans. Neither girl had a bevy of friends to keep at bay. The secrecy thing was easy. She still couldn't imagine why Mauri wanted to breach it now.

"Hey, so I'm Googling some of these words to see what comes up. Is this devil's turn a place? There was a bad accident a few weeks ago?" It popped up in a Citizen's Herald article.

Devil's Turn. It wasn't the occult or satanic rituals. Tressa hadn't connected the name and number at first. As Mauri continued with the story of teenagers failing to negotiate the hairpin turn on their way to the mine, the pieces started falling in place like a Plinko game. Chances are the accident happened at night by those unfamiliar with the winding road leading to an attraction reserved for daytime tours only. An overgrown entrance not too far past the tricky turn led to an overlooked tourist attraction that just happened to close around Thanksgiving. There was a ramp, but it wasn't the technical name. Slope 190 took you down 300 feet beneath the surface into a labyrinth of tunnels. Dark, damp, and abandoned. It sounds like a perfect place for test three.

"Do you have anything besides Theology class tomorrow morning?" Tressa asked.

"No, after Theo, I'm done for the break."

"Well, before our next road trip, we need a few things from my house if you don't mind meeting my mother and her pool boy."

Tressa pulled up the website and zoomed in on a photo of a glistening rock supported by wooden beams, leading the eye along a slick path that delved deeper into the labyrinthine depths. She recalled her school tour of the site, an old, abandoned hard coal mine now retired and restored for tourists. This attraction allowed visitors to descend below the earth's surface and experience the harsh conditions coal miners endured decades ago.

"I think we are going to stay overnight in some interesting conditions," Tressa remarked.

"What about the guide?" Mauri asked.

"I'm not sure. We'll find out when we arrive."

# Chapter Twenty

The morning fog hovered over the field, refusing to lift the curtain for a preview of the architectural masterpiece rising behind the trees. Growing up on ten sprawling acres rolling with towering pines as storybook as the cool, shallow stream marking the property line, Tressa never got tired of seeing the wedding cake-like house come into view. The bottom layer formed a beautiful, welcoming base, with stately columns supporting the entrance and a never-ending porch that demanded you sit with a glass of iced tea in the summer. The bricks reflected salmon pink in daylight, the light sea foam trim on overhanging eaves outlining the house while numerous dormer windows peered beneath their sloping cover. The home was built for a railroad magnate and his family, none of whom were Tressa's ancestors. When asked about her connection to the home's storied past, she always wished she had an elaborate story to share.

Material fluttered like passing ghosts in the lower window, and she prepared herself for the show. For as over the top as it would be, Tressa was eager for a little French-pressed coffee and homemade scones.

"You are new blood, so be prepared," she said. "We really can't stay long, but we will have to have a bite to eat before we leave with the gear. She won't let us leave otherwise," Tressa warned.

She watched Mauri walk toward the porch without taking her eyes from two small balconies, each adorned with brightly colored stained glass above the doors. "Cool," she said, with less gushing than Tressa anticipated.

The echo sounded like tap shoes in an auditorium as footsteps moved closer to the front of the house. As the pale, varnished doors swung open, her mother appeared in the usual Deborah style.

"Oh, there's my sweet girl," Tressa's mom said. She pulled her close enough to express her maternal love but left space not to wrinkle her designer silk blouse. "Look at you," she said, each word lacking endearment.

"Hi, Mom. You saw me two months ago," Tressa said, rolling her eyes.

"Well, I feel like I haven't seen you for ages." Tressa felt her mother's eyes inspect her from head to toe, her face scrunching as she reached out to fluff her hair. "Did you have a chance to try the keratin treatment I sent?"

Mauri mercifully cleared her throat, grabbing Deborah's attention.

"Oh, I'm sorry. Tressa mentioned she was stopping by with a friend. Deborah O'Malley," she said, extending a slender hand. An overwhelming wave of musky jasmine swirled around her as she flipped her impossibly straight chestnut hair, spreading it past her shoulders. Her long cream-colored sweater contrasted greatly with her deep indigo ultra-skinny jeans. Her boots added at least three inches, rivaling Mauri's vantage point.

"Nice to meet you, ma'am," Mauri said.

Deborah smiled as she motioned for the girls to head inside. "Oh please, call me Deb. I hope I don't look like a ma'am yet. I only celebrated the big 4-0 last year."

Cue the compliments. At this point, most people commented that she and Tressa looked more like sisters than mother and daughter. Mauri didn't bite, but Tressa saw her concentrating on some quick math in her head, as most did.

"Your hair is so chic," she said to Mauri as they walked toward the study. "You artsy types just always look so trendy. Tressa, maybe you should try a different color."

She noticed her mother had changed the furniture as they entered the study. Two velvet-backed chairs next to the fireplace matched the pistachio green walls, and the ornate wooden armrests nearly matched the moldings around the door. The surface of a small table joining the two chairs in intimacy gleamed with a layer of polish. Mauri raised a darkly outlined brow as Deborah fussed with the breakfast spread on the sideboard. That was the response Tressa expected.

"Now, ladies, I'm unsure if you want breakfast or just coffee, but help yourselves. Coffee is just fine for me," she said, holding a porcelain cup rimmed with a shimmer of gold. Tressa marched over to the selection of scones and muffins and placed a few pastries on the delicate plate. She searched for cream and sugar, remembering the coffee being as strong as it was thick.

"Mom, cream and sugar?" Tressa asked.

After eyeing her plate, followed by a sigh, her mother headed to the kitchen. "Sure, love. More sugar on the way," she yelled over her shoulder.

While most people regarded Tressa's frame as that of a toned and fit gymnast, her mom always pointed out that gymnasts never consumed so much sugar. "I do that on purpose," she said, pointing to the sweets. "I told her that no matter how little I eat, I'll never be as petite and delicate as she would like. But, she makes pretty good scones for growing up as a trust fund baby and graduating to this," Tressa said, crumbs spilling out of her mouth.

"Trust fund baby. Funny," Mauri said, unimpressed.

"Don't get me wrong, I love her to death, but she wasn't

thrilled when I was more interested in spending summers exploring the woods than joining the Junior League. Status and social circles replaced warm and fuzzy in this house."

Mauri awkwardly held the miniature-looking cup in her hand. She was fumbling with the delicate china when she heard the booming voice in the hall. She nearly spit out her coffee when he walked into the room.

"Hi there. I heard we had guests." Her stepdad trotted over to greet them, pulling Tressa into a hug while stopping short of sharing his post-run sweat with Mauri. He matched Deborah in height and hair color but fell short about ten years in the age department. Not to mention, he resembled and acted like any given prince from a Disney movie, but the storyline was about a prince who sold real estate with not nearly enough money to support his princess's lifestyle. Thank God for the trust fund.

"I take it that's not your dad," Mauri whispered as Ryan disappeared into the kitchen.

"No, that's Ryan," she said as they watched the high school-like display of affection between her mom and stepdad. "My dad checked out of this scene long ago, but at least she found someone to deal with her. It took her many tries, but I think she found her match. Plus, he passes the test for fitting in with her friends. My mom considers it vital to impress everyone." Tressa thought back to her childhood and the Christmas parties, peering through swags of pine and velvet red bows from the stairs while her mother floated around the room, worrying more about the breadth of her social circle than her daughter's bedtime.

Ryan poured the remainder of the coffee into his cup, and Tressa wondered if her mom would yell at him about making the new chairs sweat-stained. "So, Mauri Pierce. Where are you from?"

"South Jersey. I live with my Grandmother O'Sullivan," she said, avoiding further uncomfortable conversations.

"O'Sullivan from South Jersey. No relation to the O'Sullivans, the real estate developers?"

Mauri looked at the floor, and her empty cup clattered on her lap. "Uh, well, kind of related, I guess."

Sounding impressed for about ten seconds, Ryan continued to talk about how many houses he had sold in South Jersey, building his portfolio with every word he spoke. "So, early arrival for Thanksgiving? Maddie, will you be spending the holiday with us?" he asked while staring at his smartwatch.

"Mauri. And no, we just had to drop in to get a few things for the apartment. We are making a potluck turkey dinner at the school before everyone leaves," Tressa lied. She could have told him they were coming to remove all the furniture from the house to make a bonfire, and he wouldn't have flinched.

"Right. Well, we'll see you on Thursday. Mauri," he said, pointing his finger in a most embarrassing and cliché way before backing out of the room, obviously not paying attention to a word they said. Tressa recalled addressing Ryan as the money-hungry millennial when asked if she wanted to call him dad. Her mom never asked again.

Before rummaging through shelves of outdoor equipment, Tressa walked into her favorite area of the house—the hallway. She always appreciated the 18th-century Brussels tapestry adorning the walls and the history behind it. However, the cabinets filled with trinkets seemed more like boastful conversation pieces with a high price tag rather than mementos from a world traveler. She couldn't comment much on her mother's preference for displaying status over meaningful souvenirs.

"Wow. These look like they could be originals," Mauri said,

fawning over artwork stoically lining the walls. "I'm guessing you had some say in this."

Tressa smiled, knowing she had a hand in the Sotheby auction, allowing a few originals to hang among the reproductions. Tressa spent much of her youth taking trips with her grandmother rather than staying home. She spent hours wandering around collections of everything from Islamic Art to the work of Rembrandt. She drank in the wonder and mystery galleries and museums offered. Everything had a story to tell, and Tressa loved learning about the storied past behind every oil painting, every sculpture, and every expression of individualism and humanity. Plus, her mother constantly questioned why she liked visiting dusty old places, which increased the attraction.

The garage had no character like the rest of the house, but the organized shelves made it easy to find what they needed. A familiar perfume wafted through the garage as Tressa and Mauri shoved supplies into bags.

"Find everything you need for your dinner?" Deborah asked, arms crossed in the doorway.

"All set. I needed some tablecloths, crockpots, stuff like that." Tressa hoisted the bag over her shoulder too quickly, indicating the lack of cooking devices inside. Her mother glanced at the bag as she headed back into the foyer. Part of her wanted to explain why a tent and sleeping bags were popping out of the backpack, but they had made it this far without talking about their journey. She didn't want to jeopardize it now.

"Well, enjoy your dinner, ladies," Deborah said as the short visit wrapped up. "You know, it's nice they included you. You'll have to bring your new friends around next time. And it was a pleasure meeting you, Mauri."

Tressa backed away from the driveway as a freshly showered

Ryan strolled onto the porch. He wrapped his arms around her mom as Deborah gave her best princess wave. The late morning sun danced off the stained glass windows, making the elaborate home look like a Christmas tree adorned with two shiny, expensive ornaments. The kind of ornaments you think belong on the front of the tree, but a closer look reveals imperfections and cracks, making you want to push them to the background.

# Chapter Twenty-One

To bail them out, Tressa had a story ready in case Mrs. Swithers was privy to their overnight stay, and she planned on using a paranormal excursion or having one last adventure before the real world. Although she hadn't needed to defend the overnight jail plan, it would have been easy to talk her way out of it. She knew it sounded weak, but Mrs. Swithers could never get too upset with Tressa. The same luxury did not apply to Slope 190. The usual descent would find you traveling with a tour guide in a renovated mine car to explore 300 feet below the surface. Former coal miners or their relatives led the tours, but Tressa had no direct connections to this site, which was of great importance to the history and culture of the area. If they were caught entering the historical landmark, trespassing could be the only answer.

"Will we be freezing down there?" Mauri asked, slightly breathless.

"The temperature here is steady year-round, usually in the low 50s." The hulking bag on her back seemed to carry enough supplies to last through an ice age, adding at least 40 lbs to her weight as they trudged up the tree-covered hill toward Slope 190. While the access road led visitors to the adjacent parking lot, Tressa thought it wiser not to announce their visit.

Trying not to attract attention to their alternative route and arrival, Tressa and Mauri moved with calculated steps as if avoiding a minefield. The entrance to the retired mine yawned like a hungry mouth, ready to consume or expel its contents. Her heart pounded against her rib cage, and doubts crept in about their decision not to ask Alex to join them. For Tressa, Miner Town and Coal County Jail were familiar territory, and the layout of both areas never made her feel trapped or cornered. Though Tressa had only been on the Slope 190 tour once or twice, she knew there was only one way in and one way out for those down there. The darkness of the cavernous hole loomed as they drew closer.

"Sweet. I thought you said there were emergency lights the whole way down. I'm not sure about this," Mauri said, peering down the endless tunnel.

Rattling the industrial lock securing the gate to the mine, Tressa commented, "Lights aren't my concern." She couldn't recall much about the tour except for the metal cart at the entrance. At the moment, it seemed absurd to think it would remain open all night. Tressa shone a light on the danger sign attached to the side of the beams, realizing they would be missing test three tonight.

"Did you read this?" Mauri asked.

"I know, I know. I read it," Tressa said while pointing to the warning sign.

*Only enter during attraction hours. Fans will run overnight to release toxic gas build-up. May cause injury or death with after-hours entrance.*

"No, I'm not talking about that," Mauri said, motioning to the stand near the attraction. "I'm thinking now maybe we weren't meant to *bring someone* as a guide. Look."

Her attention was quickly drawn to the wooden box in front of her, which had opened to reveal the words "NEW GUIDES, PLEASE TAKE ONE" inscribed on it. She saw Mauri standing there, holding a pamphlet with a note attached.

"Does it say how we are getting into the mine?" Tressa asked, staring at the brochure.

"I don't think we are going into the mine," Mauri said, holding the small yellow Post-It note.



As they stood at Slope 190, Tressa felt uneasy. The surrounding wooded area made the cavernous hole into the earth, complete with toxic gas, the better option. She shivered when she followed Mauri's gaze into the tangled mess of trees and brush. The only silver lining was not being trapped at the bottom of an old coal mine, but the ominous area before them only seemed like a slight upgrade.

"I guess we're going in," Tressa said as they disappeared into the dark woods. She had been no stranger to exploring the woods in her childhood, navigating the winding paths and steep inclines with ease. But this 7,920-foot trek was different. The territory was unfamiliar, and the sense of control she once had was slipping away. Mauri, on the other hand, was engrossed in her phone screen, the light casting an eerie glow on the trees.

"Are you texting someone?" Tressa hissed.

"No. I checked our location on Mapquest to see what we should do here. We are almost at the 1.5-mile point, and I don't see anything," Mauri said, uttering the first words since they entered the woods. "I'm not going to lie. This situation is not cool," she muttered before stomping ahead.

Adrenaline and familiarity carried Tressa through the first two tests. The thought of becoming part of something money couldn't buy lost its luster as their path became as treacherous as it was dark. "Just take it slow. I don't know this area, and I'm worried about drop-offs and sinkholes," she warned.

"Drop-offs? Sinkholes? Tress, what about the fact we are in the middle of the freaking woods at night, not knowing who or what else is out here? This is really bullshit." Her mouth spewed angry words, but the waver in her voice hinted at something else.

Leaves and twigs crackled with every step as they pushed through the dense forest, the smell of pine needles and earthy soil becoming stronger. The makeshift path they followed required a constant beam of light now as roots and rocks attempted to up-end the hike. Tressa tried not to draw attention to sounds echoing in the distance, but her senses were on high alert. Branches magically appeared with every swipe of light, and she thought it best to focus on one foot at a time. Wind gusts rustled pine branches, ushering in the air as cold as a walk-in freezer. Meanwhile, Mauri once again had her head buried in her phone, oblivious to the surrounding danger. The tech device sounds contrasted with the quiet of the forest, and Tressa was more than a bit annoyed by her aloof attitude.

"Okay, this is 1.5 miles," Mauri said, throwing her hands up. "Now what?"

"I guess we are here until morning. Are you good with this?" Tressa asked, looking for the flattest ground for the tent.

"I just walked through this horror movie with you, correct? Right now, in the theater, people are telling us, 'Go back, idiots!'" Mauri said half-jokingly.

Instead of responding, Tressa unfolded the tent from her bag, struggling to pierce the ground with the stakes.

"Do you need help?" Mauri huffed after not getting a response to her rant.

"I think I got it," Tressa said as she briefly fumbled with the poles. She felt the temperature drop every minute and knew she needed to work quickly. Her tent setup skills resulted from the many adventures of camping in her backyard, which led to quick assembly. Once satisfied with her work, Tressa threw the bags through the opening. Having shelter from the wind allowed her body to regain some warmth immediately. As she unrolled the warm, heavy sleeping bags, she appreciated her mother's preference for buying the best of everything. The base of the tent crinkled as she smoothed everything into place.

"You are quite the camping connoisseur," Mauri said, not trying to disguise any hints of sarcasm as she crawled into their angular accommodations.

"Not really," Tressa said as she popped open a small lantern. "I thought we would explore underground tonight, so I came prepared," she said, tapping the LED light. "Oh, and here, take what you want. I brought snacks."

Mauri zipped the flap behind her, leaning forward to peer into the plastic grocery bag. "Pretzels, chocolate, Gatorade, nice. I'll pass on drinks unless you have a bottle of wine stashed there."

Tressa had toyed with the idea but thought it best to be fully alert for the last leg of their tour. As the wind rippled their thin nylon enclosure, she reconsidered her decision.

Tressa wriggled her way into the cocoon-like bag, every movement circulating the scent of mustiness and earth. The pumpkin orange tent reflected a warm glow, and she tried to imagine they were only a few feet from her house.

"I guess we will stay here until the sun comes up. I can't say I plan on sleeping," Mauri said, rolling onto her side with the sleeping bag grazing the tip of her nose. "Although falling asleep until it's all over would pass the time."

"Until what's all over?" Tressa asked.

"This. The night. I mean, whatever this last test is," she stammered.

Tressa didn't know what else to expect, but she did know that her calves burned from hours of hiking, climbing, and navigating trails. As she fished the last pretzel stick from the bag, she heard

Mauri sniffling.

"Tressa, thanks," Mauri said, her voice choking up.

"For what? I ate the last pretzel," Tressa joked.

"No, all of this—for you sticking with me. I don't have siblings, and if you didn't notice, I don't have the easiest time making new friends. I'm just the tall girl who should still be in high school. You, Alex, and even Professor Dawson gave me something to look forward to every day. I guess it's the fact of just being noticed."

Tressa's gaze was glued to the faint gleam in the middle of the tent floor. She couldn't tell if it was the glaring LED light reflecting off the surface or if there was another reason for Mauri's eyes to appear glossy.

"Well, I'm happy we are doing this together. I would never have been able to get out of that basement if I was paired up with someone short," Tressa said, trying to lighten the mood.

Mauri rolled her eyes and nodded toward the snacks. "Ha ha, funny. Let me see that bag," she said, trying to pick up the Gatorade bottle with gloved hands.

The two girls shared conversations about cliques they hated in school and the trials and tribulations of height discrepancies in gym class.

"And I told them I didn't care about being in student council anyway. Tress? Are you listening to me?" Mauri asked.

"What? Yeah, I'm sorry. Did you hear that?" Tressa paused, hoping and not hoping to hear that sound again. A shriek echoed in the distance, but this time it seemed closer. "That. Doesn't it sound like a person?"

Mauri stared at the sleeping bag, concentrating on the noise. "I don't know. It sounds like an animal to me."

Tressa thought about the backyard sounds she enjoyed growing up and those that always made her nervous. This sound was different, more haunting. She couldn't shake the feeling that something was out there, watching them. As much as she knew there was a simple explanation, she couldn't wait for daylight.

# Chapter Twenty-Two

Tressa awoke with a start, feeling a coarse and cold pressure against her face. Her feet wouldn't move, and her arms seemed stuck. Panic washed over her as she realized she wasn't in her apartment. The lantern was off, and the darkness enveloped Tressa, making it difficult for her to see anything. She must have dozed off, her head sliding from the warmth and safety of her flannel bag, pushed against the unforgiving rocky floor. She searched around but couldn't locate her flashlight. She realized the light wasn't the only thing missing. Mauri was gone.

An empty bottle rolled to the side, and cold air poured around her as Tressa kicked her way out of the sleeping bag and reached for the lantern. Her hands shook as light spilled on the open sleeping bag, but Mauri was nowhere to be seen. Tressa located her phone and texted Mauri. She dropped it when she heard the sound, a familiar chime muffled underneath thick flannel.

She poked her head through the small unzipped opening of the tent, like a cautious rabbit peering out of its burrow, carefully scanning the surroundings for any signs of danger. "Mauri?" her voice cracking as she whispered into the night air. "Mauri?" she asked again, but still no answer. Tressa looked up at the towering pine trees as if they could help her locate her friend. With a swoosh of the zipper, Tressa leaned forward, balancing on one knee. Her phone's slight halo of light did little to illuminate her surroundings. She couldn't recall the darkness being so oppressive as they entered the forest, but the excitement, camaraderie, and intense beams of light likely diminished most of the fear. Crawling back into the tent, Tressa pressed her elbows into her side; if she pulled her knees closer to her chest, they would become one with her rib cage. She turned on the small lantern, a starburst of light bouncing off the tent's interior. If Mauri went into the woods for a bathroom trip, why wouldn't she take her phone or lantern?

Tressa took stock of the situation and knew her options were limited. What if, in some crazy way, this was supposed to happen? Could Mauri be part of this? Was it up to Tressa to figure this out? She could call someone, but who? And explain what? Here she was, the star in her own movie, not unlike the one she had watched a few nights ago. Without further thought, she bounded out into the cold. She stooped down to zip the tent and nearly banged into Mauri.

"Oh my God, Mauri. Where the hell were you?" Tressa's heart beat furiously, and she couldn't catch her breath. "If you were going to the bathroom, you should have told me. And you left your phone?"

"Tress, I'm sorry. You were asleep, and I only ran out for a second. I had no idea I had left my phone. Come on, it's freezing. Let's go back into the tent. We only have a few hours left," Mauri said.

As they settled into the warmth of the sleeping bags, Tressa knew she couldn't go back to sleep. She checked the app, but there were no updates. The wind howled, and the light from the lantern danced inside the tent. In the distance, she heard something moving through the woods. Morning couldn't come quick enough.

Mauri leaned back on her arm, staring at the tent's ceiling, when she suddenly bolted upright. "Did you hear that?" she asked, her voice panicked.

Tressa froze, only the sound of labored breathing surrounding them until she heard it.

"It sounds like it's getting closer, listen," Mauri said. The unmistakable sound of footsteps on trampled twigs and crushed leaves grew faster and louder, coming their way.

"Someone or something is coming," Tressa whispered. Her mind raced with thoughts of everything from a bear scouting out their bag of snacks to the idea of the light of their tent drawing the attention of someone wanting more than Doritos and pretzels. She tucked her phone and flashlight in her pocket and fished in her bag for a small pocket knife. Her mouth was dry, and she saw fear mirrored in Mauri's face. She clicked off the lantern, debating on tearing out of the tent and making a run for it or waiting for the noise to go away. Instead, it grew closer but much more deliberate.

"What kind of animals live out here?" Mauri nervously whispered.

Tressa and Mauri huddled together, planning their next steps, when they heard familiar words.

"Tressa Litton. Mauri Pierce. Please exit the tent," a calm but authoritative voice called out.

Tressa, closest to the entrance, placed her shaking hand on the zipper. She looked at Mauri, who urgently shook her arm towards the front of the tent. They had few options. As Tressa crawled outside, she slowly stood up, followed by Mauri. In front of them stood four figures dressed in all black. They had hooded balaclava masks covering their faces, including their eyes. The same even-toned voice called out again, but Tressa couldn't determine if it was male or female since it sounded distorted.

"Congratulations to you both. By completing the first two tests, you have demonstrated your commitment to proving your loyalty and worthiness to becoming members of one of the most exclusive secret societies in recent years. Our organization takes pride in achieving social and economic prosperity while upholding values, ideals, and secrecy at any cost."

An awkward silence followed the recited speech; Tressa and Mauri remained frozen. Tressa shifted her weight to one foot, keeping her hand near her phone. Her fear and unease slowly gave way to a twinge of disappointment. It felt like planning a vacation for so long that you missed the excitement of anticipation when the day finally arrived. Until now, she wasn't sure what to expect on her journey, but the unfolding scene before her appeared somewhat cliché.

"The final test will not only show your resolve and dedication but also prove your total commitment to the society's goals and secrecy," the mechanical voice continued.

Tressa studied all four people, and to her surprise, one of the masked individuals seemed to be whimpering or sobbing. She watched as the person, complete with a total blackout mask, fidgeted with the bottom of their hood, but something didn't seem right.

Suddenly, a quiet female voice muttered from under the dark hood, "I'm not going to do it. I've changed my mind."

Mauri looked at Tressa, her face confused, as one of the other people forcefully grabbed the outspoken person's arm and whispered something behind their head. After a pause, the girl nodded and folded her hands in front of her.

The wind howled through the trees, and the biting cold made Tressa wish she could drape herself in the sleeping bag.

"The app will now provide instructions for the last part of the initiation. This will prove your willingness to do all that's asked of you," the robotic-like voice instructed.

Mauri and Tressa simultaneously pulled out their phones, waiting for the gray screen to give them directions. Tressa noticed one group member stepping back and holding a phone, the tiny red bar indicating they were being recorded.

"It's just a button that says PROCEED. What happens next?" Mauri asked, staring at the phone. Complete silence followed, except for the sound of a few sniffles.

"You both must accept to continue the journey," the voice murmured.

For years, secret societies were said to have bizarre rituals and rites of initiation to prove your loyalty and commitment, and this test seemed no different for the Summit Society. Tressa wished the conditions were a bit warmer and more upscale, but she thought of everything they'd been through. Enduring fraternity-style nonsense for one night would be a small price to pay to be part of something so significant. She looked at Mauri, who seemed to mirror her sentiment, and they both nodded. PROCEED.

The scream was immediate and blood-curdling, and the fully hooded figure crumbled to her knees. She was lifted and held between two of the larger individuals, her sobbing becoming louder.

"Oh my God. Wait, what just happened?" Mauri cried.

The person with the disguised voice slowly walked over to the sobbing girl and lifted the edge of the hood to reveal two glowing lights. Tressa thought she was seeing things, but it looked like she had on some kind of collar—almost something a large dog would wear.

"Our society considers trust and secrecy above all else," the person said, their voice low and ominous. "As the popularity of our organization has grown over the years, we've realized that we need a more stringent way of weeding out those who could be a liability. We only want those who are fully committed," the masked figure stated.

Tressa held her phone in a trembling hand, her eyes locked on Mauri's terror-filled gaze. She felt her stomach churn with anxiety as she struggled to process the situation. The silence around them was deafening, broken only by the rustling of a nearby bush. Tressa felt the tension in the air, her heart pounding as she concentrated on the disturbing words.

The robotic voice continued to speak, its cold, emotionless tone sending shivers down Tressa's spine. "Mauri and Tressa. By clicking proceed, you are giving our esteemed member a chance to prove her loyalty, sacrificing for the good of the society. And you, in turn, will be elevated from initiates to members—lifelong members with lifetime opportunities. Clicking PROCEED will deliver an electric shock to the altered collar our member is wearing. You will both need to PROCEED to complete the task. Continuing with this task will prove the ability to follow directions and allow a fellow member to achieve her goals."

Tressa and Mauri stared at their phones while standing frozen in place as if their devices could detonate at any second. The app's background was the familiar image of a tall, majestic mountain, its snowy peak contrasting greatly with the mournful gray sky behind it. Tressa's eyes flicked toward the hooded figure, recording their every move, her fear and confusion mounting. This wasn't what she expected.

"You'll notice the mountain and the summit," he said, acknowledging Tressa and Mauri's eyes glued to the app. "It exudes a sense of adventure and commitment to achieving new heights."

Tressa focused on the PROCEED button in disbelief. "We did not sign up for this. The first two tests, I mean, it was an adventure, a thrill, but this," she said, motioning to the girl, still being supported by the two other members. "Hurting someone? I wasn't aware that that's what this society stood for. How does that make it upscale and elite?" she said, her voice quivering.

"It's not about inflicting pain. It's about members proving

their willingness to follow any instruction and hold secrets for the betterment of the society," the masked figure said. "You've come this far. What would the public think if a video surfaced of two college seniors rebelling because they didn't get chosen for a secret society, and they tried to bolster their notoriety by trespassing, breaking and entering, and ultimately, physical assault? There could be some serious charges there. Such a shame to happen when you've already come so far."

Mauri turned her head and stared at Tressa. Her eyes reflected the same thought—they must be bluffing. But the sickly expression on Mauri's face also reflected something else. What if they weren't? What if they edited a video montage, taking everything out of context? Tressa's research into secret societies uncovered groups that pushed the physical endurance of initiates and subjected them to psychological mind games. But this seemed different. This was crossing a line.

"Are you prepared to untangle a story that could potentially damage your future, or are you ready to take the final step and elevate yourself to a level that will unlock doors to a new life?" the voice bellowed, a mix of urgency and impatience.

Tressa watched as Mauri moved her hand. She wasn't sure if her friend intended to click PROCEED, but she knew she couldn't do it. As the question seemed to hang heavy in the air, Tressa jumped back as the sobbing girl broke free from the grip of the others. She yelled something about getting out and stumbled aimlessly into the inky blackness of the forest. Only seconds passed when Tressa heard it.

A cry followed by a sickening thud reverberating in the silence of the night. Tension crackled in the air as everyone stood frozen, their apprehension palpable in the oppressive stillness before escalating to chaos and confusion. The three masked individuals rushed toward the scream's source, with Tressa and Mauri following quickly behind.

The underbrush formed a web of rope-like growth, causing Tressa to focus on her footwork to prevent falling. She scampered over a fallen tree and saw the masked figures huddled around something. Hushed whispers and arguing voices quieted once Mauri and Tressa grew closer. Without further discussion, two people hoisted a motionless body from the ground and navigated the overgrown terrain as they quickly walked away from the group.

"Wait!" Tressa yelled. Is she okay?" Tressa caught a quick glimpse of the girl, hood removed, her blonde hair streaked by a crimson stream. The glowing lights that looked to be hovering around the petite girl's neck illuminated the blood running down the side of her face. Her limp arms drooped near the ground as she was carried, her pale hands and wrists peeking from her sleeves. The swing of a blonde ponytail, the contrast of blood on alabaster skin, and a small peace sign tattoo on the girl's wrist emblazoned in Tressa's mind as the trio disappeared into the woods with the unresponsive body.

Mauri moved close to Tressa, gripping her arm. "She didn't look okay. Did you see the blood on her head?" Mauri said, her voice cracking.

A voice came up from behind them, interrupting their conversation and concern. "She'll have a pretty good headache tomorrow and a nasty bump, but she'll be okay. It wasn't a good idea to run on this uneven terrain. I told our fellow society members to take her to the car and see if she wants to see a doctor." The person turned and walked away, leaving Tressa and Mauri stunned and unsure of what to do next. It was as if they didn't spend their night in the woods, activating shock collars and pledging allegiance to some arcane society.

"What are we supposed to do?" Mauri yelled at the hooded figure.

Slowly, the person turned, pausing before replying. "Get your stuff and go home. Your test for the night has ended. We will be in touch."

# Chapter Twenty-Three

Tree branches batted Tressa's face as she darted back to the tent. She shielded her eyes with her forearm while her feet navigated twisted roots and stubborn brush. Straight forward, don't stray from the path. She heard a tear while disconnecting herself from the grips of a thorny twig. The peace tattoo on the pale hand burned in her mind. It was late November, but it could have been the middle of summer with her face on fire and hair drenched. It all happened so fast. She could hear Mauri's footsteps not far behind.

"Tress, stop!" Mauri yelled. "Why are you in such a rush?"

Tressa stopped, only feet away from re-entering the tent. "Why am I in a rush? Um, we just activated some kind of torture device, which in turn caused that girl to freak out, run, and apparently crack her head open. We don't even know if she's alive. So, quite frankly, I want to pack everything up and get home. We need to call the police."

"Whoa, whoa. I'm not sure we need to do that. We have to assess the situation here. Think about the first two tests. Would this organization have us scrambling around like we were in a scavenger hunt but then switch gears and hurt someone? I think it's all part of the test. To see how we will react." Mauri ducked into the tent, slowly folding sleeping bags and gathering her bags. "We aren't supposed to discuss anything about the society, so calling the police won't be helpful," Mauri said with a bizarre calmness.

Tressa tore into the tent, haphazardly shoving the remaining items into a backpack. She didn't have a chance to think it through, but she thought about the girl's scream, her frantic escape, and rivulets of blood pouring down her face. It sure seemed real. It seemed all too real. She grabbed her phone, ignored the app, and tried to make a call, but there was no service.

"We can't call the cops," Mauri said outside the tent, arms crossed, bags at her side.

"I know, there's no signal," Tressa said, pivoting as she held her phone high above her head.

"No, I mean, even if there was a signal, we shouldn't have a knee-jerk reaction," Mauri said, grabbing Tressa's hand.

Tressa quickly pulled back her phone and tucked it in her pocket. "Right, says the person, ready to hit the PROCEED button without a second thought. I'm done, Mauri. This is not something I want to be part of."

Tressa and Mauri grabbed their belongings and made the trek out of the woods. The air was heavy with the scent of damp earth and pine, the crunch of their footsteps trampling dead leaves and fallen twigs the only sound between them.

Mauri finally broke the awkward silence. "You know they were recording us the entire time, and I'm sure that's not the only footage they have. Think about it. If the Summit Society is as influential as they say, they could ruin our lives. Why would anyone believe us? And the girl? I think she'll be okay. They were rushing to get her out of the woods," Mauri said, trying to sound rational.

"Sure they were. They needed to cover up the evidence—fast," Tressa said, continuing her pace.

Birds alerted the arrival of predawn, and ghostly gray light settled around them, exposing the perimeter of the wooded area hidden earlier by the guise of night. She tried to wrap her head around the last few hours and imagine what she could say to the police. As they reached the clearing, Tressa knew the car was just a short distance from the tree line ahead. She stopped to look down at her phone and noticed it had one bar. She hesitated, unsure what to do next.

"Tress. I promise you, I'll be the first one to call if something still seems off in the morning. Let's try to get to the bottom of this and see if anyone from the society contacts us. Maybe they'll let us know everyone is okay, whether it was part of the plan or not. And then we'll go from there. We saw them carry her out of the woods, and it was an accident," Mauri said. "And honestly, we don't know who is involved or how far this organization reaches."

"What do you mean 'who is involved'?" Tressa asked. "As if the police could be in on something like this?"

Mauri shrugged and continued to walk. She paused, staring at something on the ground before spinning to face Tressa. "Let's just hold off until we find out more."

Tressa wasn't sure what to think, but she feared what could happen if she held off. Predawn shifted from the color of gray molten lead to delicate silver. They reached the SUV, and Tressa tossed the bag onto the back seat. Standing next to the driver's side door, she saw the white envelope tucked under the white blade, the blood-red seal pressed firmly against the glass.

# Chapter Twenty-Four

The Land Rover bumped along, announcing each cavernous pot-hole with a clunk and body-jarring jolt. Tressa's fingers hovered near the vent, the low buzz of the blower sending inviting currents of warmth along her arm. The smell of dirt and sweat filled the car, reminding her of Alex after a soccer game.

"Can you reread it?" Tressa asked, her heart racing with anticipation.

The engine whirred as they climbed the steep mountain. Mauri carefully placed the third stone piece in the cup holder. It was the final element, activating the app to give them direction. Mauri focused on her phone, again reading the message on the app.

Congratulations
You have successfully completed three tests
Your presence is requested
44 Lakeshore Drive,
Lakeshore Estates
Wednesday 6 p.m.
Secrecy still paramount

Mauri closed her eyes, letting her hands fall to her lap. She tapped her head against the headrest as if the motion would clear her thoughts.

"I told you. It was all part of it—the screams, making us believe we could administer an electric shock to someone with our phones. Come on. They tested us to see what we would do. We stayed all night. We didn't call the cops. We did it," she said, giving Tressa a cautious smile.

"We activated a system with the idea that it would administer a high-voltage shock around someone's neck," Tressa said, still in disbelief that those words could be uttered in this context. The thought of it made her skin crawl.

"Oh, Tressa. We didn't know that would happen," Mauri said as if the idea of torturing someone was no big deal.

"It looked like you were ready to hit it again," Tressa said, the thought of her friend staring at her phone, finger hovering over the button. The roar of the heater was the only sound in the car, but the silence was deafening.

"I think we owe it to ourselves to show up tomorrow," Mauri said.

"I'm sorry, but I can't get the picture out of my head. I don't know what this society considers fun, but seeing something like that has ruined the mystique of the Summit Society."

"Okay, hear me out," Mauri said, her voice determined. "I'll admit I was shaken up by the situation, but think about everything you know about secret societies. This stunt is mild compared to some of the stories I've heard—like pledges stuffed in coffins, parading on campus naked, and eating things I don't want to discuss. We signed up for a secret society, not a book club. It's about pushing ourselves beyond our limits, testing our commitment and willingness to overcome fear. We can't back down now. We need to see this through together," Mauri pleaded.

Tressa's fingers slowly regained feeling as she loosened her grip around the steering wheel. The morning had brought a different view, along with feelings of confusion and relief. The gray area in between was filled with truth supporting Mauri's statements. Despite all the ordeals, Tressa didn't want to let her down. Suddenly, her buzzing phone jolted her back to reality, and she glanced at it, resting on the seat. She must have hit send earlier when she contemplated calling for help.

A voice on the phone asked, "We've been trying to get in touch. A call has been made using this device. What's your emergency?"

Tressa's mouth wouldn't move, but she knew she needed to answer.

"Hello? Are you okay? Is someone preventing you from talking?" the operator asked.

"No, I'm here," Tressa said after what seemed like an hour. "I'm sorry. I thought I saw an injured person. It turned out to be a deer. I should have called back."

"Thank you, ma'am. Is the struggling animal still in sight? We can send a trooper or game commission to check it out," the concerned voice replied, the clicking sound of a keyboard in the background.

"No, thank you. It's gone. It must have been stunned and not injured as badly as I thought. Thank you for following up," Tressa said, her voice only slightly louder than a whisper.

Her phone banged against the cup holder as she tossed it aside. "I hope you're right, Mauri. But I'm telling you that if anything seems off with this meeting and we can't sort out the details about the girl in the woods, I'm calling the police," Tressa said.

Mauri agreed, and Tressa's wall of fear and doubt started to crumble, replaced with curiosity.

"So we still have to go to Lakeshore Estates," Tressa said, shifting the subject.

"Is it far?" Mauri asked. "I hope we can turn the trip around in an afternoon. I promised my grandmother I'd show up for Thanksgiving."

Tressa explained why the once-booming resort area was vacant. "Oh, it's not far at all. But everyone moved out years ago due to high radon levels, so it's abandoned."

"It's the perfect, secretive location, then. Do you think it's safe now?" Mauri asked.

Tressa recalled the sprawling 50's style ranches and two-story A-frames around Lake Hudson. Everyone abandoned the vacation homes quickly, and few looters dared enter due to the toxic air. Rumors circulated that radon never escalated to unsafe levels, but an investment firm ran with it when they planned on razing the structures for modern vacation townhome rentals. Financing fell through, and so did the plans for the new community and the hopes of salvaging the old.

"I need to be home for Thanksgiving, too. My mom already talked about the new dinnerware and stemware. I can't miss that," Tressa said with a laugh, trying to change the tone of the conversation.

Mauri slumped against the window, her breath fogging the glass as she succumbed to the physical and mental challenges of the past twenty-four hours. Tressa still had several miles until she could do that. For now, she turned the heat down and the music up and tried to erase the image of the limp body being carried out of the woods.

# Chapter Twenty-Five

Tressa let the water cascade over her face, the near-scalding stream attempting to chase the chill buried in her bones and soothe her senses. She blindly reached for body wash on the shelf without straying from the hypnotic spray. Dumping a small amount of suds onto her loofah, Tressa immediately thought of Alex. She must have mistakenly grabbed the dark glass bottle instead of her usual floral soap, but smelling pine and spice right now was comforting. The thought of removing herself from the warmth of the shower made her shiver, but she knew the importance of sleep before heading to Lakeshore Estates. Like ripping off a Band-Aid, she stepped out of the shower and frantically grabbed a towel. Sunlight filtered through her window, etching a small rectangle on the well-worn floor.

Sleep. No more tests, road trips, or adventures could occur without sleep. The sandwich she picked up at the deli on the way home barely satisfied her appetite, but it would have to hold her over. Lakeshore sat nearly fifteen miles from campus, so she set her alarm for 5 p.m. to have enough time to get ready. After checking her messages, Tressa was surprised that she had missed Alex's call. She had no energy or willpower to talk to him but would love a sounding board. It killed her not being able to share the events of the last twenty-four hours, but they'd come this far without sharing information, so she struggled with a response.

**T: Hey, saw you called. Busy getting last-minute things together to head to my mom's. See you after the break.**

**Heart emoji. Erase heart emoji. Heart emoji. Send.**

As Tressa collapsed on her bed, her eyelids struggled to stay open. Just then, she heard the chime of her phone. It was Alex, and his prompt response surprised her. He was usually terrible at returning messages.

**A: Give Mom a big hug from her favorite. Have a great turkey day. Talk soon. Upside-down smiley face, no heart emoji.**

The phone hit her chest with a thud before bouncing to the floor. It could have shattered into a million pieces, the floor could have opened up to a floor of lava, or Alex could have been standing next to her bed. She didn't care. Her head sunk deeper into the feather-filled pillow, and her body melded into the mattress topper. She had never welcomed sleep as much as she did now.

As she started to doze, visions of the blonde girl, the blood, and the tattoo swirled in front of her.

Tressa gasped and jolted to a sitting position, her room cloaked in darkness, the rectangle of light gone. She remembered her phone falling to the ground and sighed when she found it intact. 5:15 p.m. She fell asleep so quickly that she never set her alarm. Tressa wiped the nape of her neck, damp with sweat, Alex's woodsy scent lifting in the air since she used his soap. The egg chair slowly swiveled on its perch, late-day shadows danced on the walls, and her stomach churned from lack of food and uneasiness. The rapping at the door jolted her out of bed.

"Hey, are you okay?" Mauri said, standing in the door frame. She looked like she had gotten a complete makeover since the morning.

"Overslept, I guess. I showered before, but give me a few minutes to pull myself together," she said, running her hand through her tangled tresses.

"Okay, you know how far it is to the house, so I'm leaving that up to you. Is Alex here?" Mauri asked, scanning the room.

"He's home for the break," Tressa said while shrugging into a sweater.

"Oh, I guess the apartment just smells like him," she said, slightly disappointed. "Once this is all over, I think we should tell him. He'll never believe what we went through. I think about how I cowered walking through the haunted house last month. Look how far I've come!" Mauri rambled before turning her attention to Tressa's dresser. "Oh yeah, we should probably take this, right?" Mauri asked.

Tressa stared at the now complete medallion. Not only did three stone pieces activate the Summit Society app, but they also snugly fit together, making a virtually seamless circle, complete with the lightly carved outline of a mountain peak. Tressa was unsure if they needed it any longer, but throwing it in her bag wouldn't hurt.

"Good idea," Tressa said, ignoring the comments about revealing anything to Alex. She gave herself another look in the mirror and added a quick swipe of mascara and lip gloss.

"Ready?" Mauri asked, inhaling all the air from the room. The blend of colored strands still framed her face, but something was different. The waves fell a little softer, the lines of her makeup a little less harsh. She wore a stylish loose-knit black sweater and a pair of ripped jeans, trendy but basic. Black flats replaced her usual chunky boots, but they also replaced something else.

"Ready. Let's go," Tressa said, followed by a huge exhale. She tried to mentally prepare for whatever lay ahead and knew this could be one of the most pivotal encounters of her life.

# Chapter Twenty-Six

"Do we have to stop at the check-in?" Mauri asked.

Tressa slowed the Land Rover, rolling near the small toll booth structure. Many summers ago, the lake community tried to limit swimming and fishing for summer residents. Tressa recalled how sweet talking and a few dollars worked for most people trying to score a spot next to the sparkling man-made lake. Years of non-returning vacationers and most homes abandoned due to the supposed radon scare meant they might be the only visitors to Lakeshore Estates, save for those they planned on meeting in the first place. Not to mention, it was almost Thanksgiving.

"No, we are fine," Tressa said as she drove by, noticing the deteriorating russet-colored shingles dangling from the shed with some littering the ground. The rotting pieces snapped like twigs as the tires rolled forward, tumbling behind them as Tressa accelerated.

Compact cottages, woodsy A-frames, and sprawling ranch homes made up the eclectic mix of Dirty Dancing meets the Brady Bunch structures dotted throughout the woodsy community. Their overgrown driveways spilled forward to meet the windy road bordering the water. Simple docks with an occasional dilapidated boathouse marked property waterfront privileges. Still, Tressa noticed more sagging awnings and rusty private property signs than inviting porches with welcoming swings and other signs of laid-back lake life she remembered.

The outline of missing numbers was barely recognizable on the worn wood of the mailbox. Tressa turned onto the narrow gravel opening, hoping rocks wouldn't nick the paint as she accelerated under the canopy of trees while some limbs reached down to meet the roof of the Rover as they made their way deeper into the woods.

A house came into view, and it could have been a model home for every 1970s ranch ever built. The exterior couldn't decide if it wanted to be red brick, wood panel, or white siding. As all three mediums poured across the front of the structure, it ended with two gaping picture windows staring out into the tangled woods like barren eyes. Surrounded by green-streaked ashen aluminum, it looked more like an afterthought addition than a continuation of the home. Stark white iron posts weaved an intricate pattern of ivy and leaves while supporting the overhang above the front door. Tressa could picture the overgrown bushes once manicured into clean lines, ushering guests along the path to the entrance. Now, haphazard shrubs randomly poked through missing bricks of the elaborate wall, serving as the base for the climbing vines of wrought iron.

"Should we try the door? I guess the welcoming committee isn't coming out to meet us," Mauri said as they approached. Murky amber glass flanked each side of the entrance, making it difficult to determine what lay beyond.

Tressa stared at the corroded door flaking with paint. Standing there, she knew that stepping across the threshold could change her life, but she needed some direction before moving. Mauri's long fingers gripped her arm, and the traces of black nail polish still clung to her cuticles.

"We've come this far, Tress," she whispered. "We have to see what is on the other side. We owe it to ourselves." Mauri's hand fell to her side as she stepped back, waiting for Tressa to make a move.

Reaching up for the small tarnished door knocker, Tressa noticed something. She wasn't sure if the fluttering in her stomach resulted from having the option of stepping forward or the fact she considered stepping back. A thin sliver of light extended along the length of the door.

"I think it's open," Tressa said, her hand on the door frame. "If I knock, it will swing open," she said, her hand hovering near the door.

"I guess someone is expecting us," Mauri said, leaning forward. "Hello," she called, walking past Tressa and taking one of the most significant steps of her life.

The space provided an instant burst of warmth, a relief from the frigid time spent on the front landing. A short stroll through the burnt orange and deep oak-paneled foyer led to a kitchen adopting the same color scheme. The cramped space was loaded with builder-grade cabinets the color of congealed maple syrup, complemented by a popcorn ceiling reminiscent of actual kernels soaked in too much oil. The Formica counter mirrored the washed-out yellow of the ceiling but with flecks of sparkle. Although a throwback to the 1970s, everything stood as clean as it was dated. The self-guided tour continued to what must have been the home's focal point. Stepping past the spindled peninsula counter, it opened into a central living area. It was unfortunate the grand, arching windows looked out on a woodsy view, compared to other homes with a view of the lake.

"And what is the purpose of this, exactly?" Mauri asked, stepping down into the living room with decorative metal railings lining the perimeter.

"Have you taken Art Deco and Design yet? It was a fun class," Tressa said, walking around the retro space. "I don't know anyone with this setup, but sunken living rooms used to be huge architectural designs in the 60s and 70s. It is more of a liability since research shows people are more careless regarding three steps or less. Give them one step down, and they fumble constantly," Tressa said, hopping onto the plush gold carpet.

"The technical name is "conversation pit." It's all about being closer together, facilitating human conversation and interaction," an unannounced voice interrupted the tense silence. "Hi, ladies. I'm Helena. It's a pleasure to finally meet you in person."

Tressa reached down to massage her leg after colliding with the poorly placed wrought iron living room decoration. The heavy and expensive perfume filling the air made her think her mother was in the room, but to her surprise, a woman who looked the same age but much tinier, impossibly tiny, stepped forward to greet them. Her sleek, platinum hair cascaded over her shoulders as she walked through the kitchen, every step exuding confidence and poise. Linoleum crackled with every piercing step of her boots, and her elevated level above the recessed living room made Tressa feel vulnerable. The woman seemed to have walked off the pages of a fashion magazine. Black on black, it was hard to determine where the clingy black sweater dress ended, the opaque tights covered, and the boots reached up to. The only interruption to the dark ensemble was a cream-colored infinity scarf that looked perfectly draped around her neck and shoulders, drawing attention to her plunging neckline.

"Please, ladies. Take a seat," Helena said, motioning to the horseshoe-shaped cocoa brown velour sectional. "Please excuse the dust. We try to have meetings in a more secluded, unassuming location. One of our members generously allows us to use their vacant lake house."

As the girls settled onto the plush couch, Tressa studied Helena, wondering how someone so petite and fashionable could have been involved in the previous night's events. Tressa had reservations about meeting anyone from the Summit Society and realized it was dumb not to let anyone know where they were tonight. The only threat she felt now was the fact she felt entirely underdressed.

Mauri looked uncomfortable on the ultra-low couch, trying to adjust her position. She slid her feet back, wrapping her arms around her knees and hugging them close. Tressa noticed the glassy sheen reflecting on Mauri's lower lip, the understated gloss replacing the usual dark statement lipstick.

Tressa's mind wandered to the architectural design of renowned secret society meeting places. In her research, she recalled poring over pictures of Greek temples with their grandeur, ornamental tombs with their intricate carvings, and ominous entryways with their air of mystery. Sitting on the TV set of a 1970s sitcom led by a pint-sized femme fatale seemed out of place amid all the ancient and ominous imagery, especially given the usual male-dominated nature of secret societies. This setting was far less glamorous.

"Where did she go?" Mauri whispered, her eyes not leaving the entrance to the kitchen, the only outlet from their sunken retreat.

"I don't know about this," Tressa said. "Still not sure it's a great idea." The vision of the lifeless girl whisked out of the woods flashed in her mind. Suddenly, there was a tap-tap-tap as Helena reappeared, holding two cut crystal wine flutes with bubbly liquid sloshing over the brim.

"And here you go. Mauri. Tress-a," Helena said, singing her way back into the room as she hopped down the step into the living space. Mauri raised an eyebrow at the sparkling bubbles in the glass, but Tressa wondered again if this was some kind of trap.

"Oh, right. I apologize. We aren't used to having such a young inductee. My bad. You don't have to drink it," she said, acrylic nails clicking against the glass.

Mauri rolled her eyes, and her hair cascaded around her face as she tilted her head forward to sip the champagne. Tressa twirled the fragile stem in her hand, inspecting the contents as it swirled and burst.

"Oh, I'm sorry, Tressa. You don't drink?" she asked, clasping her hand against the fuzzy material of her dress with excessive drama.

"No, I, it's kind of early. I drove," Tressa stammered, looking for excuses to refuse an unknown drink that emerged from the dated 70s kitchen from someone she met minutes ago.

Helena must have read her mind and jumped to her feet, straightening the hem of her dress. She shuffled into the kitchen, followed by the sound of glass clinking and bottles jangling. She reappeared holding a wine flute to join them in a drink.

"Sorry. I understand. Please, I need this anyway," Helena said, her fingers fanning while she seemed to finish the drink in one gulp. "Well, now. There we are," Helena said with a head shake, tossing her shiny, smooth hair over her shoulders. She sat at an angle that gave Tressa a better vantage point. Earthy brown highlighted the hollows of her cheeks, while a shimmering bronze brought out a high luster on the apple of her cheeks. But close up, really close up, she wasn't as young as she coolly tried to portray. Beautiful, yes. Twenty-something, no. The foundation layer skimmed flawlessly over her heart-shaped face but settled in the shallow crevices around her eyes and mouth. There was no erasing that. But when she smiled, her bleached teeth glowed with the shade only described as snow-white perfection. Tressa tilted her head, returning the grin. She wondered if Helena noticed her lack of makeup.

"So, I'm sure you know why you are here, but let me give you a little background of how you got here and why you were selected," Helena said.

"The Summit Society, I'm assuming?" Mauri asked, her voice barely above a whisper.

"Correct," Helena said, leaning forward, her eyes scanning their faces. "The screening process is rigorous. Background checks and referrals are just a few tools to ensure we scout the most qualified and dedicated individuals. Of course, we look for people who meet the criteria of a specific background," she explained.

"Specific background? What would that include?" Tressa asked, tilting her head. The idea of background checks performed without her knowledge made her uncomfortable.

"Well, we need to know our potential candidates and their values align with the society's mission and goals," Helena responded as if Tressa should already have that information. "I will tell you that we were impressed. This might have been the toughest year with some challenging situations. And you two did not disappoint," she said, punctuating each syllable.

Tressa paused before asking another question. "So, what is the mission? What are the society's goals?"

Helena studied an invisible piece of fuzz on her dress, hesitating before answering. "We expect all members to preserve the heritage and integrity of the society while maintaining secrecy. The goals are to promote life-long excellence, prosperity, and financial stability for each individual who pledged their loyalty to the Summit Society."

Mauri sat at the edge of the couch, grasping her knees, her back so straight Tressa would swear a thread pulled at her from the ceiling. Her eyes, wide in anticipation, reflected what Tressa knew all along. They sold her on the idea of belonging with the first word.

Helena walked outside the conversation pit's perimeter, continuing to spew mantras about solidarity, prestige, and power, all woven together with the bond of secrecy.

"Where is everyone else?" Tressa asked, expecting others to join their initiation.

"The list of initiates varies yearly and from school to school. Some years, the pool is bigger here at Wyval, but only two brilliant women met the stringent criteria this year. The organization reaches throughout the United States, but trust me when I say your connections will reach much further. Align yourselves with our mission and goals, and your future will be secure forever," Helena said.

"And if we don't agree?" Tressa asked.

Instead of answering, the woman fluttered her spider-like lashes and grimaced as if watching an injured animal in pain.

Mauri shifted in her seat, the most uncomfortable Tressa had seen her since the journey started. Her eyes squinted as she gave a nervous smile, her expression saying, *"Don't blow it, Tressa."*

"I know this is a lot. You've *been* through a lot. But the backbone of this network is trust, and I want you to know you can start by trusting me. Let me show you something," Helena said, disappearing into the kitchen again.

"She seems okay, doesn't she?" Mauri whispered, grabbing Tressa's hand and giving it a rousing shake. "I know you're not sure, but let's listen to what she has to say. I'm only in this if you are, but let's give it a chance," Mauri said, her eyes brimming with tears. She returned to her side of the couch as Helena returned.

"May I?" Helena asked before taking a seat between the two girls.

Tressa scooted over, allowing Helena to settle between them. Her delicate hands urged the envelope to flap open, dipping inside to remove the contents. Her finger traced the outline of the first photo, stopping at the faded image of a young girl.

"Nineteen seventy-nine. Christmas Eve. We had parties for every holiday, and Christmas usually topped them all. I can remember being so excited to wear this outfit," she said, her long nails tapping the photo.

Tressa noticed the overpowering aroma of rose, jasmine, and something a little smokey as she leaned in to look at the festive picture before her. The girls in the photo wore matching styles with different prints, including the chubby-faced, curly-haired one in the center.

"My older cousins picked out those outfits, and I told my mom I wanted the same kind. She tried to talk me into something else, but I never fit in with their willowy physiques and poker-straight hair. I wanted to be just like them."

"That's you?" Mauri asked, with a bit too much surprise.

Helena laughed. "That's me. Seven years old, but I can still recall the night like it was yesterday. I remember tugging at the ill-fitting white blouse and tucking my chin-length hair behind my ears. Trust me. My cousins let me know I didn't fit in."

She continued flipping through the photos, stopping at one of Helena and a tall, slender woman who must have been her mom. She wore a forced grin, crouching near little Helena. "Oh yes, and there is my Mom and me."

Mauri nearly fell onto her lap as she leaned closer to study the picture.

"I know. We looked nothing alike. And we were nothing alike for as long as I remember. I could not fulfill my mom's idea of the perfect little girl," Helena said, staring at the photo.

"I doubt that was the case," Mauri chimed in. "It's hard to understand adults when you are so young, right?"

Helena motioned to the tissues on the end table. Folding it into a perfect square, she dabbed below her painted eyes, but her makeup must have been waterproof. "Oh, that was the case, don't worry. At that same party, I came down the stairs. The adults were just getting started, thinking all the children were asleep or had gone home with their parents. I remembered I needed to put out a plate of cookies. My mom stood near the bottom step, balancing a Virginia Slim in one hand and a martini glass in the other. Would you like to know the response to a little girl innocently asking to leave out a plate of cookies for Santa?" Helena asked.

From the incessant dabbing, Tressa knew the answer would be less than cheerful.

"She said, 'Helena, it's too late for you to be down here. And you know how I feel about you eating any cookies.' With these two sentences, she dashed any childhood Christmas magic and self-esteem."

"That's pretty rotten," Tressa said, knowing the pressure of growing up in the shadow of a glamorous mom, but thankfully not hurtful.

She stood up, tossing the manila envelope on the table. She resumed her post outside the cozy recessed layout, silver bangles tinkling against the metal railing as she leaned against the barrier. "Well, that's my sob story. And I have to say, my mother and I aren't particularly close, but we mended our past. The thing is, I'm where I am because I made my way, but I owe it all to this family – the Summit Society. They make me feel like I belong. We only choose the best with a unique talent to offer. Members who will help the organization thrive throughout the years and the world. And we chose you two, Tressa and Mauri."

Tressa wasn't sure if she should clap, laugh, or cry in the awkward silence. The monologue and theatrics didn't answer the question about the girl in the woods, and the exchange about Helena's teasing and treatment as a child seemed a little trite. Tressa left a door open so Helena could address what happened the previous night, and the lack of mention left her no choice.

"Helena, thank you for sharing that memory with us, but I have another question for you if you don't mind."

# Chapter Twenty-Seven

Helena listened intently to Tressa as she recounted the events of their last test, nodding in agreement and showing concern. Tressa was open about her worries, from her confusion about using the shock collar to her concern for the blonde girl carried out of the woods.

"I need to know if something happened. You can understand my concern." Tressa's hand hovered over the glass of champagne on the table, hesitation flickering across her face. After a moment, she grabbed it and, with a sigh, raised it to her lips. The bubbles exploded like fireworks as she guzzled every last drop, her mouth as dry as a desert. "It was so real, and I can't get it out of my head. I don't want to be part of something like that. I'm sorry," Tressa admitted.

Mauri sunk back into the cushions, her hands tucked under her arms, avoiding eye contact with Tressa.

"I was waiting for one of you to bring it up. And rightfully so. As I mentioned earlier, the tests were some of the hardest this year. I don't think any other candidates we considered would have made it through. Your toughness and tenacity will be an asset to the group. Her name is Gina," Helena said with a sigh.

"Who is Gina?" Tressa asked.

"The girl in the woods, Gina. And she is fine. Let me explain. When the panel and I designed the final test, we planned to get you into the coal mine tour location for an overnight stay. After some accessibility concerns, we didn't want to take any chances.

Instead, we said we would see how you handled being in a situation rather than an environment. A few of our members helped us set the stage."

Tressa thought back to the sobbing girl and her reaction after electric currents coursed through her body. The masked people were much taller than the girl, meaning it couldn't have been Helena that night. Tressa shifted on the couch and knew there was no delicate way to address the situation.

"So, okay. You say other society members helped set the stage to put us in a challenging situation, but it included us administering a painful electric shock to someone. I don't see how that aligns with the values and loyalty you described earlier. It's a bit demented if you ask me," Tressa said, knowing she was dashing Mauri's hopes of being in the Summit Society with every word she uttered.

"I know, I know how it sounds, but if you'd let me continue, it will all make sense," Helena said, raising a well-defined eyebrow at Tressa. "The idea was to rattle you both with the final test and initiation."

"Mission accomplished," Tressa interrupted. "I understand secret societies are known for having some bizarre initiation rituals, but we went from scavenger hunt mode to crossing the line into criminal activity? And for what? To prove we will follow the society's every instruction, no matter the outcome?"

Helena took a deep breath before responding, "Well, yes and no. The plan fell apart."

Tressa's stomach churned, and she felt the bile rising in her throat as she tried not to spew champagne. "Fell apart?" she repeated, her voice barely above a whisper.

"Yes. We planned on putting you in a situation where you thought you would administer an electric current through a collar, all with the tap of a phone. The first round was a surprise, but the second would be intentional," Helena said.

Tressa glanced at Mauri and noticed that as enthusiastic as her friend had been moments earlier, her face looked like someone about to be sick.

Mauri's voice trembled, displaying her struggle to separate morality and loyalty. "So, you wanted us to hurt someone as part of our initiation?"

Tressa continued the interrogation. "And how did you get someone to agree to be part of this? I can't imagine someone volunteering for something like this," she said, thoughts of kidnapping and coercion at the forefront of her mind.

Helena exhaled as if she was a kindergarten teacher frustrated with her students. "We give our members a chance to volunteer to prove their true loyalty if they want to increase their social status within the organization while also contributing to the initiation process. Likewise, initiates are given a chance to show they will do all that is asked of them."

Tressa grimaced, not satisfied with Helena's explanation.

"Gina was in on the plan and is an excellent actress," Helena continued, speaking a few paces slower. "We told her it was fine to be in the moment and make it seem believable. Getting up and attempting to escape would make it seem real, but no one anticipated she'd trip and hit her head. After it happened, the other society members immediately took her to the hospital, and we decided the test needed to end. Gina received care at the hospital and was released a few hours later. She is fine."

Tressa struggled to make sense of everything. They were meant to believe they were administering electric shocks, but they weren't. Gina hit her head. It wasn't the shock that hurt her. It just didn't add up.

"So, let me get this straight," Tressa said, her voice dripping with sarcasm. "You wanted us to think we were inflicting pain on someone, even though we weren't."

"Yes," Helena said, with no further explanation.

Tressa furrowed her brow. "So, Gina was fine until she tripped and hit her head?"

"Yes," Helena confirmed. "Unfortunately, things didn't go as planned, and we had to take Gina to the hospital. But we felt you proved yourselves and passed the test. It's quite simple."

Mauri picked up her glass and reclined back on the couch. Helena's story seemed to satisfy her questions, but Tressa remained skeptical.

As she stared at the floor, Tressa replayed the scenario. She remembered the feeling of horror when she thought they had hurt someone, the scream from the woods, and the sight of the limp body being carried away. It wasn't until later that they filled in the missing scene of Gina hitting her head, even though they hadn't seen it happen. It's like reading a paragraph with missing words, but your subconscious fills in the missing spaces to make it seem like it plays out normally. But nothing about this situation was normal, and Tressa couldn't shake the feeling that something wasn't right. She still had a lot of unanswered questions. What if Gina wasn't okay? What if someone had pushed her or intentionally hurt her? What if the electric shock was real and it caused Gina to collapse moments later, not a stumble over a rock?

"You might be wondering why we would want our members to inflict pain on someone intentionally," Helena said, breaking Tressa's train of thought. We've researched the ancient traditions of the Summit Society and wanted to incorporate them into our initiation process. But we wanted to avoid archaic methods like striking initiates with a ceremonial paddle, as was done many years ago."

"So the idea of an electric shock collar is much better," Tressa commented. She felt Helena was trying to cloak the situation in confusion.

"Okay, as one of our most brilliant candidates in recent years, it's ironic how this isn't resonating with you. I have to say I honor your perseverance. Would it help if I could prove Gina is okay, and you can ask her these same questions?" Helena proposed.

Mauri nodded in agreement and added, "I think it would be helpful, right Tress?"

Since Tressa took her first step inside, the room felt warmer. She couldn't help but focus on the faux brick wall lined with glass shelves and small trinkets. Celebration and induction seemed inappropriate tonight, and she couldn't unwind the knot in her stomach.

"Tressa. I sense your uneasiness with this, and I understand your concerns. I want you to know we are here for you. You will be one of us now, but it is up to each member to prove their loyalty and support, no matter what life throws at them. I know you and Mauri were slightly traumatized by all of this, and I want to help alleviate your concerns." As she finished her sentence, Helena disappeared into the kitchen.

Tressa watched the chain on the overhead light swing in the slight breeze. She thought she saw someone else in the kitchen. Her heart raced, and her eyes darted from the suspended avocado-green glass lamp to the front door, wondering if the opportunity to make their exit had expired. Her question was answered as Helena reappeared, but she wasn't alone this time.

"Ladies, meet Gina," Helena announced, gesturing towards a figure that seemed to float into the room.

Tressa's breath caught in her throat at the sight of her. Compared to Helena, the girl looked like she had just returned from a jog rather than attending an elite clandestine meeting. The rail-thin figure sheepishly nodded at them, her ice-blue eyes meeting Tressa's for a moment before settling on the shaggy carpet beneath their feet. Tressa and Mauri greeted her enthusiastically while Gina kept her hands nestled in the deep pockets of her black hoodie.

"Gina is a valued member of our society and has been involved for a few years," Helena said.

"Hi, nice to formally meet you," the girl said, looking at Tressa and Mauri. "You both did a fantastic job. I never went through anything like you did, but this was tough for me, too."

"Gina was our girl," Helena continued, holding out her hands like she was showcasing a prized possession. "The one you saw in the woods. And here she is, healthy and happy. Perhaps still shaken and recovering, but she's doing great."

Tressa could hear Mauri exhale next to her like a deflating tire.

"Oh wow. You threw us for a loop. So, are you okay?" Mauri asked, stumbling over her words. "I see the small bandage on your head," she said, pointing to the girl's forehead.

Gina gave Mauri an empty stare, and it took her a moment to snap out of it. "Oh, yeah, I guess I was playing into the scene. I thought if it looked like I tried to escape, it would be more believable. I didn't expect to trip on rocks, though. I'm such a klutz," she said, touching her forehead.

"But the collar and the electric shock? Nothing happened? You didn't feel anything?" Tressa asked.

"Oh God no. Helena explained what they were doing, and it freaked me out. Why would anyone volunteer for something like that?" Gina giggled.

Tressa wanted her to continue talking about the situation. "Because it was mentioned members could escalate their status in the society if they volunteered to be part of the initiation ceremony," recounting what they were told that evening.

Gina rocked back on the heel of her sneaker, her hands jutting even deeper in the jacket. "I'm fine. Just a little bump on my head—you know how even a tiny cut can bleed," she said, once again touching her head.

Tressa thought about the girl in the woods, her limp body swaying as the society members whisked her away. She looked at the bandage on Gina's head, and besides the amount of blood that night in the woods, the girl they saw looked unconscious. Tressa felt it was more than a small bump on the head. Things weren't adding up.

Helena walked over to Tressa and pulled her close, almost touching her forehead with hers. "I felt it important to introduce you, put your mind at ease as to what happened that night," she said. Her hands were ice cold as she grabbed Tressa's between hers. "We are going to be here for you. You are one of us. There is nothing to hide, Tressa."

The skin prickled on Tressa's neck as Helena firmly gripped her hands. "Can I ask one more thing?" Tressa said while pulling back to put some distance between them.

"Anything," Helena smiled.

Tressa turned away from Helena and faced the nervous girl. "Gina, would you mind showing me your hands?" Tressa asked.

Gina's face lost all color and turned ashen white. "My hands?" she stammered.

"Gina, my dear. Can you help ease Tressa's mind and pull up your sleeve," Helena said, her voice filled with annoyance.

Gina slid her hands from their cover, the end of the sleeve reaching down to her knuckles. Hoisting up the fabric on both armholes, she rotated both wrists toward Tressa. Faint blueish lines snaked like tributaries below the translucent skin. It was almost as if the veins were trying to escape from beneath the surface. The pasty skin stretched over little more than sinewy bones, making her look more delicate than she probably was. Gina's blonde ponytail swished as she turned her head, her arms outstretched in a pleading, almost humiliating manner. The girl's gaze shifted from Helena to the popcorn ceiling. She was alive and well, and Tressa imagined how much pain it must have caused Gina when she got a peace tattoo emblazoned on her paper-thin skin. A small puff of dust rose behind Helena as she reclined on the worn couch. The hum of the aging refrigerator echoed like a freight train. Her dress crept higher, exposing a few more inches of the short but athletic leg between the hem and boots. The tip of Helena's boot bobbed up and down while she inspected her nails.

"So, Tressa. Are we good?" Helena's face scrunched, creating rows of small lines in the makeup slathered around her eyes. Her hand clutched the back of her neck.

Tressa paused to take everything in. Usually, the day before Thanksgiving was a time for preparing at home for her mom's elegant holiday celebration. Nostalgic television specials, the anticipation of the holiday season, and some time off from school. Instead, she sat on a cheesy '70s movie set, surrounded by a diva reliving her glory days, a friend hanging on her every word, and a waif-like creature back from the dead. Tressa couldn't deny the current situation, but she still wasn't sure she wanted to surround herself with people like Helena. Mauri seemed relaxed and found no fault in the situation from last night, proving her willingness to pay any price to belong. And for that, Tressa picked up her pride from the shaggy carpet and swept it underneath. Right next to the part of her brain flashing 'caution'.

"Sure. I guess. Sorry, Gina," Tressa said, pointing to the girl's hands. "Cool tattoo, by the way."

Gina glanced at her wrist and pulled the oversized sleeves over her fragile hands. "Oh, the tattoo. Right. No worries. I understand why you would want to see it," she said, holding up a thin arm and waving it about her head.

Helena popped up, grabbed their glasses, and scuffed her way into the kitchen. Gina checked messages on her phone, and Mauri stretched her neck toward the sounds from the kitchen.

Pop. Clink. Scuff.

"Well, ladies. I hate to cut this short, but I am sure everyone has big, fancy holiday plans," she said, nodding at Tressa. "Before we leave, I insist on a special toast." She walked as if she balanced on a tightrope, bringing in four crystal flutes, bubbles escaping from the beveled rim.

"To secrets, security, and splendor. Welcome to the Summit Society," Helena declared as she handed out the slender glasses.

"What is shimmering at the bottom of this?" Tressa asked, inspecting the champagne flute more closely. A soft light danced and refracted through the effervescent bubbles, casting an ethereal glow.

Helena smiled and moved closer to the group. "Sip slowly, my friends. You'll want to hang on to that," she said, clicking her nail against Tressa's glass. Your official Summit Society medallion will open much more than an app. "Cheers, ladies."

Tressa gazed at her drink with unease and curiosity, reluctantly raising the glass.

# Chapter Twenty-Eight

The silence during the journey back home made the ride seem longer. Tressa's eyes wandered over the clusters of trees, and she caught glimpses of light shining in the distance. It reminded her of the homes tucked away behind the forest canopy, where families prepared to celebrate the holiday. Even though warm air was blowing from the vent, Tressa couldn't shake off the chill she had felt ever since they had left the lake house. The sudden transition from discussing secret societies and electric shock collars to a champagne toast didn't sit right with Tressa.

Holiday music stations seemed to be starting earlier every year, and Tressa turned down the sound of Bing Crosby's crooning voice singing *White Christmas*. "Okay, so what do you think?" Tressa asked, knowing they needed to discuss what transpired sooner or later.

"At least we each have our own," Mauri said. "Although I probably should have rinsed it," she said, her fingers sticking to the small circular memento.

"I'm not worried about the medallion. I mean Helena and everything she told us," Tressa retorted.

"Well, our main concern about the girl in the woods is addressed," Mauri said. "However, I'm not 100% comfortable with the electric shock collar thing. Her reaction seemed so real."

"I'm definitely not comfortable," Tressa said. "I know we met Gina, and she seems okay, but she denied the shock thing was real," Tressa added.

"I mean, I guess she could just be an outstanding actress," Mauri said, trying to convince herself. "Just a scare tactic. Helena doesn't seem like the type to be involved in something like that. Whatever they planned didn't work out like they wanted."

"But she wasn't there. Creating a plan and being there to see it executed are two different things," Tressa said. "And all that talk about bringing back tradition? I don't know. I think activating it through the app was real, but they never counted on Gina getting up and running. That screwed up their plans," Tressa said.

Mauri continued to look out the window, lost in her thoughts. Tressa knew how much her friend wanted this, and she actually wondered if Mauri would be willing to cross a moral line for it.

"Mauri. I need to ask you something," Tressa said, hating that she doubted Mauri's intentions. "Did you hit PROCEED on the app? The second time?"

Mauri sat up straight in the seat. "No, why would you ask that? She said we would both need to select it in the app for it to work," she snapped, her tone quick and sharp. She placed her head against the window and watched the world pass by before jolting up again. "Plus, the whole thing wasn't real, and even if it were, you know I wouldn't go through with it, no matter what was at stake."

Tressa turned up the radio, allowing *All I Want for Christmas* to replace the awkward conversation. She wished she could believe Mauri but wasn't sure either statement was true.

As they arrived at the bustling bus station, Tressa immediately felt out of place. She wasn't familiar with bus transportation and didn't know if it was Mauri's only option. Tressa hesitated for a moment before offering Mauri a ride home for the holidays. "Are you sure you need to take a bus? You can always come home with me. It's a grand affair at my house during the holidays," Tressa said, giving one last effort.

Mauri smiled at her friend. "My grandmother is expecting me, and some distant cousins are joining us. Thanks for the offer," she said, gazing at the busy terminal.

Tressa figured it best not to continue uncomfortable conversations about her home life. She looked ahead, staring at the red glow of brake lights, illuminating the parking spots surrounding the bus terminal like Christmas decorations.

Mauri reached behind the seat and hoisted a heavy bag. "Tress, I want to thank you."

"For what?" Tressa asked curiously.

Mauri hesitated before answering, staring at the floor before continuing. "I know you're not totally on board with everything. And yeah, the situation might seem overwhelming. But you must be a little curious about what doors this opportunity can open. Besides, think of what we went through together. I wouldn't stay in a prison cell overnight with just anyone," Mauri said before stepping out the door.

Over the last few weeks, the idea of staying overnight in an abandoned prison has been the least of her concerns, but she felt it unnecessary to rehash the topic again. She decided to let Mauri have her moment.

Tressa nodded and gave Mauri a warm smile. "Let's see how the next few weeks pan out. I'm willing to give it a chance."

Mauri ducked her head into the car, her face glowing with a smile to match. "Happy Thanksgiving, Tressa. I'll see you next week. Send pictures of your dinner table," she joked before slamming the door.

# Chapter Twenty-Nine

Tressa took a deep breath and savored the familiar smells and sounds of home. "Hello?" she asked, her voice echoing in the hall. She went through the hallway towards the living room, thinking about how different this Thanksgiving was from the last one. From the chaos of the previous few weeks to the warm glow of her home, it had been quite a journey. As she entered the living room, shadows danced on the walls from rows of tea lights centered in smoky amber and plum glass candle holders. The aromatic smell of cinnamon clung to her clothes and hair, and the sound of crackling logs accompanied boisterous laughter. Tressa felt at home already.

"She's home," her mother squealed, tapping her way through the foyer with her arms outstretched. The conversation continued beyond the dark paneled hallway, but Tressa wondered who her stepdad could be carrying on with as her mom embraced her in a hug. Her aunt and cousin weren't set to arrive until tomorrow morning.

Tressa's mom took her hand and whispered, "We have a surprise for you. You'll be happy about being so forgetful," Deborah said with a squeal.

Tressa was puzzled but followed her mom to the study anyway. She stopped under the intricately carved archway, studying Tressa for a response as if she had just received a pony for her birthday. Tressa heard someone cackling in the background. As the noise grew louder, she realized who the mystery guest was.

"You must have been in a hurry. You forgot this," Alex said, pointing to her school bag on the overstuffed leather chair. As he stood near the fireplace, he could have doubled as a model in a men's fashion magazine.

"Oh hey, what a surprise. I thought you were heading home for Thanksgiving," Tressa said as she hugged him.

Tressa's mom noticed her fixation on the condensation-laden tin mugs and offered to make her a drink. "I used Tuaca, cranberries, and lime," her mom said, busying herself with the preparation. "It's delicious. No time like the present to start celebrating," she said, looping her fingers through the handles, berries tumbling to the floor.

Tressa appreciated the liqueur but didn't have the heart to tell her mother she was more interested in it due to its connection to the Renaissance than as a cocktail base. She had to admit the sweet golden brandy did help the holidays run smoother. Her mom disappeared into the kitchen, and Tressa knew she wouldn't have a choice.

"It's an amazing drink," Alex said. A pale blue checkered shirt peeked out of the collar and below the fitted hem of his cobalt gray sweater. "I brought this—figured you would need it over the break. I know how much you hate to fall behind on assignments." He reached behind the matching leather couch and slid the oversized nylon backpack near Tressa's feet.

She couldn't believe she had forgotten it. "So you drove all this way to drop it off? Won't your parents be upset that you are missing Thanksgiving dinner?" she asked, trying to discern if he was staying put the next few days.

Her mom sauntered back into the room. "Nice try, Tress. I tried to get him to stay, but we can only enjoy his company overnight, and then he is heading out at dawn." Tressa knew her mom wouldn't take no for an answer from either of them, so the overnight plans were set. Her mom handed out another round of drinks. A sprig of something green tickled her nose as she took a large sip.

"Thirsty?" Alex laughed.

"Oh, sorry. Long day," Tressa said, swirling the ice cubes with the tiny straw. "So I guess you are staying the night?"

Tressa's stepdad interjected, "He's leaving first thing in the morning, right, buddy?" His tone was more like that of a college friend than a stepfather or husband. Tressa tried to stifle her laughter as she watched him eyeing Alex.

"Yep, that's the plan. But I couldn't resist having dinner and drinks with our wonderful hostess," Alex replied, resulting in Ryan pulling his wife in for an embrace. Tressa smiled as the three of them tried to one up each other.

"Well, thank you for bringing this," she said, motioning to the bag. "If you don't mind, it's been a long day. I need to freshen up before I even think about dinner. I'll be back down soon."

As she ascended the wide walnut staircase, Tressa jumped as someone grabbed her hand as she reached for the banister.

"Honey," her mother whispered.

"Yes, Mom," Tressa answered with a sigh.

Tressa's mother absently picked at the invisible fuzz on the mahogany carpet runner, running her finger along the gold trim anchoring against the wood. "Maybe spruce it up a little?" she asked, with an annoying shake of her hips.

"Spruce it up? Mom, really? I'm tired. I live with Alex. He sees me all the time in my non-spruced-up state," she said, resuming her retreat to her room.

"But he looks so cute," her mother continued.

Tressa's room reflected her love for art and her mother's expensive taste. The Old World vintage style was evident in everything, from the dove gray estate bed with ornamental carvings to the pilasters in each corner of the white-washed room, while most of the house hid behind warm wood grains, deep earth, and jewel tones. The sea of square pillows floated atop a brocaded comforter, staying in line with the color scheme somewhere between a sky filled with cirrus clouds and an ominous storm brewing. Tressa walked over to the high dresser and stared into the beveled mirror.

"Spruce it up," she said, piling her hair atop her head while studying her tired complexion. As she rummaged through a drawer, looking for eyeliner and lipstick, she realized her mom must have straightened her room as soon as she returned to campus. She found a worn guide from The Metropolitan Museum of Art, antique coins, and a small plastic frame in the corner of the drawer. Tressa studied the picture and smiled as she recounted memories from her freshman year. The black and white photo strip contained a thousand unspoken words, and it marked the moment when Tressa Litton decided to give Wyval a chance, both the school and new friendships. Over three years passed, and the sweet memories remained intact, but the trio didn't. She slid the frame into the pages of the program and pushed it back into place. Tressa put on a little brown eyeliner and sheer coral lip gloss and then shrugged into an oversized cardigan and "dressier than yoga but more casual than business" black pants. Adjusting the worn, crushed heels of her favorite suede ballet flats, she padded back downstairs.

The conversation in the kitchen revolved around caramelized onions and finding the perfect serving platters, so Tressa headed to the study. She watched the woolen sweater-clad arm reach for the frosty drink on the small table.

Tressa tried to break the ice with Alex. "So, she convinced you to stay?" she asked.

Alex jumped up, the glow from the fire making his ruddy skin tone even warmer. "Sit with me while I try to figure out what Tuaca is," he said, motioning to the couch.

Tressa tucked her legs beneath her, curling in the corner of the couch like a cat. The burgundy slip of a napkin molded around the Moscow mule cup, the words *Give Thanks* becoming darker as moisture permeated the paper. The second round tasted even better, but she needed food soon. Tressa hoped Alex couldn't tell she was keeping something from him. How she wanted to share every detail about her adventure. "I can't believe you went out of your way for me," she said with a nervous laugh. "But you know you really don't have to stay."

Alex flexed his leg, revealing printed socks matching his shirt collar. "Hey, I'm only here for the drinks," he said raising his glass, "but seriously, I wanted to make sure you had your bag over the break. I'll be out of your hair bright and early."

"That's not what I meant. And thank you, I appreciate that, the bag," Tressa said. "Nice sweater, by the way," she added, trying to sound a little less harsh.

"Hey, coming to the Litton house requires certain standards. I can't disappoint your mom," Alex said, straightening his collar.

"Oh, don't worry, you didn't disappoint. Actually, I think my stepdad feels he has some competition. It's funny," Tressa said.

Alex shifted in his chair, basking in the warm glow of the fire. Tressa was desperate to share everything she had been through, starting with the envelope that arrived at their door to the bubbling champagne she had toasted with just hours ago. The image of Mauri flashed in her mind, along with the conflicting emotions of trust and betrayal. She wanted to tell someone but knew it would ruin their chances of finally getting into the Summit Society.

"Well, I have to check on dinner. I'm starving. Do you need anything else?" Tressa asked, suddenly feeling awkward around her roommate. He turned toward her, his face bathed in the warm firelight. He didn't seem like the usual Saturday morning Alex, lounging on the couch in sweats and a concert t-shirt, watching TV.

"Dinner, kids," her mother yelled, the abrupt sound breaking Tressa's gaze.

"I do need something," Alex said.

Tressa felt a surge of unease mixed with a twinge of excitement as he leaned closer, just inches from her face.

"Excuse me. I need to grab this. Another drink is in order." He picked up the empty copper mugs and headed out of the room. He turned before he entered the kitchen and winked at Tressa.

Dinner conversation fluctuated from tomorrow's menu to the measures Tressa's mom took to acquire the two sculptures in the hallway. Alex played into each conversation, to her mom's delight and her stepdad's dismay.

"I'm bummed that I won't be able to make it to dinner tomorrow. I mean, tonight's meal was just incredible," Alex gushed. "You've got some serious talent when pairing food and wine," he said, raising a glass. Alex's praise just kept coming like a never-ending flow of wine.

"Anyone for cordials fireside?" her mom asked, face a little too flushed, proposition a little too eager.

"Babe, think of the big day we have tomorrow. We'll be up at the crack of dawn cooking. I say we get some sleep," her stepdad said, slinking his arm around her waist and pulling her close.

"You're right. The main event is tomorrow, so we should probably call it a night. We'll leave you two to it," her mother giggled.

"Mixers and liquors on the sideboard. Help yourself. Good night."

The giddiness as her mom clung to Ryan, stopping every few steps to steal a kiss, made Tressa want another drink. "Okay, this is getting awkward. Are you interested in one more?" she asked, scanning crystal decanters, syrups, and juices.

"You know what, your mom is probably right. I need to get up earlier than everyone. My parents will flip if I'm late for our dinner." Alex walked over to Tressa and pulled her close to his chest. He smelled of alcohol, smoldering wood, and pine soap. He kissed the top of her head and held her at arm's length like a parent sending their child to school. "Don't bother waking up early on my account. If I don't see you in the morning, enjoy the weekend, and I'll see you in a few days," Alex said before walking to the foyer.

"Let me show you the guest room," she said, heading to the back room on the first floor.

Tressa nudged the door and noticed an opened suitcase on the four-poster bed. Neatly stacked towels and soap sat on the bench near the foot of the bed. "Never mind, Mom was already here, I see."

"She is the host with the most. Good night, Tressa," Alex said, closing the door.

She stood in the hall, her hand on the doorframe. She paused a few minutes, but when she heard her roommate settling in, Tressa headed to her room. She thought about Alex and their relationship. They shared an apartment and spent their mornings together. They enjoyed nights of pizza, cheap wine, and Netflix. Alex was like a brother to her, knowing everything about her life, relationships, dreams, and vision for the future. It had felt that way since they met on move-in day. He filled the role of brother, roommate, protector, and best friend. She thought about their moment earlier in the night, how Alex looked sitting by the fire, his contemplative stare, and his perfectly fitted wool sweater. She knew her mom's festive drinks fueled the fun flirtation and didn't mean anything. Still, Tressa drifted to sleep with nothing but good thoughts.

# Chapter Thirty

Moonlight continued to flood her room when she heard a thud from downstairs, but the weight of the comforter beckoned her to stay in its cocoon. The fragrant smell of herbs mixed with hints of vanilla and warm bread meant her mom got an early start on the entrees and desserts she made from scratch. Tressa pulled her foot back as it touched the floor—it was freezing. As she scanned the room for her shoes, voices echoed in the cavernous foyer. Checking her phone, Tressa saw it was 4:45 a.m., an early morning or a late night. She paused before tip-toeing down the stairs, shivering from the cold as her hand fixed on the metal doorknob. Tressa heard her name but couldn't make out the rest of the conversation. The hinges groaned, but the conversation continued below, her footsteps undetected.

"Thanks again, Alex. I know she appreciated that you stopped by", Tressa's mom gushed in a sugary, sweet tone. "She can't live without her laptop."

Tressa strained to hear Alex's response, but as she leaned against the door frame and peered down the hall, she saw only two silhouettes locked in an embrace. As Alex picked up his bag and headed outside, her mother closed the door behind him. She stood motionless for a momnet, her hands resting against the doorframe.

Tressa coughed, announcing her presence at the top of the stairs.

"Oh, hi, honey. You just missed Alex. I'm sure if you run outside, you'll catch him," she said, smoothing her hair behind her ears.

"I see Alex every single day, and we talked before turning in last night. The two of you talking woke me, so I thought I'd say good morning," she said while stretching.

"Well, it's probably best. You still look a little tired," her mom said, waving her hands above her head and tugging at her hair.

"Ugh, I'm going back to bed. Wake me if you need help preparing anything," Tressa said before walking away.

She lay in bed, gazing at the intricate design on the ceiling behind the chandelier. Whenever sunlight filtered in or the light was switched on, a rainbow of colors danced on the woven plaster pattern. Though the bed was comfortable, the enticing aroma of freshly ground coffee beans tempted her to get up and head downstairs. She entered the kitchen and avoided conversation outside of place settings, updates about visiting cousins, and learning how to make cinnamon schnapps-infused whipped cream.

Later in the afternoon, dinner unfolded as anticipated. What seemed like days of preparation and fuss faded within a few hours. Her mother was a great cook, and every garnished dish looked as beautiful as it was delicious. *Like something out of a magazine,* as her stepdad described it. Candelabras supported the last of wax, and flame struggled to hold on. Empty wine glasses and crumpled honey-colored napkins interlaced with strands of spun gold littered the never-ending dining table. Conversation toggled between football games, next-day shopping sprees, and how full everyone was.

"Tressa, honey. How's your senior year going?" her aunt asked, trying to start a conversation. "I heard about the Wyval tradition and the Summit Society. Do you know anyone who got invited?"

Tressa's eyes widened as she took a bite of pumpkin pie and washed it down with a sip of Chardonnay. "Oh, the Summit Society? I don't even know if it's real, but there are lots of rumors about it," Tressa said, trying to make light of the topic.

"Oh, it's real. I heard once you are in, the perks stay with you forever. Super exclusive. I heard there were two inductees this year," Tressa's cousin Jennifer said. The only thing she and Tressa had in common was their age.

"Really? You need to tell me more about this," Tressa said, curious where this conversation would go. She was dying to know what others said about this year's candidates. It took every ounce of her being not to say anything. She loved her mother's side of the family, but she and her cousin didn't always see eye to eye growing up. While Tressa had her nose in books as an early teen, Jennifer had her nose in everyone else's business. Tressa tried to include Jennifer in her activities, like inviting her to explore the woods during family cookouts. Jennifer was never dressed for the occasion and sneered whenever Tressa suggested lending her something to wear. *I'm sure those shorts will be way too big on me,* or *I wouldn't want anyone seeing me in those sneakers,* were the typical responses. As the years passed, the time between visits also grew more distant.

"You basically get any job you want, and it's always something amazing, too," Jennifer said, her hair fluttering over her shoulders as she straightened in her seat and stared intently at her crème brulee. "Were you even aware of the Summit Society, Tressa?"

Deborah absently swirled a spoon in her cup filled with more Kahlua than coffee. "She sure does know about the Summit Society. We learned all about it when she started looking at colleges," she commented smugly.

Tressa cringed inwardly. *Don't say it, Mom.*

"It's good to set your sights high. They could select someone like Tressa," Deborah said, not looking up from her cup.

"Mom!" Tressa said, her teacup rattling as she leaned over to place it on the table.

"I mean that in a good way, honey. You have so much to offer; they'd be lucky to have your talents," she responded.

"Maybe they did pick me? You wouldn't know, would you?" she teased. Tressa knew she was treading in dangerous waters, but she also knew no one at this table would believe her even if she presented the invitation. The vision of Jennifer's expression at the sight of her boring, frumpy cousin inducted into one of the most prestigious groups in the country might be worth the risk.

"Why don't you all sit by the fire? I will finish clearing the table, and then I'll join you," Deborah said.

"I'll help, honey," Ryan chimed in. He raised his defined brows in alliance with Tressa. He hadn't said much during the conversation, but he also hadn't defended his wife nor taken any jabs at Tressa. She could have sworn she saw a few eye rolls as Jennifer and her mom droned on about purses and shoes. Maybe the pool boy wasn't as bad as she thought.

"I'll be down in a second." Tressa darted upstairs to avoid the questions of who she was texting and whether it was Alex.

**T: How'd Thanksgiving go? Make it home okay?**

**M: Good, thanks. Quiet but good. How about you?**

**T: Oh, you know, Alex showed up. My cousin is a jerk. Things like that.**

**M: Wait, what? Alex? I thought he was home.**

**T: Well, he stopped by yesterday. It's a long story. And my cousin thinks she knows everything. Typical family holiday drama stuff.**

**M: Ugh. Call me tomorrow. I want to hear all about it. I have to go to the Philharmonic.**

**T: Philharmonic? Really? Fancy.**

**M: lol. Not really.**

**T: Just wanted to let you know I think we made the right decision. You know, the Summit Society and all.**

**M: Yay. Glad you came around. *smile emoji* ttyl**

Tressa placed her phone on the ornate dresser to charge but hesitated before leaving the room. Curiosity got the best of her, and she scrolled to Mauri's last message. Despite her phone being password protected and out of reach for anyone downstairs, Tressa needed to protect their secret. Only one other person knew, and she wanted to keep it that way.

Delete.

# Chapter Thirty-One

"Ms. Litton. Can you stay after class?" Professor Dawson asked, looking over his glasses and rummaging through folders.

Tressa felt nervous and uncomfortable as she watched him shuffle through stacks of papers on his desk. Sitting at the back of the auditorium, Mauri quickly exited the room, realizing that the conversation was meant for Tressa only.

"You needed something?" Tressa said, biting her lip.

"I'm sorry. I must have misplaced your paper. The one assigned over the break. You did hand it in when you returned to campus, didn't you?" he inquired.

Tressa's mind raced back to the long weekend. She remembered her cousin's nagging and her mother's excitement when she agreed to go out for happy hour with Jennifer. Despite being surrounded by pompous classmates who always tried to compete and brag, Tressa had spent most of the night sitting in a corner, hiding behind glasses of bottom-shelf Pinot Grigio. After Ubering home and tumbling into bed, she regretted the decision, as it had resulted in a day of headache and nausea, which had kept her confined to the couch and television.

"I started it but couldn't pull it together in time. I'll have it by tomorrow," Tressa said, slinging her bag over her shoulder.

"I'm sorry, but I'll still need to deduct points," he said.

"That's fine. I'll have it tomorrow. Thanks, Professor Dawson," Tressa replied, trying to hide her disappointment. She smoothed a strand of hair behind her ear, recalling how it had taken nearly an hour to straighten the unruly waves earlier.

"Ms. Litton. Is everything okay?" he asked, looking concerned.

"Couldn't be better," Tressa said, inspecting her crimson nails under the fluorescent light.

She hurried to the top step and looked back to find her professor leaning against his desk with his arms crossed. His lingering gaze made her feel uncomfortable.

"Well, if there's anything you need or want to talk about, I'm here. I know how overwhelming your last year can be. You may think you have reached the summit, but there is much more to do before graduation. Don't lose sight of your goals," he said, returning to his work.

Tressa stepped backward and stumbled on the top step, his comment catching her off guard. "Have a good night," she stammered, scrambling out the door.

She stopped abruptly as the blast of cold air hit her in the face. "Mauri! Were you creeping outside the door?" she asked, nearly knocking her friend over.

"I wanted to hear why he wanted you to stay. Plus, I had your back in case anything else happened," Mauri said.

"Ew, what does that mean?" Tressa asked as they walked the dimly lit path.

"First of all, it means you look super cute. Your mom must be thrilled you did a little shopping," she said, linking her arm through Tressa's elbow. "Secondly, don't 'ew' me. I see how you melt like ice on a radiator when he talks to you," Mauri quipped.

Tressa couldn't shake off her cousin's sneers and comments from the weekend. She had reluctantly peeled off the couch to go shopping with her mother, hoping it would appease her until the next holiday. Her mother treated her to a new wardrobe and a visit to the day spa and salon, but it did little to lift her spirits. She had never felt such an intense need to share her thoughts as she did this weekend.

"He's too old and acting weird tonight, like making strange comments," Tressa said.

"He's acting weird because, speaking of hot and melting, that's the first time I ever saw you wear anything like that, and I'm sure he noticed," Mauri said, giving Tressa a playful shove.

"Whatever. I didn't finish my paper, but I told him it would get done tonight," Tressa said.

"Tress, you said you had straight A's your whole college career. You aren't going to fail because of one paper. We have the party tonight anyway, remember?"

Tressa and Mauri were pleasantly surprised when they received a group text inviting them to the Wyval welcome-back party. This celebration had been a long-standing tradition for everyone returning to campus after Thanksgiving, but it was invite-only. Tressa remembered Alex raving about the extravagant party in past years but never thought she would receive an invitation herself.

"Yeah, I guess I can finish the paper after the party," Tressa conceded.

"Like you need to worry about anything anymore," Mauri said.

Tressa thought about missing the paper and now ditching any more work for a party. She shifted her weight, apprehension creeping up her spine, but she gazed at Mauri, who looked like a kid on Christmas Eve. Anticipation sparkling like lights in her eyes, a mix of excitement with a dash of unknown. It was like hope dangling over your head that you'd get everything you wanted, with a bit of trepidation that you wouldn't. Tressa ran her fingers over the sharp edge of her folder before tossing it aside.

"Alright. I guess we should head back to get ready," Tressa said, switching gears. "Come over when you are ready,"

Even though Tressa was content with her current look, she still expected to be surrounded by her classmates trying to out-gloss and out-shimmer each other. She changed her outfit several times before Mauri arrived at the apartment.

"Sweet! You look good, girl!" Mauri shouted, her heeled boots tapping across the worn floor. The exaggerated hug nearly crushed Tressa as if they hadn't seen each other just hours before. "Wow, so this is what you've been hiding since I met you?" she asked, stepping back.

"I'm not too sure about this." Tressa tugged at her cropped shirt and debated changing into something less midriff-baring. She reached out of her comfort zone with darker makeup, tighter clothes, straighter hair, and higher shoes. Tressa caught a glimpse in the hall mirror. As she smudged the liner at the corner of her eyes, she heard a low whistle echoing from the other room.

"Well, hello, ladies. It looks like you are ready for the party," Alex said with a wink.

Tressa felt the squeeze on her shoulders as her roommate appeared next to her in the mirror, looking fabulous in jeans, a simple button-down shirt, and topped off with a dark gray sports coat. She felt his breath near her ear as he leaned closer to straighten a few strands of hair.

"You're a little taller there, Tress," he said, nodding at her unusually platformed feet. "Do you know where the house is?" he asked before leaving.

"Yeah, we are all set," Mauri chimed in.

"Do you want to catch a ride with me?" he asked, one foot out the door with no intention of actually waiting.

Tressa replied, "I still need a few minutes, so we'll meet you there."

"Okay, make sure you get a ride for this party," he warned.

"And why would that be, Alex? You know Mauri isn't supposed to be drinking," Tressa teased.

"I didn't say anything about drinking. This party will be lit, and there is probably not enough room to park," Alex explained before closing the door. A few seconds later, his head popped back into view. "Oh, and yeah, expect a lot of drinking." Then he was gone, slamming the door shut behind him.

Tressa considered changing but decided it would be too much trouble. In a few hours, she could chisel off the layer of makeup and retreat to sweatpants and a hoodie anyway.

"You know things are different now. We are different, Tress. It's our first day back, and we already got a party invitation," Mauri gushed.

"I think they invited all the seniors, to be honest. Nothing special about it," Tressa said.

"Nice try. You *know* things are different now, and this is just the beginning. Do you have your key?" Mauri asked, tapping her extra-long nails on the door. Tressa wondered when she had time to finish them, looking remarkably similar to Helena's.

"Yes, I do." After struggling with sliding the apartment key into her jeans pocket, she shoved it into her wristlet where there was more space. The sound of heels clattering down the metal stairs surrounded them as they rushed so their Uber driver didn't wait any longer. "Why did you tell Alex where we were going? I mean, he'd see us there anyway, but I kind of wanted it to be a surprise." Call it sibling rivalry or cool kid bragging rights, but it disappointed Tressa she wouldn't be able to see the surprise on Alex's face when they showed up somewhere he frequented.

# Chapter Thirty-Two

"Is this the right address? How far back does this take us?" asked Tressa, trying to keep her composure as she glanced at the serious-looking driver. She wished she hadn't laughed earlier, especially when he kept staring at her, looking unamused. Tressa couldn't help wondering if escaping from a moving car would be easy.

Meanwhile, Mauri leaned forward from the back seat, trying to strike up a conversation with the driver. "You seem pretty cool, but why are you so quiet?" Mauri asked but got no response. "You good up there, dude?"

Tressa felt uneasy and couldn't help but wonder how much longer it would be until they reached their destination. Was he staring at her in the mirror? As the window whirred and vanished into the large door frame of the SUV, she felt a little relief as the night air rushed in, and the welcoming glow of warm lights appeared in the distance. Tree limbs reached over the narrow road, falling a few feet short of forming a dark tunnel. The overgrown brush looked reminiscent of their cold night of camping just a few short weeks ago. Tressa tried to gauge how fast the SUV was traveling and when it could be safe if they needed to tuck and roll onto the lonely roadside.

As they pulled into the drive, she realized Alex was right. Cars flanked each side of the patterned, cobblestone driveway. It slowly descended, ending at the three-car garage on the right and the vaulted, warmly lit stone entrance ahead. Though a parade of

BMWs, Porsches, and other vehicles obstructed the view of the lake house, Tressa could see the clearing behind it, hinting at an expansive lake rounding out the property. The driver cursed under his breath as he nearly sheared off a mirror from one of the gleaming sports cars straddling the drive and lawn.

"Well, here you are," he said without turning his head. Tressa dug in her purse for a tip as she felt nails dig into her skin.

"Tips are included in the app. We're all set. Let's go." Mauri held down the hem of her barely there jean skirt as she slid out of the vehicle, focusing on the sprawling rustic but contemporary dark wood house before them.

"Well, um, thanks?" Tressa muttered before awkwardly spilling out of the car. The driver nodded, staring at the door as if he had willed it to close. Tressa stood back as the SUV rolled away, navigating party-goers and poorly parked cars. She felt more uncomfortable now than during the ride to the party. Tressa was way out of her comfort zone and felt like the invitation was a mistake. They didn't belong here. But within minutes, she found herself on the stone doorstep, music pulsating on the other side, lights keeping beat to the music.

"Ready?" Mauri asked, squeezing Tressa's hand. "First night of the rest of our lives," she whispered.

A petite brunette, her hair a perfect blend of cocoa and cappuccino highlights cascading over her shoulders, greeted them at the entrance. Her makeup smudged approximately two inches below her eyes. She extended her arms as if trying to steady herself on silver heels that added at least 4 inches, bringing her closer to the five-foot mark.

"Hey," she gushed, holding onto Tressa's arm. "Welcome to Lake View," she slurred.

"Beautiful house," Mauri said, gazing above them. The grand

cathedral ceiling boasted a mesmerizing display of twinkling lights suspended from a wooden beam that seemed to soar through the vast, open space. A sea of people crowded the room, but the wall in front of them could not be obstructed. It was most impressive—a floor-to-ceiling glass expanse separating the crowds of people from the scenic lake beyond. Landscape lighting highlighted the viewpoint from the path to the dock, where a boathouse complemented the house in the same dark wood and burnished trim.

"I'm Tori," she said, her voice a constant trickle of laughter. Her diamond bracelet caught the light above them, reflecting a rainbow prism with each movement. She glimmered from head to toe, from the tiny platinum scarf top to the delicate shimmer of what seemed like stardust against her olive skin.

"Hi, Tori. Delighted to meet you. I'm Mauri, and this is Tressa. Your party, I assume?" Mauri leaned over awkwardly as if she was talking to a child.

"Oh my God, Tess! It's like, we are the same. Tori and Tess? Get it?" she asked, cracking herself up. Tressa didn't even bother to correct her. "You haven't been here before? Are you, like, from another school?"

"We just never had a chance over the years, I guess. We are both at Wyval, but listen, we are so excited to be here tonight," Mauri said, shifting the conversation away from their nouveau status.

"Right. Love it that you are here," enunciating and stressing each word for what seemed like minutes. "Oh my God, Lindsey," she screamed. Like a dog distracted by a squirrel, she wobbled her way over to the door. As Tori reached in for an embrace of the newest arrival, the unsteady rise of the needle-thin metallic heel gave way. She tumbled into the stairs, all sparkles and stilettos, landing on the bottom step. She sat up, cradling her arm, but more desperately needed someone to tug her skirt back into place.

"Oh, come on, will no one help her?" Tressa muttered. As she saw the glint of at least three iPhones pop up, she felt she had no choice. She knelt beside Tori and helped her to a less revealing sitting position. Camera-worthy viral video moment over, the party continued as if nothing had happened. "Hey, are you okay?"

"Tess. My BFF Tess," she said, wrapping her arms around Tressa's neck.

"It's actually, um, never mind. You should probably go sit down or something. Maybe get a bottle of water." Tressa wondered how many of these parties she had hosted and how many times she hadn't had a savior at the steps.

Tori pulled herself up by the post and kicked off the remaining shoe, catapulting it across the room. "No, I need my flip-flops. That will make everything better," she said with such confidence that Tressa believed it. "Tess, Tessy," she whined. "Can you get my sandals? I will love you forever."

Any sympathy Tressa had for her faded like the makeup on Tori's face.

"Please, Tessy. They are upstairs, in the door. The first room on the right. Thanks, love." She picked up a plastic cup from the sideboard, not even bothering to check its contents before drinking it.

"What does she mean in the door?" Mauri whispered out of the side of her mouth, stifling a laugh. "Come on, it will look good if we help her."

"I have no idea. Door? Drawer? We'll just keep looking until we find shoes, I guess. And it will look good to who? She won't remember how she got a bruise on her arm, let alone remember us finding shoes," Tressa said, resigning herself to the fact they were on a mission and headed upstairs.

The darkened bedroom still seemed well-lit from enormous

windows, allowing the glow of exterior lights to flood the white-on-white walls, carpet, and furniture. Everything seemed sterile and pristine. Tressa scanned the room—no shoes peeked out from any beds or dressers. Mauri perched herself at the edge of the plush mattress, her feet grazing the floor.

"So, drawer, I guess that's what she meant," Tressa said as she tugged on the distressed silver handles from the towering dresser. "But who keeps shoes in a drawer?" Tressa wondered out loud. As she carefully closed each drawer, she found nothing more than neatly folded towels and expensive-looking linens. Looking across the room, she saw Mauri standing near the nightstand.

"Well, I didn't find shoes, but I found something. Close the door, Tress," Mauri whispered.

"Mauri, no. Let's not go through her things, please," Tressa said once she noticed the wide, stocky piece of furniture was filled with everything you would typically see strewn on top of a dresser.

"Yeah, you'll want to see this. I think our sparkly friend is one of us," the creaky hinges echoed in the vast room. Time seemed to stand still as they contemplated the contents of the drawer. Mauri held up a small round object illuminated by moonlight filtering through the window.

"But I was under the impression that it was limited to seniors and only a chosen few," Tressa said, reaching for the now familiar coin. She then attempted to discern the intricate design of the gleaming, circular medallion, which depicted a mountain with a snowy summit at its center.

"Maybe she didn't make the cut? Saved it as a souvenir?" Mauri wondered. "It doesn't look exactly the same, though. I'd say we ask her about it."

"Absolutely not! And admit we were snooping? Just put it back. We better get downstairs," Tressa said, stumbling over her words and feet. As she turned to exit the room, she noticed the giant shoe rack behind the door and glitter thong sandals dead center of the bottom row. "I guess it was a door, not a drawer," she said, tucking Tori's low-heeled but equally shiny shoes beneath her arm. "Why does anyone need a pair of shoes for every day of the year?" As she reached for the doorknob, hushed giggles and scampering feet sounded on the other side.

Mauri held up her hand. "Someone was listening to us or following us." Her expression was somewhere between resolute and fearful.

Tressa flung open the door and thrust her head into the hallway. No one was there, but they both heard it. "Maybe it was someone looking for an empty room," she said. "You know," she said, nodding toward the bed behind them.

"Maybe. It did sound like they were laughing or just giddy from too much of whatever Tori was drinking. Either way, let's get the shoes downstairs," she said, reminding Tressa of why they were on the second floor in the first place.

The hall remained clear, and Tressa shut the door as if she were trying not to wake a sleeping baby. She met Mauri at the top of the stairs, only to be stopped before stepping on the first gleaming hardwood top level.

"I saw you," the tall blonde said, popping up out of nowhere. He pointed his finger inches from Tressa's face.

"Tori sent us up to get her shoes," she said, dangling them as close to his face as his finger was to hers. "So, if you excuse me, our friend needs us," she said, escalating the relationship status of the girl they had only met less than an hour ago.

He shook his head, hair that probably hours ago was held up with a bottle's worth of product, now falling over his eye. His stark white shirt peeked out from the regal deep navy blazer, but he folded his arms like second-floor security.

"She does? You didn't seem too concerned with that a few minutes ago," he said, smirking and nodding to the closed door across the hall.

Tressa's face felt like she was eating a bag of ghost pepper chips, and her stomach turned with the same reaction. She knew it wasn't wrong to be upstairs. She held the proof underneath her arm. Prying into closed drawers of personal items was another thing. She looked at Mauri, who seemed about ten seconds away from pushing their obstacle out of the way, stairs or no stairs. He moved closer, his breath heavy with the smell of stale beer, while wafts of expensive cologne and sweat swirled around him with every movement. He grabbed Tressa's arm, pulling her close, his nose next to her ear. His fingers dug into her arm as he whispered something. She tried moving, but his grip pulled her closer, his breath heavy and nauseating.

"I know what you were doing," he said, letting go of Tressa's arm as she pulled and crashed into the wall.

"What are you talking about?" Mauri barged in between them, causing him to catch his balance with the handrail.

Tressa slipped past and stopped mid-stairs. Turning, she saw him draped over the top rail, staring at her. "I know why you were in there—both of you," he said with a wink.

As they returned to the thumping music, a symphony of squeals, singing, and laughter, they searched for Tori. Mauri stood in the foyer, both hands out in front of her.

"Wait, did he just think we were, I mean, that you and I," she said, turning and looking towards the stairs to the bedroom.

"I don't know. Either that, or he saw us snooping? Let's find Tori and get out of here," Tressa said. She had a bad feeling about the party.

In the short time since they were upstairs, people seemed a little more social, a little bit closer, and a lot more intoxicated. They made their way out to the deck off the back of the house, strings of lights undulating above them. Small groups of party-goers gathered in the recesses of a sprawling deck, seemingly oblivious to Mauri and Tressa's presence.

That's when the girls noticed Tori in the corner. She leaned against an ornamental planter, her feet propped up on the bench. The fresh air felt good but slowly crept into Tressa's bones, reminding her that winter had barely started, and her lack of a coat didn't help. Everyone wanted to attend the party, but no one seemed concerned about the host.

Tressa and Mauri sat on the bench, startling Tori. "Hey, there are my girls," she said. "And, yay, you brought my shoes. Love you both," she exclaimed, pulling Tressa into a hug.

"We can't leave her like this," Tressa communicated to Mauri without making a sound.

"Let's take her upstairs and maybe stick around until people start leaving." Mauri held up the small girl, supporting most of the weight. Tressa navigated them toward the sliding door. What she saw on the other side startled her.

With a red cup in one hand and frantically reaching for the handle with the other, a gust of warm air greeted them as Alex spilled onto the deck. "I wasn't sure if you made it, and I've been looking for you both—awesome party, right?" he asked, eyes glossier from when they left the apartment. "And I see you know Tori? The reason we are all here," he said, tousling her hair.

"Alex, my sweetheart," Tori perked up. She scuffed across the deck in her sandals, burying her head against his chest. Mauri looked away, straining to focus on the lake that seemed invisible but was only yards away.

"We were just taking her upstairs to take a break. I think our host had a little too much," Tressa said, slowly leading Tori back inside. "We will be back down in a second." Mauri took her cue and headed back inside, out of the cold.

"Okay, I'll have drinks waiting for you both," Alex said, heading to the kitchen.

The bedroom remained still and looked the same as before. Nothing was out of place, but it nagged at Tressa, knowing that rifling through the contents of the dressers was the only reason they came across the medallion. She couldn't even begin to process why Tori had it in the first place but knew now was not the time to try to find out.

"Okay, Tori, we will be downstairs and will check on you in a bit. Are you okay?"

The small form shifted under the covers, muttering about shoes and friends.

"Lanie would love you both," she murmured as Mauri closed the door.

"Who?" Tressa whispered, looking at Mauri.

"My mom, but I always just call her Lanie. She always wants to make sure I'm surrounded by the best people at the best school. And you guys are the best," she said in a sing-song voice again, exclaiming her praise for her two newest friends. "You know, she's Wyval, too. Our whole family, really."

"Your mom went to Wyval?" Mauri asked.

"Yeppers. I'm following in her footsteps, as well as my grandmother and my aunts. I had no choice. Wyval!" she shouted, pumping a fist in the air before collapsing back onto the comforter.

# Chapter Thirty-Three

**Meeting at Art League of New York**
Ranshaw, Gina<granshaw@artnyc.org>
*To Tressa Litton <lillitton@wyval.org>*

Dear Ms. Litton,

As you approach graduation and the culmination of your art history studies, we strongly encourage you to apply for the position of Gallery Director and Curator of Exhibitions and Programs. Your leadership and esteemed position would be a great asset to our program, and we look forward to hearing from you soon. Rest assured, you will be surrounded by and continually learn from the best in the business as you serve as an ambassador for The League. Please email us at your earliest convenience to schedule a visit to our gallery.

All the best,
Gina Ranshaw
Administrator for Exhibitions and Galleries
Art League of New York

**Lucas Museum Tour and Invitation**

Penna, James<jpenna@lucasmuseum.org>

*To Tressa Litton <lillitton@wyval.org>*

Dear Ms. Litton,

Congratulations on your upcoming graduation! You would be a great fit in our collections management department or exhibitions and planning. We hope you will consider us when deciding on your career choices ahead of you. When you have time, please contact me to set up an all-expense paid visit to our museum to discuss future possibilities.


All the best,

James Penna

Senior Exhibition Designer and Planner

Lucas Museum of Narrative Art


Tressa sat at her laptop, scrolling through her emails. A few messages remained unread, but the contact info let her believe they had similar content. After years of hard work, scheduling classes, studying for exams, and writing papers, the messages served as a reminder of what results to expect from dedication and perseverance. She needed to call Mauri.

"Hey, I need to tell you about what I just read in my inbox," Tressa said, breathless words jumbling together.

"Let me guess. Senior Paintings Conservator in Seattle? Or maybe the assistant director of exhibitions and collections at the Guggenheim in New York? Because those were my emails," Mauri said. "I was just going to call you."

"Oh, you got them too? It must be job postings from the career center," Tressa said, slightly deflated. She knew that many desirable positions she had seen on organizations' websites recommended master's degrees or doctorates and ten years of experience, and they all started over 100K. Something seemed off.

"Career center? Tress. What are you looking at? I would bet money it's similar to my email. I have an invitation from the director of the Guggenheim. He wants me to come out for the weekend to discuss future opportunities. The Guggenheim, Tress! I guarantee not everyone is getting this from the career center."

Tressa scrolled through her laptop, looking at some of the bookmarked pages. She knew Mauri was right. She also knew most classmates were starting to scramble to create impressive cover letters to match the laundry list of accomplishments and accolades bursting on pedigree resumes.

"Graduates don't randomly receive emails asking them to please work for their company or organization, especially with those positions and salary," Tressa said, in awe as she looked back at the unread emails.

"Not all graduates are us, Tress. It's happening. The connections, the job inquiries–it's just like Helena said. How about the party we were at? You saw the house. I'm not sure what Tori's family does, but they are doing something right. It's all connected. We are connected." Mauri said.

Tressa refreshed her email, only to have two more job inquiries pop up: Museum Curatorial Assistant at Stanford. Hartford Curatorial Fellowship in Connecticut. She had to admit that Mauri's excitement was contagious, and she couldn't help but imagine herself as part of the art world's elite. A small fraction of her brain had already visualized talking at next year's Thanksgiving dinner about restoring the latest collection she had acquired. The visual of her cousin's squinting glare and pursed lips mainly satisfied her.

"Do you want to grab dinner? I heard of a new brewery that opened not too far from here. A little bit of a drive, but I hear they have a tuna poke bowl to die for," Mauri said.

"I don't think your status will change since you aren't 21 yet," Tressa replied.

"Did you hear me? Tuna poke bowl. Come on. It's not too far from here," Mauri pleaded.

"Fine, I'll pick you up," Tressa said half-heartedly, focusing on the latest request to join a creative academic community focused on European Baroque art and French and American Impressionists. It looked out of place, nestled between sale announcements from Bath and Body Works and Banana Republic, her usual inbox alerts.

After meeting Mauri, they headed to the brewery, and only a few cars filled the parking lot surrounding the old school building. Gooseneck barn lights illuminated the entrance while a warm glow spilled from the windows lining the expanse of the brick structure. As they waited near the hostess stand, the warmth felt good, surprising in the cavernous high-ceiling room. The decor and photos paid homage to the area's local coal mining history, while beer taps extended from a wall of slate blackboards, preserving one piece of the classroom from years ago. Lo-fi music pumped into the tap room as they scoured the menu of IPAs, wheat beer, stouts, and an equally impressive selection of eclectic menu items. Tressa was glad Mauri convinced her to venture out and try something new.

"Get you started with something to drink? Or are you ready to order?" the server said, not looking up from the iPad as she waited to tap in their ticket.

"Water for me. And the Tuna Poke bowl. Tress, you can get something. I'll drive us home," she said, using responsibility instead of age as her excuse for not drinking.

"Um, same, poke bowl, and I guess I'll try the chocolate cherry stout."

"Excellent choice, ladies. That will be right out." Tressa watched as the tall blonde's ponytail swooshed behind her when she disappeared behind the bar. Within minutes, she returned with a rich-looking beer.

"Aren't you glad we came out?" Mauri said, extending her arm across the table to tap the snifter-like goblet.

"You are right. This place is very cool. You said it recently opened?" Tressa asked.

"Not too long ago. I remember seeing jobs posted around campus for servers and kitchen staff," Mauri said. "And speaking of jobs, did you get anything else?"

"I got a few emails," Tressa said. "I guess I'm overwhelmed by the sudden onslaught of opportunity. But tell me, the Guggenheim, really? And didn't you say somewhere in South Beach as well?" she said, knowing Mauri's list of offers made it more real.

As Mauri ticked off the responsibilities of working as the assistant curator at a museum in Miami, a bang of a door jolted her attention toward the bar. Their server balanced their dinner on a tray, her elbow leading through the swinging classroom door connecting the kitchen and tap room. Only it wasn't their server. As the blonde, swooshy, pony-tailed girl placed the beautifully garnished poke bowls on the table, Tressa's stomach dropped.

"Thank you," Mauri said, not even looking up, anticipating their dinner more than Tressa.

"Let us know if you need anything," the newest server said, bumping the table as she hurried back to the kitchen. Dark liquid dotted the linen napkin beside the bowl, the beer still sloshing in the glass.

"Mauri," Tressa whispered.

"Mm-mm, so good," she said, directing the fork's prongs at the tuna.

"Mauri, that wasn't our server. Someone else brought our food out," she said.

"So?" Mauri said with a shrug. "I do know this is the best poke bowl I've ever had. We are definitely coming back. Aren't you going to try it?"

Tressa stared at the door, the silhouette of two figures like a silent movie playing out behind frosted glass. The alcohol stung her throat as she gulped the high-ABV liquid as if it were water. It did nothing to ease the dryness in her mouth. She watched as the door swung open, revealing their original waitress.

"Everything came out okay? Can I get you anything else?" she asked.

Tressa wanted to ask if she could send out the person who delivered their food—and ask her what happened to the peace tattoo on her arm.

# Chapter Thirty-Four

Tressa sat at her desk, her eyes fixed on the sea of names on her tablet. She had been searching for weeks for any clue about the peace tattoo blonde that had been haunting her ever since her encounter at the brewery. The search had proved fruitless, and her stomach felt like she had just ridden a roller coaster. She had a strong hunch that something was amiss, especially after seeing Gina a few weeks ago. Tressa couldn't quite pinpoint it, but something felt off. It was like trying to solve a puzzle with two pieces that appeared to fit but didn't quite align.

Her door slammed, and Alex barged into her room. "Always doing work. I feel like you've been holed up in your room and buried in your laptop for days," he said.

She quietly closed her laptop, showing no alarm or the fact that she was hiding something. Her eyes felt like she swam for hours in a pool over-saturated with chlorine. She cleared her throat to break the uncomfortable silence as Alex waited for a response.

"Oh, you know me, I have to finish strong in everything I do," she said. "Aren't you worried about finals?"

"I think I'm fine. As long as I don't royally screw anything up next semester, I'm on track for graduation," Alex said, not seeming concerned. "Anyway, I think you should finish up. There's a little gathering on the other side of the lake tonight. Not like last week, but it should be legit. Why don't you come? I'm sure Mauri will drop by."

Tressa was aware of the party, having been in the loop about every campus event since her encounter with Helena, but the excitement was wearing off. She didn't want to make a big deal about it. "Let me see what I can finish up here, and maybe I'll join you," she said, fingers holding the edge of her laptop, hoping her half-hearted promise would get him out of her room. Her latest project had become all-consuming.

Tressa sat at her computer, her gaze fixed on the screen as she scrolled through the missing persons database. She had been immersed in this task for several days, hoping to uncover a clue about the elusive blonde with the peace sign tattoo, which had been haunting her thoughts for weeks. However, the file on the screen was dated over fifty years ago and had no connection to the girl in the woods; but instead, it became another rabbit hole into which Tressa ventured. She had no idea the database for missing persons existed, let alone was accessible to the public. The young man displayed on the screen was only a few years younger than Tressa when he went missing, and if he were alive today, he would be in his 70s. He had vanished after a swimming mishap and was never found. The thought of his family and friends holding onto hope after all these years deeply moved Tressa. Perhaps they still harbored the belief that he might appear one day, having suffered from amnesia or lost his way. Maybe after all these years, he'd realize that his puzzle piece didn't perfectly match and want to find out the truth.

Tressa glanced into the living room, where she found Alex settled on the couch with the remote. Satisfied, she gently closed the door and refocused on her laptop. As she refreshed the search engine, a familiar queasiness crept over her. Each file provided an age, basic description, date of last contact, and location. Some also had photos. Tressa studied each one intently as if trying to communicate with them through the screen. Little other information was provided in the descriptions. As she scrolled through the 'Circumstances of Disappearance,' she encountered details describing individuals of all ages and situations, from being last seen on a Greyhound bus to instances of prior sightings. Some cases involved a parent fleeing with a child amid a custody battle, seeking to disappear and remain hidden. Tressa couldn't help but imagine the heartfelt longing of those who filed the missing person reports. Other cases revealed evidence suggesting that the missing individuals had chosen to vanish, which offered little solace to their loved ones but at least confirmed their continued existence. However, the stories of a different nature tugged at Tressa's heart the most. A 17-year-old girl was last seen leaving home to meet someone from school and never returned. Her vehicle was found in a remote area, but the trail went cold there. Young children living with both parents would quietly vanish from their homes, and their whereabouts remained a mystery. Tressa closed the browser, realizing that another hour had slipped away as she delved into one wormhole after another, none of which advanced her investigation.

# Chapter Thirty-Five

The pale woman lay lifeless, arm extended, hair cascading below her while outlined in a scarlet river of blood. Watchful glowing eyes emerged from the darkness, combining both anticipation and menace. A small, dark figure crouched on the woman's chest, his expression one of annoyance and evil. Tressa stared at the screen at the front of the auditorium, and silence enveloped the class as they took in sharply contrasting light and shadow nuances.

"The Nightmare. Henry Fuseli. It transfixed, terrorized, and perplexed people for centuries. The theme of Gothic Horror is said to have inspired great writers such as Mary Shelley and Edgar Allan Poe. We go to a time in the 18th century when the Swiss painter created a dark composition known to cause great debate about its true meaning. Tell me your thoughts, whether you are familiar with it or seeing it for the first time." Professor Dawson crossed his arms, resting against a table. His eyes met Tressa's, and she was sure he was talking directly to her.

"I think the gargoyle wants her, and the horse wants to watch," a voice from the back of the room said, followed by muted laughter.

"Good observation, a theme of sexuality." The professor met the juvenile comment with a valid interpretation, stopping the frat-boy humor. "Anyone else? What do you feel when you see this?"

"I don't think she's dead," another student said. "She's dreaming or having a nightmare. The figures around her represent her fears, the crushing oppression and pressure she feels daily. The watchfulness of others." More students chimed in, discussing the mixture of horror, death, and feelings after waking up from nightmares.

"Ms. Litton, you seem to be in deep thought over this one. Do you have any input?" he asked, making her feel like she was the only one in the room.

Tressa focused on the deep hues punctuated by the light of the fair woman in the center, a golden-haired woman with her arm reaching out, evil surrounding her like she didn't have a chance. Tressa wiped her palms on her pants and stared at the papers before her as if they had answers. "I think the creatures around her are evil, capable of bad things. She looks vulnerable, unaware of what is about to happen."

"I'd like to see what will happen," the voice exclaimed with the same middle-grade humor.

Professor Dawson nodded, showing no signs of being rattled, and the image disappeared from the screen as the class ended. "Okay, everyone. We will pick up next time and go into a little more detail. You were all correct. This piece has been interpreted and described in all manners mentioned today. Ms. Litton, however, is most accurate, as it is widely said to represent our dream-like state and what frightens us. Another spin on that is that demons give us a crushing feeling, something so troubling we can't breathe, while voyeurs stand by doing nothing but reveling in our fear. The holiday break is almost here, which means the end of the semester is drawing to a close. Check with me if you have any missing assignments. I'll see you next week."

With every step toward the exit, she waited to hear her name. She knew turning around would reveal her professor's stare locked onto her like a heat-seeking missile. Mauri waited for her at the top step.

"Well, that was a little dark for the holidays. Interesting, though," Mauri said. The level of coldness escalated from bitter to biting as they made their way across campus.

"Agreed. Hey, I know it's late, but let's grab a quick coffee," Tressa said as they approached the small cafe near the end of the walkway. She needed to talk about the encounter at the brewery last week.

The jingling of bells, followed by the blast of warmth, welcomed them as they entered the nearly empty coffee shop. Tressa waited at the small table as Mauri placed two Styrofoam cups in the center, delicate wisps of steam dancing above.

"That smells good," she said as the wafting aroma of vanilla and caramel swirled around them. "So, what's up? More offers?" Mauri asked, sliding into the velour-padded booth.

Tressa did not mention the unread emails in her inbox, all from similar senders. "No, I wanted to tell you about this database I've been working with."

"Like an employment search database? Tress, really, we are good," she said, reaching across the table and squeezing her hands. "My main problem is figuring out which ones I want to consider seriously."

Tressa began, "I'm just going to tell you what I've been looking at, and I know what you will say, but just hear me out." Since the incident at the brewery, Mauri tried to brush it aside with every excuse, from *it wasn't the same girl* to *it could have been a relative*, or maybe Tressa was *mistaken about the tattoo*.

"Ugh, Tress. Are you going there again? I'm telling you, that wasn't Gina. You only saw the girl for a second when she brought out the food, and we weren't paying attention," Mauri replied.

"And I'm telling you, the girl in the woods and Gina at the brewery are not the same person. And I need to find out who that was in the woods," Tressa snapped, crossing her arms.

Mauri gripped her cup tightly. "I have a hard time understanding how you think the Summit Society would benefit by hurting one of their own. Do you think she was the sacrificial offering of the semester? And everyone gets the job of their choice, is invited to the best parties, and becomes part of a coveted lifelong network because of it? Come on, Tress. You met Helena. She's worried about nothing more than status. I highly doubt she's the mastermind behind a ritualistic cult. It's a popularity thing. It's tradition. It's our Skull and Bones."

Mauri was right. When Tressa received her first letter involving her in this clandestine journey, she spent many hours researching other secret societies. She knew the Summit Society aligned practices with other shadowy organizations, with a reputation of everything shrouded in secrecy and only allowing membership to an elite few. Secret societies were rumored to have a roster throughout the years boasting high-ranking political figures and those with prominent business influence affecting all corners of the globe. They held bizarre meetings where members dressed as skeletons and pranced around, coaxing new members to steal human skulls as a rite of initiation. On the outside, the escapades seemed nothing more than over-the-top fraternity pranks, pushing the envelope and testing everyone's moral compass. That's what historians recount and research shows, but if secret societies are as clandestine as they say, who knows what else takes place, what cover-ups happened, and who made sacrifices for the good of the organization? The Summit Society would be no different.

"For God's sake, Tress, our initiation meeting involved champagne in a dusty old lake house, hardly the setting of suspicious activity," Mauri said, crumpling a napkin and throwing it on the table. "Honestly, I'm still trying to figure out why we were chosen, but I'm not complaining. It's killing me not to tell anyone, though. Have you said anything to your family or Alex?"

"No. I haven't said a word to anyone," Tressa responded.

"What else? Come on, lay it on the line. Do you think it's a cult? The occult?" she asked, wiggling her fingers before her.

"No, Mauri. Not the occult," Tressa said, shaking her head. However, her research into some of the most secret organizations everyone heard about but no one knew about brought about the familiar twinge in her gut, the feeling you get not knowing if it's nerves or the onset of a sudden illness. She pondered whether a common thread guided pivotal decisions in history. Membership in an elite group pursuing excellence and seeking wealth, power, and prestige. A group entrusted with safeguarding secrets to protect their inner circle, no matter the cost.

Napkins fluttered off the table as a cold gust of air halted their conversation.

"Ladies, don't let me interrupt," a man said as he strode to the counter. They watched Professor Dawson rub his hands together, blowing on his fingertips while he decided on his order. "Decaf, two pumps of vanilla with a splash of soy," he said, tapping his credit card on the counter. He smiled when he realized Tressa was staring, and she nearly knocked her coffee off the table in embarrassment.

"And he's coming over," Mauri whispered.

"Fueling up before you both start working on the final semester project?" he asked, his white teeth gleaming.

"Yeah, we, uh, just stopped in after class. What are you doing here?" Tressa babbled.

"Last I checked, professors are allowed in. We don't bite," he replied.

Tressa imagined tucking herself underneath the table, disappearing as soon as he turned his back.

"Tall decaf, vanilla?" the barista yelled.

"That's me," he said, motioning toward the counter. "Well, I don't mean to interrupt, so you ladies have a good evening. And don't forget those projects. You don't need any distractions this time of year."

"Distractions?" Tressa asked.

"You know—the senior slide. Some students think they are in the home stretch and let their grades suffer. You worked hard to get where you are, so don't let anything challenge your progress. It's not worth it. I'll see you next week", he said before leaving as quickly as he had arrived.

"That was weird. 'Don't let anything challenge your progress,'" Tressa repeated once he was out the door. "What do you think he meant by that?"

Mauri tossed her empty cup in the trash and slid her crossbody bag over her head. "It means he likes you, and he attempted to make small talk outside the classroom but ended up sounding more creepy than cool."

"Haha. Very funny. Well, he's right about one thing. I have a lot of work to do. I need to start the Art History project tonight," Tressa replied.

"Good. Just promise me that you won't get sidetracked with your investigation tactics for your Criminal Justice research project," Mauri said.

Not wanting to defend her need to dig deeper into the database, Tressa changed the subject back to Professor Dawson. "Why do you think he came in?" she asked.

"Tress, I was joking. He probably wanted coffee on the way

home. Relax. I'm sure he sees seniors slack off constantly, and he doesn't want his favorite bookworm to fall into the same trap."

Tressa wasn't bothered by running into her professor at the coffee shop, but she wondered what distractions he was referring to. She watched as Mauri stopped moving and put her hand on her bag.

"It's my phone. I think there's a new message," Mauri said, plopping back onto the couch.

Tressa heard the notification sound from her phone and reached for it with a shaky hand. The two friends stared at the screen, mesmerized. They hadn't received many messages on the app lately, especially since they completed their tests. But this message was different and took things to a new level.

"What, um, what popped up for you?" Mauri asked, clearing her throat.

"Videos," Tressa replied. The app responded as it had previously, a smoky gray screen fading to reveal a small folder labeled 'tests'.

"What's this point of view? Did they access our cameras through the app? Or was someone there?" Mauri asked, studying the screen.

Tressa scrolled through each video but did not want to watch them since they had already lived through those moments. The videos were a highlight reel of both girls standing near the graffiti in the old concrete building, including the pentagram, Mauri and Tressa squeezing through the back door at the Old Jail, and then a clip of both scaling the fence. Finally, there was a close-up shot of the girls looking at their phones and Gina writhing and collapsing on the ground. If anyone saw this highlight reel, they would think it was an example of how to get arrested quickly.

Tressa stared at the thumbnails of the videos and said, "I have a feeling someone is watching us all the time, not just during our tests. Isn't it obvious? As soon as I start talking about missing person databases, criticism of the Summit Society, or the idea to share information about the organization, we get these kinds of recordings."

"Maybe that is part of it. Since we met with Helena for our official initiation, they uploaded documentation of our journey," Mauri said, trying to make excuses for the uncomfortable situation.

"Oh, sure. An edited video that doesn't give the big picture but just enough to serve as blackmail if we decide to say or question anything."

# Chapter Thirty-Six

"I can think of better ways to spend a Friday night," Mauri said, twisting the hanging chair back and forth. "Don't forget, we have two invites for tonight. How long is this going to take?"

Tressa was unwavering. "Please humor me," she said, scrolling through the prompts. "I felt we struck a chord with someone after we visited the brewery. Why would we get those videos in the app? If there is a clear explanation for it, that's fine. Until we get one, I need to do this research."

Mauri was still on the fence about the whole situation. "And keep phones locked in the car?" she asked.

"It's only while we are discussing this. It's not random to forget our phones in the car," Tressa replied, her eyes darting back and forth as she filled in the fields on the website. She bookmarked the page several times, but the form retained only some of her details. Alex had already left for a party, so they didn't need to worry about him poking around.

Mauri pulled over the puffy orange ottoman, its soft fabric sinking beneath her weight as she leaned closer to the laptop. "Okay, so what are we looking at?" she asked, trying to sound interested. The screen flickered to life, casting a cool glow across her face. "So lists of missing persons, unidentified people, and unclaimed people. Lovely," she said, the words dripping with sarcasm.

"Yeah, I know. I thought the same thing when I first looked

at this," Tressa said. "All these people, it's unbelievable," she said, scrolling through the website. She wasn't sure if it troubled her more seeing the information of those identified and never claimed or photos of deceased and never identified. Images from a morgue or coroner's office can be difficult to forget.

"And what is this? DBF? Under the unclaimed column?" Mauri's finger hovered near the screen as she figured it out. "Oh, jeez. Date Body Found." She sat back, straightening in her seat, her face scrunched as if she just bit into a lemon wedge. "Oh my God, there are so many," Mauri whispered, looking at the lengthy list.

"Alright, look, let's try to focus," Tressa said. "There is something I found yesterday. It might be a long shot, but I want to show you. Here, let me jump to the missing person section." As she refreshed, it pulled up the general search again.

"Look at all those young people. What the heck?" Mauri asked, hands clutching her face. The light reflected from the laptop screen, her eyes glistening.

"I know, it's bad. But if you click on some cases, it indicates things like a custody battle or runaway situation. Even though it doesn't make things much better, at least you know they aren't all random kidnappings," Tressa said.

"Or murders," Mauri added.

"Or murders, right?" Tressa agreed. She needed to decompress for several days after poring over file after file of individuals, some including personal information such as tattoos or cartoon characters on their backpacks. Someone had to miss all these people, whatever the reason or circumstance. Tressa prayed she would never need to consult this website again.

"Let's talk about the girl we saw that night in the woods," Tressa said.

"You mean Gina?" Mauri interrupted.

"Gina, but not Gina," Tressa said. "And let's say for the sake of argument that it wasn't her." When she realized Mauri wouldn't interrupt, she continued. "So if the girl carried out of the woods was hurt, or worse, and someone wanted to cover it up, isn't it possible she could be missing?"

Mauri inhaled deeply, her palms digging into her thighs as she lurched forward. She exhaled and stared at the screen before her. "Just tell me what you found or how you found it."

Tressa wasn't sure if her idea was far-fetched. She needed to explain how she got to this point. "Let's say the Summit Society had someone involved in the initiation, even if they agreed to it and volunteered. They would probably ask for the help of someone they knew who wouldn't question what they were doing," she explained.

"Probably, someone who goes to Wyval? Wouldn't we have heard about a missing person from our school? Come on, Tress."

"Not a current student. Alumni. Wyval Alumni and a member of the Summit Society. It's the only way they can trust someone to be involved."

"Right. Let me get out my little black book of all previous Society inductees. How would you ever figure that out?" Mauri asked.

Tressa knew that was where things could start to unravel. She knew Helena and friends could choose anyone to assist them, but chances are it would be someone local, or local enough, to meet them on a dark November night, entering the vast tangle of woods.

"First, I scoured news stories and even obituaries, locally and surrounding states," Tressa said.

"Oh, Tress. This is too much."

"No, listen. I'm confident I would have found something. If a young girl like that died unexpectedly or especially from unusual circumstances, any local news outlet would make it a top story. There are no stories, no obituaries."

"In this immediate area, but your alleged "dead girl" could be from anywhere in the country," Mauri said, pushing her thumb into her eyebrow. "But go on."

"Look here. I entered some search criteria into the website for missing persons." Her fingers slid effortlessly across the keys, hammering away at the info she had come to know so well by now. With a bit of exaggeration, Tressa hit enter.

Mauri squinted, but Tressa knew what she was thinking. It yielded fewer results than she anticipated. "Wow, I expected more, I guess."

"I know, right? Entering the date range when they were missing, approximate age and hair color narrows it down. And then we can even do more," Tressa said, ranking the list of states in order. "So Pennsylvania, obvious choice. But note the surrounding regions, like you said, in case they are from the general area."

"Six? Really? Only six names?" Mauri exclaimed.

"Crazy, right? And I have already contacted three of the families. The circumstances don't match up. Two never went to college; one mom broke down and confessed that she would run away from their home if she could. I haven't gotten in touch with the others yet." Tressa sat back and looked at the screen. As soon as she said it out loud, she knew she needed to contact those other families immediately.

Mauri held the back of her neck, looking to the floor as if it would open magically and reveal answers to everything she was thinking. "Tress, what if none of this is connected? What if it's just a coincidence?"

"What if it's not? I'm telling you, Mauri. The girl at the restaurant was Gina, or whoever we met at the lake house, but it's not the same girl carried out of the woods. And there is no tattoo on her wrist," Tressa insisted.

The steam heat hissed, followed by the echo of a clang. Mauri returned to the chair, swaying back and forth. While waiting for a response, Tressa aimlessly scrolled through the faces of those missing and unclaimed, pictures of jewelry and shoes found, anything to help with identification. Despite the heat in the room, she couldn't shake the chill running up her spine.

"So we are almost in our last semester of college, with positions in the art world falling at our feet, and we are going to act like criminal justice majors all of a sudden?" Mauri said with a sigh. She stared out the window before returning her gaze to the computer screen. Finally, after several minutes, she jumped up, her hands on her hips. "Okay, let's do it. Who are we visiting first?" she conceded.

"That's what I wanted to hear," Tressa said. "We need to take a little road trip to the Jenning household."

# Chapter Thirty-Seven

As Tressa and Mauri followed Mapquest's directions to the Jenning home, they felt a growing anticipation.

Mauri glanced at the GPS and asked, "You haven't talked to anyone at this address?"

Tressa replied confidently, "No, but I've done my research and have a backstory for each case. Just let me do the talking."

As they stepped out of the car, a wave of excitement washed over them as they approached the Jenning home. As they made their way towards the porch, wind chimes filled the air, creating a discordant melody that only added to the anticipation. The air smelled of gasoline and winter as Tressa carefully weaved past the ATV parked near the porch. Her attention was drawn to the iridescent sea shells hanging near the screen door, their gentle tinkling like the sound of rippling water. Mauri stayed a step back, taking in the sights of the rundown porch. Hinges squeaked as Tressa pulled back the door, bits of screen fluttering as she reached out to knock. Before her knuckles met the worn wooden surface, she jumped as a face appeared in the small window.

"Can I help you?" The petite woman who appeared between the two doors looked older than Tressa expected for the mother of a college student, with a slumped posture and drab, ashen strands of hair tucked inside the collar of her robe.

"I'm sorry, I was looking for Karen Jenning. Sorry to have bothered you," Tressa said, slowly retreating from the door.

"You got the right place. Let me guess. You are one of those reporters or wanna-be internet-famous types. Can I help you with something that doesn't involve an interview? I'm done commenting because no one will listen to what I have to say," the woman muttered.

Tressa studied the woman's eyes and noticed the bold emerald color surrounded by swollen redness. While her skin was sallow, few wrinkles and a smooth complexion belied the idea she was older. Her thin hands looked childlike as she dug her thumb into the opposite palm repeatedly. The symphony of chimes rattled around them, the pre-sunset amber glow falling on the fields, their surroundings growing dimmer. They had the right place but not the right time. Mauri stepped forward.

"Mrs. Jenning. My name is Mauri, and you met my friend, Tressa," she said. "We don't want to bother you, but we wanted to ask you a few questions about Rachel. I hear she was a great artist."

Tressa spun around, surprised to hear Mauri's voice, especially talking about Rachel Jenning.

"You know my Rachel? You know what happened?" Karen asked, opening the door a bit wider.

"That's just it. I heard about what happened, and if we could get some information from you, we might be able to help," Mauri responded.

The wind picked up, causing the chimes to clatter and sway erratically. Mauri pulled her light jacket close under her chin while Tressa shoved her hands deep into the pockets of her jeans. Karen glanced over her shoulder, her hand still grasping the door.

"No, it's not a good time," Karen whispered, her voice shaking as she repeatedly turned around and stared into the house.

"Oh, okay. Well, we need to get back soon anyway, and it's pretty cold out here," Mauri said, trying anything to get into the rundown farm home. "We promise not to stay long."

Karen tapped a worn bedroom shoe on the corner of the screen door and crossed her arms. "I guess so. But I only have a little time." She squinted, the remnants of the day giving her complexion a soft golden hue. She didn't step aside to allow Tressa and Mauri to enter the house, but she didn't walk away.

"So, tell me a little about your daughter. What was her major at Wyval?" Mauri asked, trying to keep Karen talking.

"Theater Arts. And a minor in Sculpture. She's a talented girl. Beautiful, talented girl." The words made Karen's face soften a bit.

"And she graduated a few years ago?" Mauri continued.

"Top of her class, destined for big things," Karen said. "There was a little drama her senior year, and she got wrapped up with some nice-looking teacher, but it was a passing phase," Karen said, rubbing the sleeve of her faded robe.

"What kind of drama? Was everything okay?" Mauri asked.

"Oh yes. You know how it goes. A student gets infatuated with their professor. It didn't last long. He made sure of that, thankfully. That's not what I'm worried about. I'm afraid about the other people she associated with," Karen said.

Tressa felt a burning in her chest, hoping the rickety post would hold her weight as everything seemed a little off-kilter. She managed to squeak out a few syllables. "Other people? What people? From the college, Mrs. Jenning? Was Rachael in any special clubs?" her voice wavered.

Instantly, Karen's eyes welled up with tears, and she let out a sniffle and a few gasping sobs. Within seconds, pounding footsteps echoed behind Karen. A voice bellowed from within.

"Mom. What are you doing? I said no interviews." As a ruddy-faced boy approached his mother, his blond buzz cut stood out against the background of the dimly lit hallway, his looming presence dwarfing Karen's small frame. His anger melted into pity when he noticed tears streaming down his mother's face. "Let's get you inside," he said, guiding her away from the door.

"Wait. I mean, hi. I'm Tressa. We didn't mean to upset her. We go to Wyval, and we just thought we could help," Tressa said, stretching on the tips of her toes to get a better look into the house.

"We are good. Don't need any help." The porch shook in an angry crescendo as the door slammed into the frame. Tressa expected to see shards of wood at their feet.

"I guess that was Rachel's brother, Andrew. I don't suppose we can get him to talk," Mauri said, taking a step back.

The girls retreated from the porch and headed to the Land Rover. Sitting in the confines of the vehicle, away from the buffeting winds providing some relief, Tressa wondered how they got to that point. Any traces of daylight dissipated, and the sadness of the desolate land around them mirrored that of Rachel's mother.

"Dare I ask why you know so much about Rachael? And you know her brother?" Tressa asked, skepticism creeping in like the cold winter air.

"I don't know him. You aren't the only one who can search a database. Rachael isn't missing. She's probably in New York getting away from that mess," Mauri said, nodding to the farmhouse. "She's not our girl."

The road unraveled before them, snaking its way back to campus. Tressa couldn't get the woman's look of despair out of her mind or the eruption of rage from the brother who ended their conversation. But neither troubled her like the details surrounding the mention of drama with a professor.

# Chapter Thirty-Eight

Tressa found herself in a bind. The end of the fall semester arrived like an unexpected guest, but she knew it was due to her lack of preparation. While she spent time studying missing person databases, reading about the origins of cults, and investigating whether the several job offers she received were legit, she let most of her assignments slide. Now it was crunch time, and to make matters worse, the reminders of Christmas seemed to be everywhere, adding to her stress.

"Studying again? Come on, Tressa. It's our last Christmas as roommates. You can't break tradition," Alex pleaded, sitting in the center of the couch with weathered moccasins peeking out from an oversized, fuzzy throw blanket. The smell of slightly burnt butter and cocoa hung in the air, punctuated with a fragrant smell she couldn't quite place. Alex leaned forward, with creamy liquid spilling over the edge of a porcelain mug.

"Drinking hot chocolate? How festive," Tressa said, peering into the mug.

"Hot chocolate with a kick," he winked. "Burnt microwave popcorn, spiked cocoa, and *Christmas Vacation*. How can you resist?"

"Alex," she whined. "I have so much to do. This is the first time I've been this far behind in my entire school career. I have no shopping done, and the end of the semester and Christmas will be here in a second," Tressa said as she slumped on the couch.

"You are buried in your laptop most hours of the day, you miss no classes, and I'm sure your Mom will take care of whatever shopping remains." He tried to disguise the long neck of the white glass bottle as he generously topped off a steaming mug on the counter. She knew it was useless to refuse, so she let the thought of ten-page papers and violent crime statistics slip away as quickly as the warm mug fell into her hands. Warm coconut-scented steam filled her nostrils.

"First, my mom doesn't buy all my presents. Secondly, is there coconut rum in this?" She leaned against the back of the couch, sipping quicker than she should. "Okay, that's fantastic." The table-top aluminum tree shimmered with vibrant hues from a rotating wheel below, creating an elaborate light show. Tressa reminisced about finding an aluminum tree in the attic of her childhood home, feeling it added a retro holiday magic. However, her mother didn't like it and traded it for tall, pre-lit artificial trees. It was Tressa's first year at school, and she felt a little homesick when the small shiny spot of nostalgia appeared on her desk, compliments of Alex. The tree bore witness to many nights of drinking and partying since then.

They nestled into their favorite corners of the couch underneath cozy throws. Tressa could hear her mother's voice, "*That Alex is such a great guy. I can't believe you are just friends living in the same apartment.*" While most mothers tend to be overprotective, Tressa's mom approached their relationship with the familiarity of a sorority sister.

"I might not sit through the entire movie, but I'll hang out for a while," Tressa remarked, getting swept up in the festive ambiance.

Scrolling through the holiday movie selection, Alex sported a knowing smirk, realizing she wouldn't decline. As the familiar jingle filled the air, accompanied by animated opening credits dancing across the screen, Tressa found herself enveloped in a sense of relaxation she hadn't experienced in weeks.

"I have to admit, this is nice," she commented, setting the cup and saucer on her lap as the movie began. "I needed this break. Thank you."

"See, I know what's good for my Tress. Just relax. You have nothing to worry about," Alex said, reaching over to tousle her hair.

"I don't know about that," she said. How she wished she could tell him more.

"You'll breeze through next semester, and job offers are pouring in. Your main dilemma should be choosing between the museum curator and gallery manager positions. First-world problems," Alex teased.

Agreeing with a nod, Tressa shifted her focus to the screen. "I was thinking of asking Mauri to join us, but she was busy," she added.

Raising his eyebrows, Alex strolled over to the counter to refill his drink, extending the bottle of rum toward her.

"No, thank you. I'm fine. Have you seen Mauri today?" Tressa asked, feeling anxious after not receiving any responses to the texts she had sent earlier. She was eager to share the latest findings about another individual on their list. The recent disappearance of Tarah Cavanaugh, followed by her reappearance a few days later after a cross-country excursion with her much older boyfriend, allowed Tressa to mark off another person from the list. She was excited to share the news with Mauri and eager to learn about any new developments following their visit to the wind chime farm last week.

"Yeah, actually, I did run into Mauri. She seemed pretty

friendly with Mr. D," Alex replied.

"Mr. D?" Tressa said, her face feeling warm, her throat tight.

"Mr. Dawson, Professor Dawson, whatever you call him, I didn't want to disturb their conversation, if you know what I mean," Alex said.

"I don't know what you mean. Where were they?" Tressa asked. She felt her face flush as she tried to keep her composure.

"I take it you are also a Professor Dawson fan," Alex teased.

"No. I was trying to get in touch with Mauri today, that's all. We usually chat in the morning, but I haven't heard from her."

"She was standing outside his office, showing him some papers. It is the end of the semester. I'm sure she's feeling the crunch, too."

"True. Let's just finish the movie. I'm getting tired," Tressa said. In ninety minutes, her mood plummeted like someone coming off a sugar high–or a hot chocolate high. She placed their glasses in the sink, and Alex stopped her before she retreated to her room.

"I'm glad we got to carry on our tradition. I mean that," sensing her change in mood.

"Me too," she said, and their eyes met in a lingering gaze before she entered her room.

Her phone chimed before going to bed. Mauri finally got back to her. She said she was tired after spending too much time on a paper at the library. Tressa lacked the energy to respond and engage. Scrolling through her unread email, she clicked on the invitation to visit the upscale gallery in Manhattan. *Ms. Litton, we would be honored to speak with you regarding the position. Please contact me at your earliest convenience,* read the email she received only three hours ago. Countdown to Christmas sales, end-of-semester reminders from Wyval, and a cryptic link to update her nonexistent Venmo account filled out the rest of her inbox, except for a bold message that popped up only seconds before. She hovered over the sender, DjandyJ, the header enticing her with CAN WE TALK?

Hi Tressa – Sorry our meeting was kinda rude a few weeks ago, my fault. There's something I need to show you. I know you were looking into my sister's disappearance and all—if you want, you can respond or text me at this number.

Without overthinking or wondering how this person got her email, she tapped the numbers into her phone, surprised to get an immediate response. Her heart pounded in her chest as wavering dots immediately appeared. It seemed like hours for his response to pop up.

**T: Hey, got your message. What's up?**

**Unknown: I wanted to show you something related to my sister's disappearance. Can we meet somewhere?**

**T: Too busy to run out. But do you want to call me?**

**Unknown: Nevermind**

**T: Wait, maybe later next week.**

**Unknown: Maybe. I dunno. It's probably not a good idea.**

Within seconds, her screen went from a back-and-forth chat to an incoming call. Tressa didn't hesitate to answer, but the voice on the other end of the call sounded muffled.

"I'm sorry, I'm having a hard time hearing you," Tressa said, her whispered tone not helping matters, but she didn't want Alex overhearing. "Andrew?"

"You can call me Andy," he said, the volume increased but still barely audible.

"Andy. Hi. Listen, I'm sorry if I upset your mom and you. We,

I mean, I am researching your sister's situation, being from Wyval and everything."

"Yeah, you and half the town. We get many self-made investigators looking for social media likes rather than trying to help," Andy said, his voice raspy.

"Well, believe me when I say I am trying to help," Tressa said. After almost a minute, she held the phone away from her face to confirm the call wasn't dropped. "Are you still there?"

His heavy breathing made it sound like he was walking uphill or working out. "Can I trust you? This isn't a YouTube thing you are doing? Cause I swear, if I find this picture all over the internet," he said, his voice crescendoing into something more fitting the day she saw him at the house.

"Hey, Andy, wait. You are the one who reached out to me. I thought I could help," Tressa said, images of the lifeless blonde flashing behind closed eyelids. "Wait. What picture are you talking about?"

Andy must have moved the phone away while continuing to talk. She could barely make out the words. "I spend some nights as a DJ, parties, and stuff. I know a lot of people in the industry, and they know about my sister. A buddy of mine sent this only a few days after she went missing."

Without risking putting the call on speaker, she asked him to hold a second while she checked her messages. The picture was fuzzy and not in focus. Tressa noticed a group of people but couldn't make out any of the faces.

"I got the picture, Andy, but what am I looking at?"

He sighed, "Upper right, zoom in. The couple standing by the couch."

Tressa examined the phone closer, her clammy fingers sliding as she tried to enlarge the image. A wave of nausea washed over her when she realized who it was.

"You know him, right? The teacher? That's my sister next to him. I think she ran away with him," Andy grumbled.

Tressa was at a loss for words. She had seen him only hours ago in class and noticed how he looked at her, but she didn't hate it. She felt flustered whenever she spoke to him, but not in a terrible way.

"Tressa? Are you still there?" Andy asked.

"Yes, I, um, yes. That looks like him, that's for sure. But maybe it's not. Your mom said there was drama with Rachael and Professor Dawson when she was in school?" Tressa asked. The room seemed to tilt, and she tried clearing her throat to erase any signs of alarm.

"I dunno—you don't know my mom. She had her own problems after we lost everything. Sometimes I don't know what to believe," Andy replied.

*Lost everything.* It was clear her new confidant thought Tressa knew way more than she did.

"Andy, I'm sorry, I'm not following you. Who lost everything?" Tressa asked.

Andy exhaled another heavy sigh before he continued. "We had a bad run for a while. Things were pretty good when my sister was still at Wyval. Our farm was doing well, and then the gas driller came and told us what they discovered on our property. It was an offer we couldn't refuse. Money started pouring in, and it's like our lifestyle changed overnight. Rachael was tooling around school in a fancy new car with friends to match. Then Dad passed away suddenly. The agreement we had with the gas company had everything in his name, and things got screwed up when he was gone. They said they no longer had permission to drill, and everything ended. The contract, the drilling, the money. It seemed to end just as fast as it started. We lost our house, and you saw where we live now."

Tressa tried to digest all of this, the tip of her foot pushing against the floor as her chair thudded against the wall. "God, Andy. I'm sorry about all of this. And now your sister is gone, too?"

"Yeah, it sucks. At least if we could find her, it might bring some of my mom's sanity back," Andy said.

"Well, Andy, if I find out anything about the professor, I'll be in touch. Sorry, there's nothing I can tell you now," she said, glad he couldn't see her guilty expression. "One more thing: Do you remember your sister being in any clubs at Wyval?"

Andy paused. "I don't know about any clubs or anything. I know when things were going good, it was good. Right before graduation, Rachael started receiving all these awesome job offers. I have to say I was a little bit jealous. But when the bad luck came through, it really came through. Even if she's not with that professor, I wouldn't blame her for wanting to run away."

Tressa could hear Alex rattling around in the kitchen. She peeked out her door, and she attracted his attention instead of having him ignore her. The Christmas tree in the corner flickered like a rainbow, its multicolored lights reaching out to touch her bedroom. Alex stared at her phone, clutched in her hand.

"Who is that? Mauri? Tell her she missed an awesome Christmas movie party," he whispered, lingering by the door.

"No, it's my mom," she mouthed, pointing to the phone.

"Hi, Mrs. Litton! Maybe I'll see you over the holiday," he yelled while closing the door.

Tressa closed her eyes, grateful he retreated to the couch. She crept back into her room, gently shutting the door. "Sorry, Andy. Listen, I'll see what I can find out and get back to you. Again, I'm sorry about everything that happened, and hopefully, we'll hear something."

Tressa crouched into a ball, letting the chair slowly undulate. She had hoped her research would unveil some connections, but never in a million years thought this was the direction it would take.

# Chapter Thirty-Nine

"Good news, everyone. We're nearing the finish line. For those who have handed in all of their assignments, all that remains is the final exam. For those who still have outstanding papers, see me if you want the chance for partial credit. As Abraham Lincoln said, 'You cannot escape the responsibility of tomorrow by evading it today.' I'll have the final review ready by Friday. Let's wrap this up so we can all relax and look forward to the holiday break."

Class ended fifteen minutes early. The lights dimmed, and Tressa checked her phone. She watched as Professor Dawson struggled to shove his laptop and folders into his worn, leather bag. Scarf draped around his neck and coat tucked in the crook of his arm, he skipped every other step as he beelined to the exit. As she turned to watch him disappear at the door, she watched as Mauri made her way down the steps.

"Hey, sorry I didn't get in touch with you yesterday. Crazy day," Mauri said.

"What was that all about? The professor bolted out of here," Tressa said, thumb pointing to the door.

"Maybe he had to meet someone at his office. Who knows," Mauri said.

"Oh, I'm sure you are very familiar with his office hours," Tressa said.

"Wait. What are you talking about?" Mauri said.

"I needed to talk to you yesterday, but you never got back to me. Alex said he saw you hanging out at Dawson's office, and you were, well, it seemed," she said before Mauri cut her off.

"It seemed like what? Listen, Tress. I wasn't aware I had to check in with you or Alex." Mauri's hair, now a glossy, monotone mocha hue, bounced against her puffer coat as she headed back up the steps.

"Mauri, wait. There's something else I wanted to tell you—about the research."

Mauri reached the door and paused before entering the chilly December cold. "I don't want to hear anything else about your stupid research right now, and if you must know, I was talking to Professor Dawson about some of the jobs I'm considering."

The lecture hall was empty, but Tressa still felt uncomfortable having their conversation echo through the cavernous space. Trotting up to meet her friend, she whispered when reaching the top step. "Why would you say anything to him? I thought part of the deal is to not speak about it."

"Like you care!" Mauri yelled. "Whenever I mention going to check out the museum in New York or calling for an update on the position on the West Coast, you don't want to hear about it. Why can't you be happy for me? Why can't you be happy for yourself? It's okay, Tress, to be happy."

Tressa paused, thinking of the right way to respond. "You know I care. I care about everything going on for both of us, but right now, I only see it as a distraction. I talked to Andy, Rachel's brother, the one from the farm. There may be a connection between her and Dawson. I'm not sure what's happening, but he seemed to be in quite a hurry tonight."

Mauri bit her bottom lip, her gaze shifting to the carpeted landing. The mention of Rachael and the professor slowed her pace. "I don't think it's anything to worry about," Mauri said. She scanned the class before continuing. "But let's not talk about it here, okay? I'll call you later. Maybe we can meet for coffee." She turned to the door, but before she ventured out, she faced Tressa. "Did you get a gift?"

"A gift? For who?" Tressa asked.

"Not for who, from who. Didn't you receive a box at the apartment?" Mauri asked.

"I haven't, but I also haven't been back at the apartment in a few hours. Who is it from?" Tressa asked curiously.

"Oh, if it's there, you'll see." The quiet swoosh of the door ushered in a gust of icy air as Mauri left the auditorium.

Tressa retrieved her books and scampered out of the hall. The wind permeated her coat and chilled her to the core, spreading like ice water in her veins, her cheeks becoming numb. The well-lit path lined with ornamental grasses and shrubs snaked through campus, her usual route home. Usually, the walk was relaxing, but tonight, Tressa only noticed dark recesses and shadowy areas where someone could hide. She thought of the missing persons' database, the entries and information of girls who disappeared while going about their everyday lives. Turning to look over her shoulder every few seconds, she slid her phone out of her back pocket to answer an incoming call.

"Hey, Tress. Oh, wait. Where are you? It sounds like you're running," Alex said.

"No, I'm heading home. Just a weird night, and I was creeped out walking back, I guess," Tressa said.

"Are you okay?" Alex asked with legitimate concern in his voice.

"Yeah, I'm fine. What did you need?" Tressa asked, wondering if he had called after hearing from Mauri.

"Oh yeah, right. Well, when you get back, you'll change your tune. There is a huge gift waiting."

"How do you know it's a gift? What if I ordered something?" Tressa asked, realizing the words were a little too snarky on delivery.

Alex stammered, "Oh, for Christ's sake, Tress, there's a box here for you. I don't know what the hell it is, but it has your name on it. Be careful coming home."

She thought staying on the phone with someone would make her feel better, but she felt even more uneasy.

As Tressa stepped into her apartment, she noticed a large cardboard box sitting on the coffee table in the living room. After taking a moment to defrost and catch her breath, Tressa planned on opening the package in her bedroom, even though the door to Alex's room remained shut. With the box nestled under her arm, she tiptoed into the room to avoid announcing she was home. As she removed the tape, she discovered the box was filled with delicate white and gold tissue paper. At the center of the package was another beautifully wrapped box adorned with a silky ribbon and glittery gold print.

It could only be from one person, but she wondered why her mom had it sent to school rather than making a big display in front of guests over the holiday. The stationary felt heavy in her hands, exquisite and formal. With the font and color matching the gleaming ribbon, Tressa folded back the card, but the inscription was not what she had expected. The fanciful script danced across the stark white background, "Tressa, a pre-holiday gift. So glad you are part of the family. Love, H~"

Frantically tossing the crumpled packing aside, she eased the box onto her bed. The lid glided smoothly from its fitted counterpart to reveal a bag. Tressa reached in and held up the leather messenger bag, pale gold rivets punctuating the black-satin finish, delicate links connecting a matching leather strap. The dimensions and interior pockets lent themselves to be one of the most rich-looking messenger bags she had ever seen — the stitching elegant, the feel buttery soft. Tressa slung the strap over her shoulder and snickered when she saw her reflection, clad in a worn sweatshirt, yoga pants, and expensive bag.

**T: Hey, so I got my package.**

**M: I figured you'd get one. From Helena?**

**T: Well, H, so I am assuming.**

**M: Dior? Sable colored?**

**T: Dior. Black.**

**M: Check the price?**

**T: I did not. Assume you'll tell me.**

**M: 5K. And hey. Sorry about everything before. Still want to meet up?**

**T: How about early breakfast instead?**

**M: Sounds good.**

Tressa tossed her phone next to the box, the leathery smell of luxury hanging in the bedroom. She carefully packaged the bag and placed it under her bed. She wondered about the actual price tag that came with this gift.

Exhaustion took hold of her, and she could have sworn her eyes closed for merely minutes. Lids still struggling to stay open, she wrapped herself in the down comforter, staring at the ceiling and trying to make sense of the gift. The sliver of gray slowly crept through the curtains, the subtle but undeniable light betraying the presence of night. It was already morning. And, of course, there was the singing.

Tressa and Alex had an unspoken agreement regarding getting ready before classes. It was more of a daily scramble with three roommates. This year's staggered schedule and Alex's desire to work out when most living things were still sound asleep allowed Tressa a bit more shuteye, not requiring a hurried morning rush. Alex didn't have a terrible voice and belted out tunes like a rock star in the shower. The squeak of a faucet and the end of a melody prompted Tressa to fling the blanket to the floor, the drafty apartment ensuring she was awake. Without the need for morning small talk and explanations, she waited a few minutes before hearing the familiar morning routine continue, knowing Alex would head out soon.

"I'm leaving, Tress. Talk to you tonight," he yelled, door slamming behind him.

In a hurry to leave, Tressa decided on a hat rather than washing her hair and, more importantly, waiting for it to dry. She knew the walk to the coffee shop was short, but wet locks turned frosty quickly. She and Mauri arrived at the same time.

"Hey, good morning," Mauri said, sliding into a booth. She must have been on the same wavelength. She piled her hair in a messy bun, something Tressa couldn't pull off since her wayward curls never conformed to that style. Dark smudges danced underneath her eyes, remnants of the night before. "I'll go order. Coffee and egg sandwich okay?"

"Yeah, fine," Tressa replied. She watched as her friend leaned against the counter, staring at the menu, but she already knew Tressa wanted an English Muffin, toasted, egg fried, and her coffee with two sugars and light cream. The light crowd allowed a quick turnaround, and Mauri returned promptly with their breakfast.

"Here you go," Mauri said, carefully placing the steaming cups and paper-wrapped sandwiches on the table.

Tressa noticed Mauri's worn, olive green messenger bag slumped against her hip. "So, no new bag this morning, I guess?" Tressa said, motioning to the frayed cotton satchel.

Mauri looked at it as if she had forgotten it was there. "Oh, this? Yeah, a far cry from Dior, right?" her face instantly brightened, and her scowl softened into a playful smirk. "I mean, when would we be carrying bags like that anyway? Can you imagine, on campus?" she continued, relief washing over her when she realized the conversation would not be hostile. It would be like a calling card attracting too much attention.

Tressa gushed into everything she wanted to tell Mauri since yesterday. "First, let's talk about Professor Dawson. You know our girl from the farm, Rachael? I told you her brother reached out to me. He seems to believe there was a connection between his sister and Professor Dawson." Tressa went on to show the pictures and explain Andy's concern. She watched as Mauri hesitated several times throughout the conversation, catching her breath and stopping her comments before they even started. Tressa knew she wasn't sold.

"I don't know, Tress. We know the professor pretty well, but that family is kind of weird. What if the brother, Andy, has something to do with her disappearance? It would be easy to blame someone else."

"But the pictures, I'm pretty sure it was him. And *that* doesn't make sense. Why would he be with her? A student." Tressa watched as Mauri absently swirled the contents of her cup but failed to comment. "Well, how did your meeting with him go anyway? Did he have any good advice?" Tressa asked, not wanting to venture into accusatory territory again.

"Well, he thought it was terrific that these opportunities presented themselves. I only went to his office to ensure nobody else overheard our conversation. He had no opinion on it either way. It almost seemed like he wanted to rush me out of there, if I'm being honest. He seemed a little uncomfortable or preoccupied," Mauri said.

Tressa could tell there was something else, her friend's tired eyes trying to disguise a tsunami of true feelings waiting to unleash its fury.

"Well, what do you think about the bags? My mother would be overjoyed if she saw it draped over my shoulder, but you know it's not my style."

Mauri smiled, and Tressa could tell her friend was relieved they had changed the subject from Professor Dawson.

"It's obviously from Helena and is nothing more than a gift. The holidays are around the corner, so I don't think it's unusual. Something that will look perfectly in place after landing a job at a popular museum or gallery," Mauri added.

This comment solidified the fact that Mauri didn't share Tressa's suspicions. Flashy purses, bubbling champagne, and grandiose plans were working their magic. Tressa knew she needed to tread lightly.

"Nice gesture, I guess. But you can't send blackmail videos one week and a Dior purse the next. I still can't rest easy until I find out the story with Gina. I told you about my list and checked a few more leads that came up empty. There is only one more name from the list I'd like to look into, and I'm sure it will end the same way. It will just put my mind at ease."

Her phone chimed.

**Mom: Tree trimming party tonight. Invite Alex and Mauri.**

"Are you interested in sorting through ornaments that probably cost as much as the Dior bags? I almost forgot that tonight is my mom's annual tree trimming, cocktail drinking, and shopping bragging party. She does this every year, but it's kind of a fun tradition. I know it's during the week, but it will be worth it. Want to come? She'd love to have you there," Tressa said.

"Sure, it would be a good change of pace. Are you going to ask Alex?" Mauri questioned.

Tressa paused but thought how this was their last Christmas season as students before leaping into the real world, wherever that took them. She felt they needed to embrace nothing more than friends, drinks, and ornaments right now.

# Chapter Forty

Deborah O'Malley was well-known for her love of luxury, which is evident in her taste for entertaining and decorating. Her opulent lifestyle was reflected in the decor and style of her home, which resembled something out of a Hallmark movie or could have inspired a Thomas Kinkade painting. Tressa mostly nodded in agreement when her mother spoke about her lavish purchases, such as a set of imported Bohemia stemware or a hand-knotted Persian rug, but she wasn't necessarily impressed. However, when it came to Christmas, things were different.

Deborah's enthusiastic greeting filled the room, "Hello, I'm so glad you could make it on such short notice!" The flirty tie waist of the cherry-red satin blouse fluttered as she scuffled over to greet friends before family. Her flared black pants stopped short of her ankles to reveal matching pointed mules that said casual but classy. The sparkle dangling from her earlobes and adorning her finger rivaled the spectacle surrounding them. But Tressa didn't care. She took it all in as if it was also new to her.

"Mrs. O'Malley, this decor is straight out of a magazine. Actually, better than any magazine," Alex complimented, admiring the fresh pine garland, playing into Deborah's decorating skills and ego.

On the boundary between friendly and flirtatious, Tressa wondered where her stepdad was as she watched her mother gently cradle Alex's elbow, guiding him to the sideboard to select from the variety of drinks. Mauri cupped the small crystal glass filled with smooth, creamy liquid and a dancing cinnamon stick. Fresh pine effortlessly draped across the mantle, and the deep fireplace housed crackling logs with a warm glow that matched the miniature lights woven through the rich forest green of the garland. A ten-foot tree stood tall and proud, rich candy apple red and shimmering gold bows elegantly attached to each branch.

As if he read Tressa's mind, her stepdad strategically positioned himself between his wife and Alex, giving a hearty laugh as ice cubes clinked in the glasses.

"So, what is left to decorate? I thought this was a tree-trimming party," Mauri asked, gazing around the festive room.

"Well, it's more of an excuse for a get-together, but my mother has a smaller tree near the foyer that still needs decorating. She'll bring out the boxes of Lenox ornaments after dinner."

"This is a lot of stuff to put away after the holidays," Mauri muttered.

The light dinner, as her mother described it, left Tressa full, not wanting to do anything else but lounge in front of the fireplace.

Frank Sinatra crooned in the background as her mother arrived with the velvet-lined boxes. "Now, kids, just be careful and anchor each ornament. You know they are—" she said as Tressa cut her off.

"Very delicate," Tressa said, preventing her mother from pointing out how costly they were.

Tressa felt the weight of the ivory porcelain snowflakes in her hand as she carefully hung them on the tree. Alex continued to talk sports with her stepdad, seeming more and more like frat brothers with every drink they poured.

"Hey, Mauri. Do you all decorate like this at your grandmother's house?" Alex asked, slightly slurring his words.

Tressa felt her face flush and uncomfortably tried to clear her throat as she yelled over to him. "Alex!" she scolded.

"I mean, do you have a million Christmas trees around the house? Fancy ornaments?" Alex laughed.

Tressa was aware of Alex's behavior when he had a few drinks, but she knew he wasn't the type to be mean or belligerent. She prided herself on never making others feel inferior for any reason; it was quite the opposite. If it weren't for her mother revealing their situation during Alex's first visit, Tressa would never have spoken about their family's fortune.

An ornament dangled from Mauri's fingertips as she looked for the perfect branch. "We don't do a lot of decorating, or celebrating for that matter," she said, precariously letting the pricey decoration swing close to the tip of her muted gray acrylic nails.

Tressa knew it. Alex had struck a chord with Mauri and she seemed uncomfortable. Underneath the twinkling lights, the soft aura of glinting gold outlined everything in the room, and the swirling scents of pine, bergamot, and cinnamon filled the space around them. The crackling logs in the fireplace produced a soft, comforting sound that mixed with the melody of the Christmas channel playing in the background. Despite the festive atmosphere, Mauri looked distant and unimpressed as she stared at the poinsettias lining the stairs as if counting every leaf. It could have been the faint ribbons of smoke escaping from the fireplace or one too many drinks, but Tressa could have sworn Mauri's eyes were glistening. She walked over to Alex, grabbing his elbow much differently than her mother did earlier. As she leaned closer to hide the anguish in her voice, the pungent smell of his soap mingled with single malt repulsed rather than enticed her.

"What are you thinking? How can you be so rude? You know

this is over the top. Everything my family does is over the top, but I thought we could enjoy this. The holiday. The atmosphere. Not shove it in someone's face to show them what they don't have," Tressa hissed.

"What they don't have?" Alex laughed. "Tressa, dear, you have no idea. Maybe you don't know Mauri as well as you thought."

"Well, I do know what it is like to feel uncomfortable. You, *dear,* just accomplished that," she retorted.

Alex stumbled backward, the flickering candles casting dancing shadows on the walls as he bumped into the end table. Tressa's mom quickly busied herself with clearing glasses while her stepdad disappeared. Sinatra's smooth and effortless crooning continued to echo throughout the room, filling the silence left by the abrupt commotion. Meanwhile, Mauri lowered her head and turned to walk out of the room, her movements silent and graceful despite the tension in the air.

"Mauri. Wait. I need to apologize for Alex's comments. It's just the scotch talking. I did not invite you here to show off. I wanted to share it with you."

"It's fine," she said. "My grandmother and I don't go all out for the holidays. Not anymore."

"I'm the one who is sorry, okay?" Alex interjected, his rosy cheeks matching his hair. He rolled up his taupe woolen sweater, white shirtsleeves peeking out beneath. "I'm sorry if I joked about how an heiress might decorate for Christmas," Alex said, setting his glass on the table with a little too much force. It didn't shatter, but the jolt caused the ice cubes to tumble onto the highly waxed mahogany table. Deborah walked back in, partly because she was curious about what caused the tree decorating party to go up in flames and to check the status of the $300 double Old-Fashioned glass.

"Tressa, I'll show your guests to their rooms. Everyone will be staying tonight," Deborah stated firmly.

"Fine," Tressa conceded, fully aware of her mother's penchant for showcasing her hospitality skills. "I'll be up in a few minutes, too."

The high-backed chair shielded Tressa from seeing anyone else in the room, but it sounded like everyone else headed upstairs. It was just her, downing the last of the burning alcohol from the Waterford crystal and visions of an heiress dancing in her head. Her eyelids grew heavy as she reclined on the couch, and warmth crept through her body. She wanted to get some water and Advil before falling asleep, knowing it would make her morning a little easier. As she told herself she would go into the kitchen in five minutes, she succumbed to the cozy warmth surrounding her and the effects of her last few drinks. Tressa's breaths grew slower and more even as she drifted off to sleep, but a theme continued in her dream, reflecting something darker weighing on her mind. Visions of the woods, the glow of the collar, and the guttural scream were things Tressa imagined when she closed her eyes. She pictured herself in the woods, trying to escape something or someone, but twisty roots nipped at her feet, challenging her to walk without falling. Tressa couldn't run, her feet heavy as if anchored with cement blocks. She kicked her foot wildly, unable to free her feet and move away from whatever was following her.

"Tressa," she repeatedly heard. "Tressa," it grew louder as something tugged at her foot.

She sat up quickly, the velvety throw tangled on her feet, her mother standing near the edge of the love seat.

"Tressa, wake up. I wasn't sure if you were going to school or not. Alex already left." Her mother grasped onto an oversized mug. "I made you some coffee," she said, extending the steaming cup.

"I thought everyone just went upstairs. Aren't they sleeping?" Tressa said, feeling disoriented as she looked around the room.

The fire had long gone out, and the brilliance of the Christmas lights dimmed. Weak sunlight filtered in, but not enough to illuminate the rows of poinsettias or the luster of glittering garland— the warmth and magic from last night extinguished. Sitting up quickly resulted in a slight tilt of the room, and her stomach felt queasy, but she took the coffee from her mother. A few fireside drinks last night did not answer her problems, but Tressa was thankful to be somewhere other than the dream she had escaped.

"I didn't want to disturb you last night. I figured you were okay with a blanket on the sofa," her mother said softly.

The events of the previous evening vividly replayed in Tressa's head. "Where are Alex and Mauri? Are they going to class? And wait, how did they get home? I knew a mid-week party wasn't a great idea," Tressa said, rubbing her forehead.

Her mother tucked her legs beneath her and dissolved into the welcoming leather chair. She twirled a stray tendril between her finger and thumb, calmly replying to Tressa's questions. "Mauri is upstairs changing clothes. I think she said she's not worried about missing class. Alex asked Ryan for a ride. They left a few hours ago." She stood up and walked over to the couch, lifting Tressa's feet and sliding beneath them to join her on the loveseat. "I'm not sure what happened last night, but I don't think you should be so hard on Alex."

There it was. Her mom was always worried about Tressa ruining her chances of having a boyfriend, especially Alex.

"You don't get it. Alex was rude, and he made Mauri uncomfortable. There was no reason to make her feel like it was a privilege to be here."

Her mom squeezed her feet before getting up and busying herself by plugging in the strings of lights, returning the room to a warm glow. "I don't think she felt that way, believe me."

Tressa rubbed her brow, pushing the heel of her palm against her eye to clear away any remnants of sleep. How could she forget? "Oh, that's right. An heiress. What could he have possibly meant by that?"

"I think you will have to ask her," she said, staring toward the foyer. Mauri stood under the festooned archway with her bag over her shoulder.

"I'm ready whenever you are," Mauri said, her voice tired and her tone solemn.

The journey back to campus felt like a cross-country trek, with the vibrant autumn hues giving way to a somber, drab backdrop. An occasional home interrupted the landscape, lawns littered with smiling snowmen waiting for evening to come alive. Christmas music seemed to be on every station the entire ride home. As they neared campus, Tressa turned down the radio.

"Hey, so that was a little weird yesterday. Sorry about all of that. I don't know what Alex was thinking," Tressa said, gripping the steering wheel.

"No worries, it's fine," Mauri replied, head turned to the window, intently studying the barren branches as they cruised closer to town.

Fewer cars populated the parking lot, a sign of the semester wrapping up. A blast of icy cold immediately filled the space around them as Mauri opened the door. Swinging her feet to the ground and clutching her bag, she paused, her back still turned to Tressa. Finally leaving the car, she held onto the frame and turned back to face Tressa.

"I know you have a lot of questions, and I wish I had never told Alex in the first place," Mauri said.

"Told Alex what?" Tressa asked.

"I don't want to get into it, but the long and short of it is, my grandfather was a successful real estate developer in South Jersey, vacation homes and such. Anyway, my dad followed in his footsteps, and things were good. After a car accident took both my parents, it was just us—me and my grandmother. It will be almost ten years next week. Needless to say, celebrating Christmas isn't our jam," she said, biting her lower lip and staring at the leather seat.

"Oh, God, Mauri. I'm so sorry. I had no idea," Tressa apoligized. The thought of constantly persuading her friend to come to a tree decorating party made her feel even worse.

"Like I said, it's fine. I don't talk about it much. It gets old. When I came to Wyval, I saw it as a way to escape the stigma of being the poor little orphaned rich girl, people always talking about when I would inherit all the money. Wyval gave me a new identity, a new start where no one knew my past. I wanted to belong somewhere because of who I am." She looked over her shoulder, hoisting her bag onto her back. "But look, it doesn't matter. I'm going to head to my apartment and pull myself together. Maybe I can salvage a class or two before the end of the day. I'll see you later?" Mauri said, her eyes glistening as she gave a small wave and walked away.

As the car grew colder, Tressa remained frozen in her seat. The two people she had considered her closest friends now seemed like strangers to her. On top of that, she wasn't prepared to finish the semester successfully for the first time ever. But there was something else weighing heavily on her mind. Tressa couldn't shake the feeling that someone from that night in the woods wasn't okay, and she had a strong sense that someone was missing her at that very moment. Despite the potential threat to her friendships, chances of staying in one of the most elite societies, future opportunities, and even her own life, Tressa was resolved to discover what had happened. She knew she had to uncover the truth, no matter the cost.

# Chapter Forty-One

Tressa breathed a sigh of relief as she stepped into Slocum Hall, grateful for the hustle and bustle of students and staff milling about. Offices lining the hallways were filled with laughter and chatter, and some had long queues of students waiting to discuss their grades. As she walked down the hallway, she checked the time on her phone to make sure she wasn't too early for her appointment with Professor Dawson. Room 104 looked unoccupied, even though the small placard indicated office hours had started at 2 p.m. Tressa cupped her hands against the narrow glass pane, confirming the vacancy. Just then, the harsh slam of a door and the jangling of keys nearly knocked her off balance.

"Oh, hello, Tressa. I was just about to head into my office if you'd like to come in," Professor Dawson said, reaching past her to unlock the door. His arm brushed against hers, and she noticed he smelled crisp, like winter, and had an ever-present lock of wayward hair falling over his eyebrow. She thought he seemed nervous as he struggled with the lock. His bag hit the door with a thump, sliding down his arm awkwardly, the keys still a musical jumble. "Sorry, this always gets stuck. Here we are," he said, sighing in relief as the door swung open.

As she walked into the cramped, dimly lit office, a gust of heat hit Tressa like a wave. The waning afternoon sun filled the space with only a hint of light, and Dawson reached over to turn on the small brass desk lamp, adding a warm glow to the room. Files spilled off his desk, and papers covered every inch of space. A narrow bookshelf hugged the wall, groaning with the weight of art compilations and coffee table books. A collection of baubles and small sculptures added an air of curiousity to the office.

Dawson noticed her surprise as she turned and sharply sucked in a breath as if all the air in the room had suddenly been taken away. "I know. Fuseli. It's an odd choice to brighten up this little room. I received it as a gift years ago. Whenever we discuss this during the semester, it garners the most interest. Students seem mesmerized when they see it."

Tressa walked over to the painting and again realized how much was happening in it. Her heart thudded in her chest as she focused on the pale woman draped across the bed, the only point of light in the agonizingly dark and evil figures surrounding her. She shuddered and rested her hand on the seat across from Dawson's desk.

"Please, take a seat. What can I help you with? If it's about class today, you didn't miss anything. I gave everyone a chance to catch up," he said, unwinding the deep maroon scarf from his neck.

The door remained open, and Tressa could hear voices carrying on down the hall. It eased her to know they weren't alone. She knew she would be safe no matter the direction of the conversation.

"I, um, I'm not here to talk about class. There is something else I wanted to discuss. You know, Mauri and I," she started before being interrupted by Dawson.

"Ah, Mauri. She came to see me the other day to discuss some of her options."

"Options?" Tressa asked.

"After school, her job options. She has quite the opportunities at her fingertips. I'm not surprised. Bright, talented girl," he said.

"She told you? About the job offers?" Tressa wondered how much he knew but didn't want to offer more than he needed.

"Yes. She told me about the gallery and moving to the West Coast. I imagine you will have the same chances," he said. His focus shifted to his monitor, furiously clicking the mouse. Tressa tried to interpret the meaning behind his comment.

"Same chances? She told you that?" Tressa's voice came out as a garbled squeak before she cleared her throat. "I mean, job offers for me?"

He paused scrolling through the screen before him, and looked at Tressa. The shade of his eyes was a deeper blue under the warm light but with the same intensity. "Tressa, you are very talented as well. I know you'll receive similar opportunities. Give it time."

Tressa swallowed hard, and her ears clicked as she did it again. She would die for a bottle of water. "Right. So that's why she came here the other day?"

Dawson moved his hands away from his keyboard with an exaggerated plunk. He fidgeted in his chair, with the wheels squeaking below him.

"That's what she came for the other day, Ms. Litton," he said, enunciating each word. "What is it you came here for today?" he asked, his voice teetering between playfulness and annoyance.

"Actually, there's something I wanted to ask you. I'm trying to get in touch with some former students, you know, some job connections, and I was wondering if you knew Rachael Jenning?" Tressa watched all the color in his face drain, abruptly pushing away from the desk.

Dawson walked over to the door, shutting it more forcefully than expected. "Ms. Litton, we both know you are not looking to Rachael Jenning for job leads. Why don't you tell me what's going on," he said, arms crossed.

The heat felt overwhelming, and Tressa felt on the verge of panic and nausea. She knew other students and teachers were only feet away, but would they even notice her cries for help? Were they the only ones remaining on the floor? The air was thick with Dawson's woodsy scent but mingled with the aromas of the cramped office—sweat, old paper, and pencil shavings. A sudden slam of a door in the hall made her jump. Should she ask to open the door? She decided to keep her phone accessible on her lap.

Tressa had to be careful to get information about Rachael. She couldn't mention searches for missing persons, meetings with Helena, or high-end gifts. Instead, she got straight to the point, letting out a long exhale before continuing. "Rachael Jenning is missing, and someone sent me a picture of her at a party, and you were in it."

"What connection do you have to Rachael Jenning?" he asked as if Tressa's presence at a college party was in question. "And let me guess—did you get it from her brother?" Dawson asked.

"I'm not the one needing to explain myself. I do know Rachael's family is worried sick, not knowing if she's okay."

"I can assure you she's okay," Dawson said, his voice bordering on a sarcastic chuckle.

It could have been the heat in the room or the thoughts swimming in her head about not getting out of the office, but Tressa felt her ears ring and the room tilt. She stood up, moving closer to the door.

She fidgeted nervously on the heels of her boots as she spoke to Dawson. "I met Rachael's mother and promised I'd help find her. When I saw the picture, I knew you were in the background. So here I am, wondering why a former student of yours is missing and why you were at a party with her."

Dawson studied Tressa intently, tapping a pencil against his manicured hands as if analyzing a complex work of art. "How did her mother and brother seem when you met them?" he asked.

"What do you mean?" Tressa asked hesitantly.

"They come from a wealthy family that had fallen on hard times. I sympathized with Rachael's problems a few years ago and tried to give her advice, but she took it the wrong way and thought it was something more. There were nights she waited for me after class and followed me everywhere I went. Despite her situation, she was a talented girl, and I suggested she pursue her passion for theater by heading to a big city like New York."

Tressa interrupted Dawson. "Was?" she asked.

"Was, is, I don't know. I couldn't tell you where Rachael is now," he replied.

"I thought you said she's okay. And how do you explain the college party?" The quivering in her voice subsided, making it easier to continue questioning.

Dawson threw his pencil on the desk and propped his foot on his knee. "I am guessing she is okay. If she got away from her crazy family and took my advice, she would probably be thriving. And you are wondering about the college party, right?" he asked.

Tressa nodded.

"Was there a sign in the background identifying one of the campus frat houses?" Dawson asked.

"Well, no. But it looked like a lot of people, and clearly, you were both in the image," Tressa replied.

"What if I told you I was invited to a dear friend's art gallery launch, surrounded by our colleagues and peers, and Rachael was the one out of place?"

His question hung in the air, keeping Tressa at a loss for words, as he paused before continuing his defense. "While I had faced some scrutiny in the past, I'm glad the university recognized the truth of the situation. I'm not sure what Rachael went through, but she's an adult and can make her own choices. Hopefully, she will leave her family behind and start a new life."

Tressa noticed beads of sweat on his brow, and she moved abruptly out of the way as he reached for the door. The office chair squeaked as he fell back into the seat, heat escaping from the room and a feeling of relief rushing in.

"Tressa, listen. I told Mauri the same thing. It's the end of the semester, and you possess talent beyond your years and opportunities most students can only dream of. Finish out this semester, enjoy your senior year, and don't worry about problems that don't exist." He swiveled in his chair, staring at the small collection of picture frames, avoiding eye contact with Tressa.

"Well, I guess that's that. Thanks for helping clear that up. I'll be sure to turn in my final paper this week. Do you want the door closed?" Tressa asked, awkwardly ending the conversation.

As Tressa's hand gripped the edge of the door, she noticed his gaze on a framed picture teetering on the edge of the shelf. The dim lighting and distance prevented her from focusing on the exact images, but she could make out a happy golden retriever and a stunning woman with long blonde hair in the frame. Tressa wanted to get closer to see the details but Dawson held up a hand, a signal acknowledging or dismissing her from the small office.

When she removed her hand from the doorknob, Tressa quickly unlocked her phone and scrolled through her contacts until she found Mauri's name. She hit the call button, and Mauri's face appeared on the screen after a few rings.

"Hello?" Mauri answered, her brow furrowed.

Tressa knew she had caught Mauri off guard. They communicated daily but rarely via phone calls, let alone FaceTime.

"Oh, hey. Where are you? I'm surprised you went to class," she said, squinting at the camera view.

"Sort of. I'm on campus. I just finished talking to Dawson in his office." Tressa wanted to address Mauri's one-on-one meeting with their professor but realized her friend could ask her the same thing. She shifted her focus to something more pressing. "I wanted to get back to the list."

"The invite list?" Mauri asked. A screenful of her hair flashed before the camera as she dipped to grab something from the floor. She returned, propped on one elbow, holding a black postcard, the font shimmering and reflecting overhead light. "I assume you got one, too? I thought this was the reason for the call, wondering who else would be invited.

"Invited to what?" Tressa replied.

"You haven't been home yet. I'm sure you have one waiting. New Year's Eve at the lake house. It's a personal invite from Helena." She held up the gleaming rectangle, the words "Celebrate the New Year, the New You, the New Life" scribbled on the bottom in metallic marker.

"Oh great," Tressa said, trying to mask her lack of enthusiasm. "That's weird—everyone will still be on break."

"That's just it, thus the question about the list. I don't know what to expect. Anyway, what are you talking about?" Mauri asked.

Tressa described her visit with Dawson and her concern for Rachael. She reiterated the details and realized it sounded reasonable. An infatuated student trails a professor who gives her enough attention to let her think he is a shining knight to take her away from family problems. The picture could have been taken anywhere, and nothing indicated the location except for what she was told.

"I never thought Dawson would cross the line with a student.

He's smart and knows how to relate and encourage his students while staying professional," Mauri said, sounding dangerously close to the line, serving as his cheering section.

"I'm not one hundred percent sold on all of that. I'm not sure what I'm convinced about, but before Christmas, I need to talk to the last person on my list. I need to confirm it's not her, Mauri." Tressa knew it was a long shot, but it fits the limited criteria she looked for—missing girl, age range, blonde hair, within the general area. "I need to know. In the profile, it mentioned she worked at Country Crossing Mercantile. I'm going there tomorrow. Do you want to go?" Tressa asked.

Mauri brought the screen closer to her face. "I understand why you want to go, but I'm maxed out right now. There's just too much to get done in the next week. Will you be okay by yourself?"

She didn't expect Mauri to go with her but hoped she would. The bond that cemented so strongly in just months seemed to fade in a few days. Overcoming obstacles and facing challenges, but now, the friendship seemed to have lost its luster.

"I'll be fine. I'll let you know what I find out. Talk to you tomorrow." Her fingers were frozen, and she struggled to tap the cold glass to end the strained conversation.

"Hey Tressa, wait. Promise me two things. First, be careful; second, if this doesn't pan out, you'll stop searching," Mauri said.

"Thanks, I'll call you tomorrow," she said. Before tucking her phone in her pocket, she realized the Summit Society app showed there was a message. After seeing the videos, she had not checked it lately, but now she couldn't resist. There were no new messages, so Tressa checked the folder. The videos were still there, but a few new pictures were added, including a close-up of Tressa's face frozen in terror at the haunted house and, most recently, a picture of Tressa walking along a familiar path on campus. She realized that someone was watching, listening, and making sure she was aware.

# Chapter Forty-Two

Tressa didn't mind stopping at Country Crossing Mercantile, even though it was over an hour's drive from her home. The information noted in the missing person database showed Kayla Calefson worked there at the time of her disappearance, so Tressa hoped to get some info. A few wide, worn steps led Tressa to a sprawling front porch, a row of weathered rocking chairs serving as sentinels to the historic home. Bells chimed against the old wooden door as Tressa gently closed it behind her.

"I'll be out in a second," a voice chirped as Tressa walked around the old farmhouse store. The slightly uneven wooden plank floor groaned with every step as she browsed shelves of homemade goods and trinkets. She peeked around the corner and noticed a small deli counter with a swinging door behind it. The air carried the scent of freshly unwrapped banana bread, but her moment was interrupted by a loud bang.

"What can I get ya, my dear? Cheese? Smoked ham? Pickles?" the small, curvy woman said. She rested her ample hands on the deli case, beaded bracelets clinging to her wrists.

"Oh, no, I'm fine. Nothing from the deli, thanks," Tressa said, staring into a dimly lit case. "I hoped you could tell me about someone who worked here. Did you work with Kayla Calefson?"

Tressa's question seemed to have an immediate impact on the woman. Her full, berry-glossed lips parted, but she seemed unable to move or speak.

"How do you know Kayla?" she said, breaking the awkward

silence.

"We both went to Wyval, and I heard about what happened. I was hoping to get some information," Tressa said, her voice wavering slightly.

"You were friends with Kayla?" she asked skeptically.

Tressa watched as the woman went from cheerful to suspicious in minutes. "We weren't especially close, but like I said, we were at the same school, and I thought I could help," Tressa replied, trying to appear sincere.

"You and dozens of other reporters. Or TikTok users, or whatever it is. I know, fifteen minutes of fame and all, but at what expense? Her mother is beside herself, and I promised not to send anyone her way. So, if there is nothing I can help you with here, you'd best be on your way."

Tressa felt disappointed as the woman responded with suspicion rather than compassion.

"I hoped you could answer a few questions, and maybe I could help with yours," Tressa said, not giving up hope.

"Who said I had questions?" the woman snarked.

As she contemplated sharing the information she had, Tressa's heart raced with anticipation and fear. She knew revealing too much could change everything. Hissing steam, the squawk of radio talk show banter resonating from the storeroom, and the low hum of the refrigerator case filled the silent void, the direction of the conversation hanging heavy in the air.

"Listen, I'll be honest with you. I'm sorry, what did you say your name was?" she asked.

"I didn't, but it's Terri," she said, arms crossed against her chest.

"Terri. I'm Tressa, and I didn't go to school with Kayla, but I am a Wyval student," she said.

"I knew it. Like I said, if there's nothing I can help you with,"

she said, making her way over to the door, a cue for Tressa to follow.

"No, wait, please, just hear me out. I will graduate from Wyval
in the spring, and something happened to me. I can't get into it,
but I know something's not right," Tressa said, her voice cracking
and her eyes filling with tears. Tressa watched as Terri reached for
a box of tissues and offered them to her without looking, seemingly moved by her vulnerability.

"I guess I can spare a few minutes," Terri whispered, gesturing
to a small table near the deli counter. "Let me make sure we don't
get any interruptions," Terri said as she headed over to turn the
'closed' sign before locking the door.

"Let me tell you about Kayla. She's the sweetest girl you'll ever
meet. She used to come by when she was younger, saying how she
wanted to work here. But with a family like hers, she never needed
to work anywhere."

"A family like hers? What do you mean?" Tressa asked.

"Oh, her daddy had money—old money, from what I know.
I never asked how he got it, but I can assure you Kayla wouldn't
have to worry about working at a deli counter to get through college, even though she still wanted to," Terri said, motioning to the
case behind them. "Anyway, she came around asking for a job, and
the owners knew her parents, and well, that's how Kayla started
here. Although you may not have known her too well, she was
a people pleaser who just wanted to feel welcome and be part of
whatever was happening. I think of her as a little girl, running up
to the candy counter, her brown curls bouncing around with all
that energy."

Tressa's mind was racing as she listened to Terri's story. "Brown
curls? I thought Kayla was blonde?" she asked, trying to understand everything.

Terri nodded. "Most recently, yes. Kayla was always a cute little kid, but you can say she was a couple shades short of beautiful. Then, it was the summer of her senior year, and things changed. She changed."

Tressa was intrigued. "Changed?" she asked. "Like appearance or how she acted?"

Terri leaned in, a serious expression on her face. "Oh, she was still our sweet, friendly Kayla, but her parents pushed her to Wyval. She was nervous about college. Then, one day, Kayla showed up for work, hair as blonde as a Barbie doll, with stunning makeup and matching clothes. It's like she grew up and transformed overnight."

"So she had this transformation. Lots of girls go through that," Tressa said.

Terri shook her head. "That wasn't all. Once she got into college, she acted differently. Our Kayla seemed more concerned with her appearance than ever. She worked fewer hours at the store and got all wrapped up in school and stuff. She started running around with these flashy types—it wasn't the same Kayla."

Tressa felt a burning in her chest. The anticipation of waiting for Terri to finish her story made her feel like she could combust.

"I've been researching missing person cases, and there seems to be an increase of missing girls from wealthy backgrounds," Tressa said. "You said Kayla's family has a lot of money?"

"What, do you think it's like a ransom or something?" Terri asked, walking over to a winter wreath display. She stood with her back to Tressa, her gaze focused on the assortment of faux foliage. As she placed her hand on her forehead, her body shuddered.

Tressa's hand was inches from Terri's shoulder when the woman whirled around, her face streaked with tears and smudged makeup. "Terri? Are you okay?" Tressa asked.

"Ah, dammit," Terri said, her voice quivering with a combination of sniffling and snorting. "You bring up money, and it really gets me. That's all Kayla worried about. Worried about being able to pay for things."

"I thought Kayla didn't have to worry about money? And you said she didn't work much," Tressa said, her face scrunched in confusion.

"Well, things changed pretty quickly. She started asking to work as many hours as possible, saying her career depended on it." Terri dabbed at her face with a tissue before continuing. "Her parents *used* to be pretty well off, but I guess assets weren't managed well after their divorce."

Tressa's heart sank. "Kayla's parents are divorced?" she asked softly.

"Don't worry. I know what you're thinking. Neither of them did anything to Kayla. They're not like that. They're good people. Her mom was so proud when she started at Wyval. The divorce was a rough patch for her."

"When did the divorce happen?" Tressa asked.

"I don't remember exactly. Maybe Kayla's sophomore or junior year?"

Tressa's mind was filled with visions of the lake house, Fendi bags, and posh parties that some people would do anything to be a part of. Terri disappeared into the stock room and returned with a cardboard box.

"This box contains some of Kayla's things. She was here so much that she left a lot of her stuff in the back. I don't know if there's anything in there that can help you, but I hope you can help find her," Terri said, lightly patting the lid.

Tressa felt guilty as she gingerly searched through the box, a representation of who Kayla is. Or who Kayla was. A tube of vanilla lip balm, an expired Wyval ID card, loose change, and a hand-woven scarf. Tressa picked up a small frame and looked closely at the image of a smiling girl with her arms wrapped around her friends. That's when she noticed it.

"Terri, did Kayla have any tattoos?" she asked, already knowing the answer. A high-pitched ringing filled her ears as she struggled to hear the woman's response. Feeling like she was going from frigid to on fire in minutes, she tugged at her jacket, longing for a bottle of water and steadying herself against the counter.

"Hey. Are you okay?" Terri asked. Tressa's face must have given away how she felt.

"Yeah, I'm okay. Really, I'm fine. Maybe just a bottle of water?" Tressa asked.

"Sure, here," Terri said, handing Tressa a bottle from the cooler. As she started to feel more stable, Tressa sat on the small stool next to the counter, waiting for Terri to continue.

"But, oh yeah. You asked about tattoos. That was a thing for sure," Terri said, followed by a low whistle.

"What do you mean it was a thing?" Tressa asked.

"Kayla came into the store to show me her tattoo. Her mom wouldn't let her get one until she turned 18," Terri said, nodding. "I didn't think it was a big deal. Actually, it was appropriate for Kayla. Oh, wait, that's someone rattling the door. I'll be right back," she said before hurrying to the front of the store.

Tressa's hands trembled as she reached into the box and pulled out the picture. The girl in the center had a beaming, wide smile, but Tressa's gaze was immediately drawn to the peace tattoo on her arm, peeking out of her long-sleeved tee. Tressa pulled out her phone to take a quick picture. Her hand shook as she zoomed in, her jaw dropping when she noticed something else. As she pushed aside some papers, something blue glinted from the bottom of the box. The medallion felt cool in her hand, but her face flushed with warmth like the embers of a smoldering fire.

# Chapter Forty-Three

As Tressa tried to focus on the road, she realized she was driving almost 20 miles over the speed limit. Quickly, she pulled back, released her fingers from the tight grip on the steering wheel, and turned down the heat—it became unbearable in only a few minutes. Her mother's voicemail greeting repeatedly echoed, with no return calls. Tressa had some questions regarding Wyval. She knew it was an esteemed school from which to receive an art degree, but she wasn't sure that was Deborah's end goal for her daughter. She wondered if a desire for elite social status and endless career prospects drove her mother's yearning for Tressa to attend Wyval. The thought of Helena, a woman like Tressa's mother, crossed her mind. Would Deborah associate with someone like Helena, or would they compete with each other? As she tried to remember Helena's age, her mind instinctively turned to an internal calculator.

The thud was loud and shocking. The Land Rover careened off the road, and Tressa tried to gain control before abruptly stopping in a ditch. She couldn't tell if someone had hit her from behind or if she had hit something. As panic set in, she grabbed her phone and then struggled to open the door. After what seemed like an eternity, she managed to tumble out of the car, feeling like she was moving in slow motion. Standing on the slanted ground, she tried to catch her breath and figure out what to do next. She discovered that her front tire was destroyed, and she didn't have the expertise to change it. Desperate, she tried calling and texting her mom, Ryan, and Mauri, but none responded except for the last person she tried contacting.

The small Honda rumbled up behind the Land Rover. Tressa watched as Alex searched for something in the back seat of his car. She checked the time on her phone, surprised at how quickly he made it to her location.

"Thanks for coming," she said, her hands deep in her pockets, hiding from the biting cold. Alex began to arrange some tools on the ground, and the only sound surrounding them was metal clinking. They hadn't spoken much since the tree-trimming incident.

"No problem. Can't leave you stranded out here," he said, crouched down near her tire. A strip of bare skin divided his black puffer coat and gray joggers.

"Thanks again." Tressa focused on the road for passing cars, the silence awkward.

"Oh wow, this looks like it might be the culprit," he said, pointing to the frayed tire.

"Is it a nail?" Tressa asked, leaning closer.

"A nail?" Alex chuckled. "It looks more like a railroad tie. Let me get the spare."

"I don't recall seeing anything. Just heard the loud thud." She failed to mention her mind was elsewhere when it happened.

Tressa wondered if she could have run over something at the Mercantile but couldn't imagine missing something that big in the front of the store.

"Okay," Alex said several minutes later. "You are all set," he said, admiring his work.

"I really appreciate it, Alex," she said, staring at her phone.

"Are you sure you are okay to drive? I don't mind leaving my car here and going with you," Alex said. "You seem shaken up."

"That's silly. I'm fine." Usually, jokes about bad driving or not knowing how to change a tire would fill the strained silence they found themselves stuck in. There was only the hum of the occasional passing car, giving some relief to fill the void.

"I'm headed out as soon as I get home. I was in the process of packing up when you called. Only a few days until Christmas, and I haven't even started shopping," Alex said, leaning on his open car door. "I guess I'll see you after the break? Have a nice Christmas, Tress. And enjoy your New Year's party."

"Who told you I was going to a New Year's party?" Tressa asked.

"Mauri told me. We were hanging out before, and I asked about her holiday plans. I wanted to make sure she wasn't offended or anything, you know, at your mom's house," he said. The issue with Mauri feeling slighted at Tressa's house seemed like it happened years ago.

"Merry Christmas, Alex," she said, walking over to the Land Rover, secretly wishing they were getting into the same car. She adjusted the mirror, fixed her hair, looked at her phone, and rummaged in the glove box. Once she navigated back onto the road, he followed her for several miles. Seeing Alex in the rearview mirror gave her a sense of reassurance, but she couldn't help but feel lingering anxiety and unease about how she got into the situation in the first place.

As Tressa returned to her apartment, Mauri finally got back to her.

"Hey, I just saw your texts. Are you okay?" she asked.

"Yeah, I'm fine, but let's meet for coffee," Tressa instructed. She needed a jolt of caffeine as much as she needed to share her new information.

# Chapter Forty-Four

A candy cane slowly melted into the steaming liquid, and Tressa twirled the holiday stirrer until her fingers became red and sticky. Mauri sat across from her, her gaze fixed on the table, looking pale as the whipped cream piled high on her hot chocolate. Tressa did not mention that Mauri had met with Alex, the incident at the tree-trimming party, or the meeting with the professor. All she could think about was the peace tattoo and what else the Summit Society hid from them.

Mauri sighed as she reclined on the crushed velvet sofa, vibrant violet pillows propped beneath her arm. The lack of students and nearly vacated campus allowed them to snag a seat in the coveted cozy couch section in front of the gas fireplace.

"So you really saw it? A peace tattoo?" Mauri said, trying not to act unnerved.

"Clear as day. I think the blonde girl in the woods was Kayla," Tressa said.

"But that doesn't mean she's dead. She's just missing, right?" Mauri asked.

"It means I saw a girl in the woods with a peace tattoo who looked in bad shape when she was carried out. And then someone pretending to be that girl. They are keeping something from us," Tressa said.

Mauri sat in silence, staring blankly across the room.

Tressa told her how she found the medallion in the box of

Kayla's things, but she didn't share information about the pictures received earlier. If she and Mauri were on the same level of this initiation, her friend would have received similar blackmail photos. Maybe Mauri received pictures of herself and felt the same way about sharing them with Tressa. Or perhaps she hadn't received any at all.

"I don't know. I guess we should confront Helena," Mauri said unenthusiastically. "I don't imagine any of our job offers will remain on the table," she added.

"I'm not concerned about job offers. There's a lot more to worry about," Tressa said. "But look, we can come up with a plan on how to deal with Helena. However, Mauri, there's something I need to ask you. If you don't want to talk about it, it's fine, but I need to know."

She watched her friend unwind a hand-knit scarf from her neck, carefully placing it on the couch. She reflected on everything they had gone through – navigating crumbling buildings, spending a night in prison, and the adventure in the woods. If it hadn't ended in the situation they were in now, Tressa would look back on it all as a memorable journey that led to a strong friendship. These experiences should have made any senior feel like they were in a dream, particularly at Wyval. The excitement of being part of something bigger, unlocking opportunities to land a career that would place them in elite circles for the rest of their lives, and most of all, belonging to something almost untouchable and exclusive – belonging to the Summit Society. However, right now, Tressa didn't know who to believe or who to trust.

"Shoot. What is it you need to ask me?" Mauri asked.

Tressa sipped her drink, the whipped cream now swirling into a creamy mixture of chocolate and peppermint. "It's about what happened at the tree-trimming party."

"Look, Tress, it's fine. I told you not to worry about it," Mauri said with an exaggerated eye roll.

"I wanted to ask you about the O'Sullivans," Tressa continued.

Mauri shifted on the couch, fumbling with the metallic tassel on the pillow, avoiding Tressa's gaze.

"You said you live with your grandmother, and your parents passed away," Tressa stated.

"True. My grandmother raised me," Mauri said, intent on studying the rivets of the upholstered couch.

"But the name, O'Sullivan. Your dad was a real estate magnate, correct?" Tressa asked.

"Yep."

"So that means," Tressa said before Mauri cut her off.

"Yes, that means my dad came from old money. My grandfather started it as a small seaside real estate company and grew it into something bigger than you can imagine. My parents were part of that, and the O'Sullivan name was associated with all things rich, glamorous, and philanthropic."

"But your name?" Tressa continued while figuring out the answer.

"Is my mother's maiden name. After my parents passed away, my grandmother did not want me to be known as the rich little orphan girl. More so, there were threats even when my parents were alive about kidnapping me as a baby for ransom."

"What?" Tressa asked in disbelief.

"Yeah, I know—crazy, right? I contemplated changing my name back to honor my dad and grandmother, but she convinced me it would attract too much attention no matter what path I took. She was right. I wanted to carve out my place in this world because of who I am, not because of what I came from," Mauri said.

Tressa could see tears welling up in her friend's eyes, and it was then that she realized they had more in common than she thought. The extraordinary level of wealth may not have been the same, but Tressa knew how she felt. She couldn't get past the ransom aspect of the situation, though.

"If you don't mind me asking, how much is your family worth? I mean, if they were worried about kidnapping and ransoms," Tressa asked, not expecting a reply. Mauri tapped away on her phone and turned the screen toward Tressa.

"That was on the Travel Channel," Tressa said, looking at a picture of a sprawling seaside mansion. Three of her houses could fit on the property's footprint. "And that was one of the houses your family sold?" Tressa asked, her eyes wide.

"That house is where my family lives," she said, sitting back and sipping her coffee.

Tressa thought of the few times Mauri was at her house, how she wondered about her friend, and what Mauri thought when she saw Tressa's house. Foolish doesn't even come close to how she felt at that moment. They always say you don't judge unless you walk in someone else's shoes, but you never expect them to be that much bigger.

"So it looks like there is a more common denominator for receiving an invitation to be part of the Summit Society," Tressa explained. "It makes a little more sense now—it wasn't so much as being the right type or trustworthy. It's how we fit into this bigger picture of people with bigger bank accounts," Tressa said, thinking out loud. Images of the girl with the lake house, the parties they attended, Helena, and the gifts swirled in her mind.

"But what about Rachael and the broken-down farmhouse? That's not a cash connection," she said.

"Not now, but it was. Remember the story of the gas drilling cash flow at the beginning of her college career, and then it dried up? Maybe she was a good fit to start, but things changed."

Mauri paused, leaving something on the tip of her tongue. "Maybe that's why she moved away? I know her brother and even Professor Dawson think the people she was hanging out with had something to do with it. It could have all been a coincidence?" Mauri's face lit up as she spoke these words.

"It could be. I haven't worked that all out. But the common denominator follows the money. And we fit right into that role," Tressa said.

A look of alarm crossed Mauri's face. "Oh, my God. You don't think it's possible that Helena -" Mauri stopped short of finishing her sentence.

"At this point, I'm not sure what to think. However, we will be attending a New Year's Eve party in a week, and Helena has some explaining to do."

# Chapter Forty-Five

Christmas decorations dominated the decor of every room. Since Tressa's last visit, her mother extended the holiday explosion throughout their home–pointsettias lined the staircase and popped up on every end table or shelf, glittering gold swirling adornments poking their way through the forests of green and red. Tressa picked up a nutcracker from the mantle, its fierce expression daring her to look back.

"Mom, this is new, too," she said with a hint of exasperation.

Her mother smiled as she arranged more fresh pine on the mantle. "You know you love it as much as I do. I remember when you used to disappear beneath the folds of the tablecloth, taking ornaments and garland to create your own festive wonderland."

Tressa chuckled, "I was probably hiding from you trying to force me to wear some crushed velvet nonsense and uncomfortable shoes." Tressa was always her mother's final touch in the decorating process, after setting the tables, wrapping presents, and hanging fresh wreaths.

"And you still fight me, my pretty girl," she said, kissing her cheek, following with a typical backhanded compliment. "You never got the care package I sent?" she asked.

Tressa remembered the box that arrived a few weeks ago. The long sweater looked cozy, but it was a little too bright and scratchy for her taste. She remembered thinking that her mother should know she hated wool. The sweater was neatly folded in layers of fragrant tissue paper and secured with a black velvet bow. Its accompanying price tag rested on the sleeve.

"I did, thank you. Alex enjoyed the goodies as well," Tressa replied.

"Oh, good. Did everything work out okay with Alex after last week? I've worried about it ever since."

Tressa saw this as an excellent opportunity to segue into a different topic. Amid all the small, twinkling lights, mountains of gorgeously wrapped presents neatly stacked under the tree in the study, and the clinking of glassware near the sideboard, Tressa was focused on the next holiday. It wasn't that she loved New Year's Eve more than anyone else, but this year would be different. She hoped to get some answers or at least a better explanation. But for now, she hoped to shed some light on another troubling issue.

"Let's sit by the fire, Mom. I've been dying to try your new eggnog recipe," Tressa exaggerated, hoping to divert her mother's attention from any other potential concerns.

"Of course! I just bought new glasses," she said, hurrying into the dining room. She returned with a slender decanter and placed it on the table next to the petite etched glassware. Her silver earrings swayed gently, catching the light of the flickering fire and casting a warm glow on her face. Tressa noticed how happy she seemed—with her holiday decorating triumph, her social status, and her young husband. Tressa pondered, was she happy with her daughter?

The overpowering smell of rum and a hint of cinnamon filled Tressa's nostrils as she lifted the glass to her mouth. "This smells good," she said, continuing to play the game.

Deborah leaned toward her and asked, "So, how did the semester end?" Tressa noticed her mother staring at the fire, absently twirling a long, dark tendril of hair around her finger. It felt like the conversation was just another task on her never-ending to-do list, but her heart wasn't in it. The dancing flames of the fireplace held her attention more than their conversation.

"There is something I wanted to talk to you about. And I don't want you to get defensive." This caught her mother off guard since Tressa wasn't sticking to the script of holiday and school small talk.

"Oh, sure, what is it?" she asked, straightening her posture and turning to face her daughter.

As she nervously fidgeted with her fingers, Tressa asked, "Do you happen to know someone named Helena?" Her eyes were fixed on her mother's face, scanning for any hint of surprise or alarm. Despite her mother's talent for putting on a good show, she always had difficulty hiding her emotions. Tressa had seen her give away surprise parties and spoil Christmas gifts with her expressive face, but she could not read anything this time.

Her mother, a bit confused, responded, "I'm sorry, who is Helena? Is she a friend of yours or someone Ryan knows?" Tressa realized that the conversation was going in the wrong direction. Her stepfather was younger, and her mother always kept that in mind. Tressa noticed a light shade of red reflect off her mother's face, even though she wasn't facing the fire.

"It's someone from school. I was wondering if the name rang a bell. Nothing to worry about, Mom," Tressa said, raising her eyebrows. She ran her finger around the smooth rim of the glass, a slight stickiness keeping her finger somewhat attached. She thought she saw her mother exhale as she sank into the couch.

"Why did you want me to go to Wyval?" Tressa's question hung in the air, waiting for her mom's answer.

"Well, you know I've always wanted the best for you, sweetie," her mother replied.

"I understand that, but I'm asking, did you actively seek out Wyval, or was a recruiter involved? Why Wyval in particular?"

Tressa's mother seemed uncomfortable and hesitated. "What's with these questions? Is there something wrong at school? You are so close to graduation, Tressa. What could have happened? And all of these job offers—my God, the latest one at the art gallery in New York," her mom said, then she immediately covered her mouth with her long, slender hand, regretting what she said.

"I didn't tell you about the opportunity in New York."

"Sure you did," Deborah said, trying to sound confident.

"No, I told you about the museum in Connecticut and the West Coast opportunity but nothing about New York." Tressa waited for a reply but watched as her mother left the room, returning with more eggnog and adding a more than generous amount of rum.

"I think you are going to need this," she said, holding the liquor bottle. "Tressa, my dear. I want you to know that I love you very much, and everything I do is for you," she said, her words sweeter and syrupier than the festive drink.

Tressa took a sip but quickly pushed the glass aside, feeling the burning sensation in her mouth. The room suddenly felt warm, and her stomach churned. She had been contemplating this conversation on the drive over, but now that the moment was here, she was afraid of what she might discover.

In a trembling voice, she asked, "Please tell me you don't know Helena." Tressa couldn't bear the thought of her mother being involved in what happened in the woods or her mom associating with someone like Helena.

"Tress, I truly don't know who this Helena is you keep referring to, but what is it you want to know?" she said, flipping her long hair over her shoulder and propping her chin up with her hand. Her cherry-red nails glinted in the firelight.

Despite feeling breathless, Tressa knew there was no turning back once she started asking questions. She decided to begin at the very beginning. "So, obviously, you have heard of the Summit Society," she asked her mother.

Deborah ran her long acrylic nails through her sleek hair and asked, "The Summit Society? Do you mean the elite group at school? Is it a legitimate group?" The words seemed to cause her pain with each syllable.

"Mom, yes. Oh my God, you do know all about it, I can tell. Is it because of you I'm part of this?"

Her mother's face turned red, and she seemed to struggle for words. Finally, she spoke, her voice barely above a whisper. "I, um, well, yes and no. It's complicated."

"Please tell me what's going on. I have a right to know," Tressa said. Tears threatened to spill from her eyes, and her throat felt tight.

Her mom walked over to the mantle and smoothed the pine swags before turning to Tressa, her eyes glistening. "Tress, you are such a smart girl. I know you'll do big things, and I swear to you, I want the best for you. You've accomplished so much on your own and are much smarter than I was in school. Seeing how easily things came to you often made me jealous."

"What does that have to do with the Summit Society?" she asked.

"I knew money wasn't going to be a problem for your education, and I had no issues taking care of that, not to mention your academic achievements and scholarships paved the way anyway. However, if there was anything else I could do to ensure your future success, I would do it without any hesitation. That's when I heard rumors about a secret society at Wyval. This could help you with the social aspect of things, allowing you to connect with the right people and secure your future." Deborah's eyes sparkled with excitement as if she just announced something extraordinary.

Tressa thought of their meeting at the lake house, the focus on money, everyone trying to outdo each other at any cost. She wasn't sure they were the connection she needed.

"Who do you mean by the right people? And what do you have to do with the school?" Tressa asked.

"Nothing. We just checked a lot of the boxes they normally look for. Of course, there was no guarantee, but you would have a pretty good shot. I did what I could to get you to your senior year and only hoped you would be selected. Do you know how exclusive it is? And it's not just students from Wyval, so the competition can be fierce. Money is part of it, but the chosen ones must prove their loyalty and trustworthiness. It's not just about the money. Otherwise, everyone would pay their way in," Deborah explained.

"Okay, so you mentioned the money. Can you tell me more about that?" Tressa asked her mother.

Deborah returned to the couch, refusing to make eye contact with Tressa, and explained that they had made an initial donation to the university as a benefactor. Their financial advisor informed them that a few prominent board members inquired about their economic standing and assets, which had led to further discussions about their wealth.

"So you never really met with anyone?" Tressa asked.

"Tress, I swear to you. This whole process was word of mouth. I couldn't even guarantee the Summit Society existed. I couldn't point out who runs it if I saw her in a line-up."

Tressa's doubts persisted. "Her?" Tressa asked, not sold on her mom's lack of connections.

"Her, him, whoever. I'm telling you, I never met with anyone said to be associated with a secret society, and no one ever promised you would be given consideration. I spoke to enough people in my social circles who seemed to know about the rumors. Donating to the university was a good thing; if you attended and weren't chosen, nothing was lost on my end. I figured it was worth a shot," Deborah said.

Tressa's mind raced with thoughts of all correspondence from Wyval. She remembered getting all the voicemails that wouldn't stop until she returned the calls. Emails flooded her inbox like spam until she responded. The weekly letters and brochures were addressed to her. She only thought they were persistent, and it worked. It wasn't until her freshman year she heard rumors about the Summit Society, but she never gave it much thought.

"So what you are saying is that everyone associated with the Summit Society comes from wealthy families," Tressa said.

Her mother looked at the floor before meeting Tressa's eyes and nodding.

"And there's Mauri. I guess her family, the real estate business, got her in," Tressa said.

Her mom sat close, the smell of Chanel and perspiration strong. "I don't want you to look at this like a bad thing. Our money may have gotten you considered, but you proved yourself worthy through four years. That's something to be proud of. Think of the opportunities in store for you." Her mother squeezed her hands until the tips of her nails created small crescents in her skin.

"What do you mean about proving myself for four years? What did I do to prove myself besides my grades?" Tressa asked.

"I don't know, sweetie, but you did something to impress them. Although I never talked to anyone who ran the Summit Society, your foster informed me about your selection. Ryan and I were thrilled when we heard the news. I couldn't say anything at the time, but I'm just happy I was able to give you this opportunity," she said, her eyes welling up with tears.

"What do you mean by foster? A person?" Tressa asked.

"Yes, your foster was someone assigned to watch you throughout your years at the university, ensuring you were on the right path and still met the stringent qualifications for initiation," her mom explained.

"And that my financial status remained the same, I guess," Tressa added.

"Well, that, too, but also academic and social benchmarks," Tressa's mom said.

"Mmm," Tressa said, not sounding convinced. Although she was sure she knew the answer, she had to ask the pressing question.

"And who was my foster watching over me all these years, Mom?" Tressa asked, afraid to hear the answer.

Deborah lightly touched her shoulder before squeezing it. "It's Alex."

Electricity coursed through her body. Tressa wanted to run out of the house, unsure if she wanted to cry, scream, or hit something. Memories of the past four years swirled in her head like a tornado. She tried recalling orientation. Were the signs there from the beginning? She could stay in a dorm, but when the opportunity to land an exclusive apartment near campus arose, she jumped on it. Tressa recalled her mom's push to take advantage of the extra space and privacy, even though it still meant sharing with two other students. How could she be so stupid? Why would a new student be allowed to live in that scenario during freshman year, especially in a co-ed scenario? A chill crept through her body as she thought about her former roommate, Jess.

"What about Jess? What happened to her?" Tressa asked.

"Jess? I don't know what she's doing now except that she transferred from Wyval. Honey, listen. I don't have as much information as you think. You decided to go to the university regardless, so when the living arrangement presented itself, I figured you'd appreciate more space. The landlord promised me it was coveted housing, and we should jump on the opportunity," her mom explained.

"Who was the landlord? And jump on the opportunity? So your freshman daughter could stay with a guy she barely knew?" Tressa thought back to the early days, the awkwardness of having new roommates, let alone a guy. But everything fell into place within weeks. The apartment gave each of them enough space while having the option of hanging out together, close friendships she never had in high school. Her feelings for Alex wavered between big brother and freshman crush, but big brother always won. She thought about the movie nights, staying up until 3 a.m. talking about goals, classes, and life. How having Alex for a roommate was the least likely and best match ever. Now, Tressa wondered how much of their friendship was genuine, if any.

"What about Jess? She met the financial criteria, too, I guess?" She walked over to the mantle, the nutcracker grinning at her like she was the only one not in on the plan.

"Many students came from families with a secure financial landscape, but not everyone fits the mold to become part of a secret society. You possess something they like, honey," her mother said. She walked behind Tressa and placed her head on her shoulder, the show of emotion a little too forced.

"We possess money. Lots of it," Tressa said, avoiding eye contact with her mother.

"No. From what I heard, no one knows the specific criteria. It takes certain character, intelligence, trust, and loyalty. If you demonstrate these things, you have a better chance. Alex was only there to guide you and encourage good choices," Deborah said as if her daughter had signed up for student council.

Tressa thought about her mom's bizarre affection toward Alex and his familiar tone whenever Tressa mentioned her mom. It all made sense in a disturbing kind of way.

"Well, Mom. Bravo. You can tell your friends that your daughter was selected into the most exclusive, prestigious secret society. The only problem is, it won't last," Tressa announced.

Deborah stood up, twisting the hem of her cardigan. "What do you mean?"

"Once I explain the situation to Mauri, we will get out of the Summit Society as soon as possible," Tressa said.

"I don't understand. I thought this would make you happy," her mother said.

"I don't want to be part of something that values money over life. You truly have no idea." Tears rolled down Tressa's face as she headed to her room, stopping at the top landing.

**T: Hey, we need to talk.**

She paused, waiting for a response but not expecting one. The deep mahogany banister felt waxy, and the lingering smell of lemon and cleaning solution replaced the gentle blends of Christmas on the first floor. A small tabletop tree twinkled at the end of the dark hall—a reminder of the holiday throughout the entire house. Tressa stared at her phone while hearing hushed whispers from her mom and stepdad floating from the living room. Tressa felt like she had only scratched the surface of what was going on.

# Chapter Forty-Six

"Maybe he's busy doing things with his family for the holidays. It's possible, right?" Mauri asked.

"We both know Alex always has his phone next to him. He saw the message," Tressa replied, eager to see Alex in person and ask him some important questions.

Shoppers bustled through the mall food court, looking for post-Christmas deals before the upcoming storm. Mauri played with the straw in her cup, jabbing away at the ice. "Did you hear they are predicting over two feet of snow?" she asked. "I wonder if that will change plans for the party."

"As long as the party is happening, we are going. I need to talk to Helena," Tressa said.

Mauri shrugged. "Oh, and you know it's not at the lake house where we met Helena, right? It's the party place, Tori's house. Her parents are on a ski trip in Vienna, so she told Helena she'd host."

"Oh, good. I'll feel more comfortable confronting her if the party is like the last one. Large parties can give the best cover." She took a bite of her burger, the salt and grease a welcome change of pace from lavish holiday food. She followed Mauri's gaze to a group of teens near the pretzel stand. "How did you know it changed? The party?" Tressa asked.

Mauri snapped out of her daze, her attention returning to the noisy surroundings. She shook her head and shifted in her seat, nearly knocking her cup off the table. "Sorry, what was that?"

"How did you know the party was changed?" Tressa repeated. As she waited for a response, she pulled up the app to see if she missed any notifications, but there was nothing new.

"It was in the app. You didn't get the updated info?" Mauri said, fumbling with her phone. "Here, look," she said, turning the screen to Tressa. A simple message was displayed, indicating the party address and time.

Tressa pulled up the app to see if she missed any notifications, but there was nothing new. As she clicked on the close-up of herself in the haunted house, she was about to show it to Mauri but thought it best to keep it private. They seemed to receive different information from the society, with Tressa's a bit more unnerving. "Strange, I don't seem to have any updates," she said before sliding her phone in her pocket.

Mauri crumpled the straw paper between her fingers and leaned in to speak. "There's something I need to tell you about the Summit Society," she began.

Tressa felt a flush of warmth spread across her cheeks. Her burger sat like a lump in her stomach, with the rest of the food suddenly unappetizing.

Mauri's voice was heavy with guilt. "Ever since you talked about that girl at the brewery, it's been on my mind," she admitted. "I tried to bury it, and I've been selfish. I was blinded by the promise of something bigger than me, an easy path in life. But then I saw the databases."

"The databases?" Tressa echoed, confused.

Mauri leaned forward, her voice low and intense. "You remember those missing person files we were looking at in your apartment?" she asked. "I did some digging myself, and I'll tell you, it's overwhelming. Every case number, every file, it's someone." Mauri's eyes glinted with sympathy and determination. "If the girl we saw at the brewery isn't the same one we saw in the woods, then we need to find out where she is. You are right. We can't just sit here and do nothing."

Tressa wasn't sure if the new information she shared helped change Mauri's mind, but she was glad her friend decided to take the blinders off when looking at the situation. "You are wrong about something," Tressa said.

Mauri looked over at her in surprise.

"The Summit Society is not bigger than you. You, just as you are, are bigger than the whole lot," Tressa leaned and whispered.

Groans of disappointment rang out around them as an announcement came over the loudspeaker, indicating the mall would close early due to the storm. As they headed to the parking lot, the sky seemed busy gathering ominous gray clouds, any ray of late December daylight erased by the snow-laden horizon. There was a different cold in the air, the bone-chilling type that seeped into the heaviest of jackets, the snuggest hats, and gloves.

"So I guess this really is the calm before the storm?" Mauri asked, staring at the darkening clouds above.

Tressa slipped into the Land Rover when she heard the chiming ringtone. It wasn't a message—it was a call from Alex.

"Hey," she said, wanting to say everything at once but unable to say anything.

"Hey. Tress. We have to talk, but I'd rather do it in person. Do you want to meet at the apartment?" Alex asked, his tone somber.

Blizzard-like conditions weren't forecasted to start until overnight, but you could never trust Northeast weather. Besides, Tressa tried getting in touch with Alex for days, and suddenly he made contact. She needed to see him.

"Um, sure, I'll see you soon," Tressa said, not revealing to Mauri who called. As they pulled out of the parking lot, Mauri didn't ask either. She needed to confront Alex alone.

"You can drop me off at my apartment. I want to get my stuff together so I can get home," Mauri said. "Don't worry, I have a ride," she said, not offering additional information.

Tressa couldn't worry about her friend's travel plans right now, and when she glanced at the clock, she realized she needed to make up some time. She needed to reach her destination before Alex to have a clear idea of what she was getting herself into.

Once Tressa dropped Mauri off, she hurried to the apartment building, which appeared deserted due to the holiday break. As she walked into the apartment, she felt a sudden chill. Her phone buzzed, alerting her to a new message on the app. It was another picture, but this time she wasn't alone. Tressa could also spot Mauri in the image, confirming that someone was keeping a close eye on her, and only hours ago. She rushed to the door and locked it, feeling breathless and uneasy. The air seemed heavy with the weight of the silence, the only sounds being the click of the steam pipes and the buzz of the overhead light. She sat at the kitchen table and waited. Besides the newest picture, there were no texts and no calls. Maybe there was something wrong with her phone? She never received Helena's message in the app, and she received nothing from Alex. When a blizzard warning popped up in her alerts, she decided it was time to return to her mom's house. Dealing with listening to her mother beat the alternative of getting stuck in a snowstorm. As she walked down the hall, she paused to make a final attempt at messaging Alex. After no response, she headed to the car, pausing before every corner, looking in every doorway. Confident no one was lurking outside the building, she sprinted to the SUV, checking the backseat before driving away.

A squall of flurries whipped through the air, obscuring the landscape as she headed home. Tressa knew the worst was yet to come. She tried to concentrate on driving through the snowy conditions, but she had so much to unpack in her mind with the new situation she found herself in. She was sure Alex wouldn't miss another party at the lake house—especially if instructed by Helena. Tressa wondered about Alex's role. Her academics never posed a problem, and he knew that. He even joked about how she was at the top of the class. Financial stability? Being friendly with her mom and stepdad kept him in the know, and one visit to her house would verify all was well on that front. The social aspect? Maybe that was why he encouraged her to go out and meet new people, but it always had to be the right people. Or perhaps they wanted someone a bit backward, who would relish and embrace the idea of being welcomed into the secret society—someone who would do anything to pledge their loyalty and trust no matter the circumstance. It's too bad they misjudged her.

# Chapter Forty-Seven

Tressa positioned herself in front of the fireplace, enveloped in a fleece blanket. The fire crackled as the heavy snow created a blank white canvas outside the window. She repeatedly checked her phone for the latest weather updates, hoping the system would move out by the weekend. She had every intention of attending the New Year's Eve party.

"Hey, Tress. Mind if I sit?" her stepdad said, plunking down without permission.

Tressa pulled her knees closer, shrouding herself beneath the blanket. She was perfectly fine relaxing alone in her cozy spot. Ryan rarely sat down for a chat, at least not with Tressa. His universe revolved around her mom.

"Your mom told me a little bit about what's going on, and I wanted you to know that you shouldn't be upset with her," Ryan said, his voice low and serious.

As he continued to talk, Tressa found it difficult to take his advice seriously. He had never tried to assert authority over her, but she did not need a pseudo-father figure in her life. Tressa had a hard time taking any advice from someone who had walked the halls of a college campus a little more than ten years ago. She didn't hate Ryan but resented the awkwardness and was never quite sure of his intentions. As she focused on her phone, she became increasingly confident that her mother put him up to this.

"I'm fine, Ryan," Tressa said, staring at the fire.

"No. Your mom told me about some of your questions, and I think I owe you an explanation," Ryan said.

Tressa felt a sharp pain in her neck as she abruptly turned to focus on her stepdad. His dark hair, the color of a strong espresso, swooped to the side, skimming the top of his bold eyebrows. She understood why her mother fawned over him, but on most days, she viewed him as an annoying older brother.

"Your mother mentioned how some people she knows gave her the scoop on the Summit Society. It's not a bad organization to be part of, you know," Ryan lectured.

Tressa couldn't believe they were having this conversation. It was bad enough that her mother seemed so disappointed when she told her she would bow out, and now Ryan, too? She watched as he smoothed his red plaid pajama bottoms and stood up from the couch. His waffle tee clung to his biceps as he reached over the expansive coffee table to grab the decanter and glass. His chiseled jaw twitched as he focused on pouring the perfect measure of whiskey before returning to the couch.

"So, no comment, I guess?" Ryan asked. As the room remained silent, he continued. "Look, I'm just trying to help keep the peace here, and I promised your mother I'd talk to you. He took a long gulp of his whiskey, shivered, and placed the glass on the table. "Will you at least listen to what I have to say?" he asked.

Tressa shrugged her shoulders, assuming she had no choice.

"What do you think of when it comes to secret societies?" he asked.

She rolled her eyes and shot him a look. Tressa didn't think she'd be grilled like she was in a sociology class, but she figured she'd play along to see where this was going. "It means belonging to something exclusive and secretive while proving that you are worthy and loyal," she said as if reciting an answer in a classroom.

From her experience over the last few weeks, she knew it involved a lot more, but she had no intention of getting into lengthy explanations with Ryan.

"Fancy. What about the main reasons behind the creation of these secret societies?" Her stepdad continued with his questions.

"Ryan, come on," Tressa said, tossing the blanket from her lap.

He waved his hand in a spiral, urging her to answer.

Tressa continued his game, but the words came out in a rush. "Religious, political, crime, social status, wealth, power. Things like that," she replied, hoping to end the Q&A session.

"Right. So most people are intrigued by the power and wealth aspect, wouldn't you say?"

She bit her lip and focused on the glow from the fireplace. She thought about the emails inviting her to interviews for some prestigious positions. "What are you getting at, Ryan?" she asked, curious about the direction of the conversation.

"Well, like your mom, I know the people in those social circles, and she's right. The Summit Society can provide both, but it wasn't always like that," he said, sparking some intrigue in Tressa.

"Really?" Tressa suspected he had already had too much whiskey tonight. She wanted the history lesson to be over, but she also wanted to see what he was trying to accomplish. To be honest, she may have sounded a little harsh.

"I just think," Ryan continued, "if I give you a little backstory on it from my angle, you might be a little more understanding."

Tressa's legs swung off the couch with a heavy thud as she propped her elbow on the armrest, bracing herself for what her stepfather had to say.

"Did you know that the Summit Society has an interesting history? It didn't start with any ties to Wyval or any other university. It began as something entirely different," he said, piquing his stepdaughter's interest. "You've heard of the Molly Maguires, right?" he asked.

Tressa could have responded to that in about ten sarcastic ways, but she bit her tongue. She wondered if he paid attention to anything she ever said, including her job at the old jail. "Yes, I'm familiar," she said slowly. "The society started in Ireland—they were farmers defending land rights and fighting unfair taxes," she said.

"That's right," Ryan said, impressed. "Until immigrants moved to the United States, working in this region in the coal industry. Same thing, the Mollies formed labor unions to protect workers from oppressive mine owners. Some of the organization broke off into even smaller, more secretive factions."

Tressa let Ryan continue since he seemed excited to give her information she already knew—except the part about the smaller organizations.

"The Summit Society was one of those spin-off groups. As the years passed, it changed from farmers to miners and eventually business owners. At some point, one of the wealthy business owners attended Wyval, and the association was born. It branched out to other universities nationwide, but the origins are rooted here," Ryan explained.

"But it still comes down to money, right?" Tressa asked, cutting to the chase.

"Well, it does, somewhat. But there's preferential treatment for certain people," he added. "I told her that with your Irish heritage and great academic record, it would give you a better chance. Best-case scenario? You are chosen as one of the Summit Society. Worst-case scenario? You get a great education."

Tressa weighed this information and wondered why Ryan was suddenly interested in her future. She figured this had to benefit him somehow, and he was also nervous she was going to screw it up.

"Anyway, I don't want you to be mad at your mother. She only wants you to have the best opportunities with promises of a successful future. We both want that for you," Ryan said. "But, anyway, that's all I got. I think I'm going to head upstairs. I'm tired. Please don't be so hard on your mother, okay, kiddo?"

Tressa could not believe he had just said kiddo.

"Will do. Thanks for the info." Tressa watched as Ryan disappeared upstairs, still wondering about his true intentions. She couldn't shake off the feeling that something wasn't right and wondered if he knew the current values of the Summit Society embodied those of the original Molly Maguires. Murder.

# Chapter Forty-Eight

New Year's Eve. The weather forecasters were wrong, as almost three feet of snow fell over a few days. The snow crunched under the Land Rover's tires, and Tressa navigated the SUV through the narrow passage that someone cleared down the center of the drive. She had not heard back from Alex, but she wasn't surprised. Mauri had promised to meet her at the party, and they had the most significant New Year's resolution of their lives to fulfill. As Tressa drove, her bag fell off the seat, and her glittery flats tumbled to the floor. As she reached the edge of the circular drive, a man dressed in all black approached the driver-side door.

"Good evening, ma'am," the attendant greeted, gesturing towards the plowed area designated for parking. "It's valet service tonight," he added, his hand on the door. Tressa slung her tote over her shoulder and handed him the keys, ready to make her way into the grand end-of-the-year gala.

Before leaving, the attendant called out, "I think you'll need this too." She turned around and picked up the black and silver sequinned mask, the inky black feathers fluttering onto the pristine snow near the walkway. The mask was the only requirement for entrance to the exclusive event.

The party was a repeat of the one held only weeks before, but everything had a silver sheen this time. The room was filled with tuxedos and short shimmering dresses, each accentuated with exquisite masks. It all seemed fitting—everyone hiding behind a sparkling image. Tressa scanned the crowd and found no sign of Alex, Mauri, or Helena. The music pounded, and reflected light showered a small parquet dance floor with geometric shapes. Snow would not hamper anyone's plans tonight as guests adorned in Mardi Gras-type masks poured through the front door. Tressa had rehearsed her speech a thousand times. Her goal was to give Helena a chance to come clean before involving the authorities, as that would be the end result anyway. She knew she had to do this for Kayla and anyone else who may have been hurt by the Summit Society or even worse.

As she pondered her next steps, Tressa headed to the bar, the area of the house reminding her of a trendy nightclub. Colorful bottles of every shape and size lined glass shelves, the dim lighting casting a sultry glow. Edgy artwork decorated each side of the bar, and the gleaming marble countertop was a work of art itself.

The bartender interrupted her thoughts, "Drink? Specialty of the host," he said, passing along a long tapered flute, its bubbly goodness supporting a few floating raspberries and mint sprigs. "Oh, and ma'am?" the bartender asked before Tressa walked away, "Don't forget about the masks," he said, touching her wrist.

Tressa thought about the night in the woods and the masked society members. She stared at the bartender, studying his eyes, wondering what he was trying to tell her until he nodded at the black and silver mask in her hand.

"Oh, right, thank you," she said, the carbonation burning her nose as she downed half her drink. She stopped, wanting to be coherent when confronting Helena. She positioned the satiny mask over her eyes, fitting in with the layer of surprise and intrigue. As she made her way through the crowd, the smell of candle wax, heavy cologne, and sweat was overwhelming, and the hum of conversation and laughter mixed with the pulsing beat of the music.

Tressa touched the feathers on her mask, realizing she blended in with this group in a sense of unity and anonymity. She knew that was where the similarity with these people ended. She searched the room for Alex or Mauri and saw a woman with a vibrant jewel-toned peacock plume reaching above her mask. As she drew closer, Tressa's heart skipped a beat as she recognized her. It was Helena.

"Hello, my dear," she said, hurrying over and leaning in for an air kiss. "I'm so happy my girl is here." Helena looked stunning in her body-hugging electric blue mini dress. Her talon-like nails grasped the glass as they moved towards the staircase, away from the pulsating speaker.

"I'm meeting Mauri and hopefully Alex. Have you seen them?" She searched the wall for the thermostat, tugging at her rounded neckline, wishing she wore something sleeveless. "Is Tori around, the host? I think I overdressed for the party," Tressa said, wondering why the heat would be on blast for a party.

"Oh, you look adorable, don't change. Would you like to get some fresh air? It is quite warm in here," Helena suggested.

The duo walked outside. Surprisingly, the deck and walkways were cleared of all signs of a snowstorm. Outdoor heaters flickered, the warm, glowing light outlining couples hiding away in the recesses of the shadows. Although the cool air felt refreshing, it couldn't alleviate the fire burning in Tressa's face and neck.

"Come walk with me," Helena said, linking her arm to hers. "I hear you want to talk, so tell me, how is everything going?" she asked, her petite arm holding on to Tressa's with surprising force. "I hope you liked your Christmas gift," Helena said.

"Oh, yes, the bag. It's very nice," Tressa responded.

"I'm also aware you received several emails. The hardest part of your job search will be deciding which offer to choose. It sounds like you will be good to go after graduation," Helena said, tapping

Tressa's arm.

Tressa hesitated for a moment before speaking up, pulling away from Helena's grip. "Yes, I mean, no. Helena, I don't think this is what I want."

The petite woman paused, and the strings of lights cast unflattering shadows on her face. Her cheekbones looked sunken in, and her eyes were surrounded by crepey skin. "I know it's a lot to take in, but you must understand you are one of us now. You are part of a legacy, a forever family. The Summit Society will always be here for you—we promise to take care of each other," she said.

"Really? What about Kayla? In the woods? I see how you took care of her," Tressa said, changing the direction of the conversation. She felt like a weight was lifted off her chest, addressing the issue that had troubled her since they left the woods that night.

"Oh, Tressa, Tressa. I knew it would come back to that. We've been through this. It was Gina in the woods, it was Gina at the lake house, and it was Gina you saw at the brewery," Helena said in a sing-song voice. "What other proof do you need?" she asked.

Tressa tried to stay on track with her planned speech but had trouble focusing on her words. "And another thing, she said, swaying back and forth, trying to keep her balance. I want to know what the story is with the shock collar. Was that real?" Tressa asked, watching Helena come in and out of focus.

"Tressa, dear. You don't look so well. Maybe we should go inside," she said, grabbing Tressa's elbow. As they returned to the house, Helena led her to a couch. "Now, don't go anywhere; the fun is about to start," she said with a smirk, disappearing through the kitchen. Tressa looked around the room, but still no signs of Alex or Mauri. She grabbed her phone but couldn't remember her code. She stared at the screen until everything went black, and screams surrounded her.

A few flickering candles illuminated the walls, distorted shadows playfully dancing. Tressa knew she should get up before Helena returned, but her legs wouldn't move. As other partygoers scrambled around her, she tugged on the corner of someone's silver satin floor-length gown.

"Hey, are you okay?" the girl asked, staring at Tressa. "We all have to leave," she said, disappointed. "Worst New Year's Eve party ever, right?" she asked, brushing Tressa's hand off her dress. "Maybe you need an Uber?" she asked before walking away.

Tressa fanned herself and wiped the sweat from her brow. She wondered why people were concentrated in the foyer. It looked like a concert, a sea of cell phone screens glowing in the crowd, although the music had stopped. She reached out a hand and tried to stand before collapsing back to the couch. As she settled back in the cushions, Helena's face appeared only inches from hers.

"It seems the heavy snow has caused power outages in the area over the last few days, and Tori's house isn't immune. And sadly, the generator doesn't seem to be working. I announced to everyone they had to leave. Such a shame on such a big night," she said, her face frozen in an exaggerated pout.

Tressa could barely sit up now, and all she wanted to do was lie on the couch—the room was spinning.

"Come on, let me take you to Tori's room so you can rest until everyone leaves," Helena said, leading Tressa up the stairs.

Tressa's feet seemed to float as she reached the landing, and everything was out of focus. As they walked into the pristine bedroom, Helena grasped Tressa's arm, the pain the only thing she could focus on. "I'll be back once we get all these guests out of here. You have a decision you have to make. And in case you are wondering, yes, it was real," she hissed before closing the door.

Tressa stumbled through the darkness before collapsing on the bed. As she reached for her phone, her world went completely black.

# Chapter Forty-Nine

Tressa's eyes slowly opened as she struggled to make sense of her surroundings. The moonlight was shining through the window, illuminating everything in a white glow like she was surrounded by snow. She recognized the place—it was Tori's room. As she tried to sit up, Tressa's head pounded, and she felt sick. She couldn't remember drinking anything after the bubbly cocktail earlier. Her last memory was struggling to climb the stairs, feeling like her feet were moving through mud. She searched the room for her phone, but it was nowhere to be found. Panic set in as she tried to open the door and realized it was locked from the outside, but that wasn't the only thing she noticed.

Cold metal constricted her neck, sending a surge of primal fear through her as she realized what it was. Tressa frantically clawed at the edges of the collar, her fingers trembling as she attempted to find a latch or catch that would release her from its grip.

The house was silent, except for the clicking sound like heels on marble in the distance. It had to be Helena. Tressa wiped her palms on her dress and tried to calm her breathing—she needed to focus on getting out rather than obsessing over the collar. The room was adorned with flowing pearl-white curtains concealing two windows overlooking a steep drop to the deck below. Her eyes darted around the room, searching for anything that could be used as a weapon. Without hesitation, she ran into the en suite bathroom to continue her search. Her eyes fell on the small ornate window as she scanned the gleaming white and silver space. It had a tiny hinge, barely visible to the naked eye. Without a second thought, she locked the bathroom door and climbed onto the edge of the tub. Her heart raced as she realized the bathroom was above a sloped roof. She could jump down and escape if she could squeeze through the window. Suddenly, she heard the doorknob rattle.

"Oh, Tressa, dear. I expected you'd be sleeping. Can you come out, please?" Helena asked.

Tressa knew it was now or never. "Just a second, I needed to use the bathroom," she said in a tired voice.

Without wasting more time, Tressa hopped onto the clawfoot tub and quickly pulled herself up to the window. She got half her body through the tight space, relishing the freezing air. Suddenly, there was pounding on the door.

"Tressa!" Helena screamed. "Open this door!"

Tressa knew she had to act fast. She slid out the window with one push, landing on the sloped roof. The ice and snow prevented her from stopping, and she braced herself as she slid. Peering over the edge, she tried to gauge the distance to the ground, all while the icy wind numbed her skin. Behind her, the pounding on the door became louder, and Helena's voice angrier. She leaped, and her shoulder crashed into icy resistance before giving way to a soft pile of snow. The restrictive collar tugged at her neck, and Tressa's heart raced as she expected to feel a jolt at any second. Standing up and trying to get her bearings, she realized she was at the back of the house. As she hobbled toward the deck, Helena appeared at the door. Tressa knew that her only option was to head towards the lake.

Helena called out. "Don't bother running—the lake is behind you. And I need you to see something," she added.

"Oh, I don't need to see it. I can feel it," she yelled into the frigid air, grabbing her neck. Tressa looked out at the lake, wondering if it would be safe to cross the ice to access the woods. She wondered if the valet would have left the keys in the car.

"I'm not talking about you. I'm talking about Mauri," Helena replied with a hint of mischief.

Tressa's heart skipped a beat. Up until this point, she never considered Mauri could be in danger. She wasn't even sure what role she may have played leading up to this moment. "Where is she?" she asked, her voice trembling.

Helena smirked and walked closer to Tressa. "Come on, silly. Let me show you," she said, holding out a phone. "I think you'll be shocked."

As Tressa approached the deck, she noticed the entire house was engulfed in darkness, except for a few flickering candles. Helplessness washed over her as she moved closer, and Tressa's head was pounding.

"Check out the app!" her nemesis said with too much enthusiasm, handing Tressa her missing phone.

Her fingers trembled as she tried to unlock it and open the Summit Society app. Finally, it sprang to life, and she saw a new notification.

"Go ahead, open it," Helena gestured to the phone.

Tressa clicked on the folder, expecting to see a picture of herself from the night's events. Instead, she was greeted by a live video feed of Mauri's location. Tressa squinted at the phone, trying to comprehend what she saw. She struggled to catch her breath as she watched two glowing lights moving on the screen.

"It seems like we only have room for one initiate after all. And if you click on the bottom of the screen, you'll see a familiar button," Helena said with a sly grin.

Tressa's hands shook as she scrolled down to find the button that read "PROCEED." Suddenly, the horror set in as she remembered what Helena had told her earlier.

Tressa's heart felt like it was going to explode. "So, the situation in the woods. We did administer the shock, didn't we? Is that what made her fall?" she asked Helena. "And why? Why would you make us do something like that?" she asked.

"This year, I decided to make things more challenging by raising the stakes. For existing Summit Society members, it was a chance to elevate their status or pay off their debts. As for new members, it was an opportunity to demonstrate their loyalty," explained Helena.

"And blackmail, I guess. I saw the edited videos, which made it seem like everything Mauri and I did was criminal," Tressa said.

Helena tilted her head and shrugged, saying, "I guess authorities would see it that way."

Tressa's mind reeled as Helena's words sank in. She felt a sickening sense of disbelief, her eyes darting back and forth between the woman and the phone screen.

"It would have been fine, but things did not go as planned. She messed up," Helena said.

"Who messed up?" Was it Kayla?" Tressa asked. Her breath came out in quick, white puffs. Despite the chill, Tressa could feel sweat beading on her forehead. She waited for Helena to answer.

"There was never a Gina in the woods that night," Tressa said in frustration, coaxing her to respond.

"Oh, please. I realized you figured that part out. That's why we monitored you—in case you did anything foolish. We had eyes on you the whole time," Helena replied, dismissing Tressa's concerns.

"You killed her. You killed Kayla," Tressa shouted.

"I killed no one," Helena screamed. "Kayla was just as much a part of this organization as anyone else. It's not like I'm to blame for her family's financial troubles, which made it difficult for her to keep up with the alumni fee. Unfortunately, it's one of the stipulations," explained Helena.

"How much?" Tressa asked.

"What do you mean how much?" Helena asked.

"How much does it cost to be a part of this? I mean, isn't that what the Summit Society is really about? You pretend it's about heritage, tradition, and academic achievements, but it's just about money," Tressa said.

Shadows danced around them as the moonlight reflected off the barren trees, the wind intensifying the numbing cold as Tressa's fingers started to lose sensation.

Helena sighed. "How do you think we can afford these parties and lavish gifts? Or pay organizations to secure job opportunities? It's all from the alumni fee," she explained, showing no remorse.

Tressa was taken aback. "You never mentioned anything about alumni fees. All these tests, the app, and the medallions are just distractions, aren't they? A smoke and mirrors scam allowing you to take advantage of rich kids who are desperate to fit in," she said, her words laced with bitterness. "It's all about the money," she added, tears streaming down her face.

Helena's voice wavered as she spoke, "It's not just about fitting in and money. What we share is much more than that. It's a bond that has been nurtured for generations. We are the Summit Society—a coveted group that everyone aspires to be a part of. And you, Tressa Litton," Helena screamed. "We pursued you for years, believing you were perfect for our group. And now you want to destroy everything. It was an accident— a goddamn accident. I am not going to let one night ruin everything we built. I invite you to our world, my world, and this is the thanks I get."

Tressa was stunned by the woman's outburst. As the darkness seemed to press in on her and the cold seeped into her bones, Tressa thought about Kayla being carried out of the woods. She needed to know the truth, no matter how painful. "She's dead, isn't she?" Tressa asked. "Kayla had second thoughts about going through with it, and then she panicked and ran," she said.

"I told them to take her to the hospital, but unfortunately, it was too late. It was an accident. I couldn't let that ruin everything we built up," Helena said, trying to justify her actions.

Tressa's mind raced with thoughts about the collar and Mauri. She couldn't believe she was forced to choose between her friend and her future. "So, what now?" Tressa asked, trying to keep her voice steady. "Are you saying there's only room for one inductee? I get it. You want me to click PROCEED to hurt Mauri," Tressa said, her voice trembling with anger and disbelief.

As she spoke, Helena raised an eyebrow and pursed her lips, seemingly unfazed by Tressa's reaction. Her silhouette cast shadows on the snowy backdrop, and the moonlight bounced off the dazzling sequins on her dress. Tressa knew Helena had to be freezing, but she stood stock-still as she stared at Tressa.

"Oh, my God. You want to kill her," Tressa said, realizing what was happening. She watched Helena, wondering how someone could go from sending designer purses to causing death by electric shock.

"I had planned to eliminate both of you when Mauri began poking around. I knew that you both had the potential to ruin everything. However, I've decided to let you make a choice. Let's find out who is truly committed to joining the Summit Society." A subtle glow reflected on Helena's face as she furiously punched her fingers on her phone. "And now, my dear Tressa, I must say, you too look glowing tonight," Helena said with a laugh.

Tressa's eyes darted around, noticing the sickly green glow below her chin.

"I've had both of these altered, and the highest voltage setting is now even more powerful. Tressa, say hi to Mauri. Mauri, say hi to Tressa," Helena said, turning her phone.

Tressa squinted at the screen, the glowing lights not moving, the outline of her friend kneeling on the ground.

"You will both have the opportunity to hit PROCEED. Let's see who acts first and wants it more," Helena said.

"Neither of us will," Tressa said, backing up toward the lake. She looked over her shoulder, the moon reflecting off the frozen lake. She was sure that running across the corner of the lake would take her to the edge of the woods, but she needed to find out if the ice was solid. She also wondered if frigid water would deactivate the device holding her hostage.

"We'll see about that," Helena said, "you might be surprised."

The lake was perilously close to the snow-covered pathway, marked where the staff had stopped clearing during the party preparations. Helena's heels slipped on the snow as she struggled to keep up with the retreating girl. "Someone will be here soon," Tressa said, trying to delay the inevitable. "I'll tell them every-thing—about Kayla, the money, everything."

Helena chuckled lightly. "Well, since I turned off the power to the house and sent everyone else home, and Tori is currently away with her parents, it looks like it's just the three of us here- Mauri, you, and me," she explained, tapping her phone as she spoke.

Helena inched closer to Tressa, her hair fluttering in the wind. She navigated the slippery surface cautiously, and Tressa's heart raced with fear. She was running out of time and land.

As Tressa held onto her phone, she contemplated calling for help, but she knew Helena could probably kill them both.

Helena noticed Tressa's hesitation and held up the screen

showing the feed monitoring Mauri. "Don't even think about it," she warned. "I'll activate it in a second, and there's no one around to help her. Or you."

Tressa's mind raced as she tried to come up with a plan. "I know someone who could be here in minutes. He's probably on his way already," she said, hoping to buy some time.

"Who, Alex?" Helena asked, followed by sinister laughter.

Tressa's heart sank at the thought of Alex being involved. "What about Alex?" she asked, afraid to hear the answer. "Don't try to tell me he was in on it, too," she stammered.

"Alex? Yes, he was involved, but not in the way you think," replied Helena. "He only wanted to help you get where you needed to be. After all these years, I think he developed a soft spot for his fellow redhead. He had no idea about Kayla's accident. When he found out, he was as shocked as you are and happened to have a little accident of his own."

Tressa's eyes widened in horror, "What kind of accident?" she whimpered.

"Well, when he found out about Kayla, and then I found out you wanted to talk to him, I made sure he never made it to the apartment," Helena said, her voice lowering to a whisper.

"You killed him too?" Tressa cried.

"I told you I never killed anyone. I decided to let nature take its course and not interfere. The blizzard was perfect timing. Perhaps he encountered car trouble during the storm, but I'm confident he'll be found once the snow thaws," Helena said with a smile.

The mere thought of Alex being in danger made Tressa feel light-headed, causing her to fall to her knees. As she struggled to get back up and stumbled towards the path, Helena grabbed her arm, forcing her to lose balance, and both of their phones fell into the nearby snowbank. Despite the sharp rocks digging into her hands like glass splinters, Tressa focused on the house in the background. She had to retrieve both phones and get to the house to find Mauri and Alex. Tressa needed to save her friends.

Tressa reached for a tree, the bark digging into her hand as she pulled herself up.

Suddenly, there was a thud.

A searing pain surged through Tressa's head like a lightning bolt, causing her ears to buzz like an electric current. She instinctively reached up, thinking her collar was activated, but instead, her hand was immediately covered in blood after touching her head, a stark contrast to the surrounding snow. As she stumbled backward towards the lake, she noticed Helena approaching with something in her hand. Out of nowhere, a male voice echoed in the distance, followed by heavy footsteps pounding on the walkway. Helena spun around, and Tressa knew it was her chance. She bolted to the lake's edge and carefully walked onto the ice. As she inched farther along, she picked up her pace, focusing on the trees in the distance.

Tressa was just a few feet from the shoreline when a loud crack echoed beneath her feet. Her heart pounded as she tried to run faster, but the cracking sounds grew louder. The ice started to give way, and she could feel the cold water seeping into her shoes. She attempted to keep her balance, but it was too late. The ice broke apart, and she plunged into the inky blackness. Struggling to keep her head above water, Tressa gasped for air as the cold numbed her senses and body. Desperate to save herself, she reached for nearby reeds and ferns while her thoughts drifted toward Mauri, wondering if she would be okay. She sank deeper into the icy cold water and fought with everything she had to come up for air. Then, she noticed someone approaching the edge of the lake from the nearby trees. Assuming it was Helena, she felt hopelessness wash over her, knowing that it was unlikely anyone could save her now. As she gasped for air, Tressa found it difficult to tell if her arms and legs were still moving. She gazed up at the night sky, where the stars shone brightly, oblivious to the turmoil below. As she tried reaching for something to grab onto, she knew she wasn't coming back up if she went under again. She closed her eyes, her arms floating out to the side. Suddenly, she was jolted out of the water as someone grabbed her by the arms and dragged her to the shore.

Her feet bumped along the path as she was pulled to a clearing. Her vision blurred, and the frigid air against her wet skin made it seem like her limbs would crack. Her muscles felt stiff, and her chattering teeth made it impossible for her to speak. As she reached up to the figure looming above her, she felt something wrap around her before being carried away. Her head bobbed against the person's chest as she struggled to stay awake. Tressa opened her eyes and realized they were nearing the lake house. She attempted to kick her feet, but the person pulled her closer. As they passed the outside deck, she saw a brilliant blue crumpled figure curled into a ball only feet away from her, writhing on the ground. She wondered if this could be one of the society members following Helena's commands, only to find an end like Mauri and Alex. Her world became fuzzy, and she had no strength to fight or think. As her eyelids fluttered, she looked up to see the dark chocolate hair fall over determined, blue eyes. Tressa realized who saved her. Professor Dawson.

# Chapter Fifty

Tressa's legs felt trapped, and her movement limited. She struggled to sit up, but the blinding fluorescent lights overhead and a throbbing headache made it challenging to focus. The scent of antiseptic mingled with the sweet aroma of roses filled her nostrils, and muted chatter and beeping machines surrounded her. Suddenly, Tressa heard a familiar voice, and a firm hand grasped her arm.

"Hey, hey, relax, Tress, it's okay, " a voice murmured.

As she squinted, trying to make out the person sitting next to her, Tressa felt a tingling in her fingers and a searing pain in her arm. She clutched the rough fabric covering her legs and sank back onto the pillow. Looking around the room, she recognized the palette of wild colors surrounding her friend's face and a warm smile.

"Hey, Mauri. Are you okay?" Tressa asked, staring at her friend.

"Much better than you. They said this will fade," Mauri said, tugging at her turtleneck.

Tressa noticed a faint red mark encircling her friend's elegant neck. "Oh no, was that because of me? Did I do that?" Tressa asked, trying to recall if she accidentally tapped her phone, causing Mauri's injury. "Or was it Helena?"

Mauri laughed. "No, it wasn't you or Helena. After arriving at the party, I had a drink while waiting for you to show up. The next thing I knew, I woke up in a dingy basement with a terrible headache and a shock collar around my neck."

"Like Kayla's?" Tressa asked, remembering the blonde girl in the woods.

"Yes, like Kayla's," Mauri said while squeezing Tressa's hand. "Helena may have modified the shock collar to deliver high voltage, but it was still made of weak material. I thought I was going to snap my neck at one point, but I finally managed to break free. I'm okay, though. Let me text your mom and tell her you're awake. She went to the snack area and asked me to find her if anything changed," Mauri said, patting Tressa's bed.

As Tressa tried to recollect the night's events, they all seemed like a blur: the party, the drink, and then falling through the ice into the freezing water. Suddenly, she remembered something important. Her mouth went dry, and her heart raced wildly.

"Oh no, no, no, no. Alex. Oh my God, Mauri, wait, please don't go. You don't know. We have to find Alex," Tressa pleaded, tears welling in her eyes. She felt a sudden wave of nausea and tightly gripped the bed rails, trying to calm herself down.

"He's just two doors down from you, Tress. You and Alex are the ultimate roommates. You're both in the same hospital," Mauri informed her, pointing to the door.

Tressa tried thinking about what Helena had said. "But didn't Helena kill Alex?"

"Well, she tried something. Alex's car broke down on his way to your apartment. He got disoriented in the blizzard, and someone stole his cell phone. He made it back to his car before the storm got really bad. Luckily, someone else ventured out on the road that night, too. Like you, he's being treated for frostbite, but he will be okay," Mauri said.

Tressa closed her eyes, a wave of relief washing over her. The thought of Alex lost and alone in the blizzard sent shivers down her spine. She rubbed at her temple and felt a tightness in her scalp.

"Yeah, that, too," Mauri said, pointing to Tressa's head. "Helena tried to knock you out and hit you in the head with a piece of a broken deck spindle. You needed a few stitches, but it could have been much worse. I guess her swing wasn't that good, or you are more hard-headed than I thought," Mauri laughed. "It will take longer to recover from the frostbite."

Tressa remembered the biting cold and feeling paralyzed in the icy water before being pulled out. She shuddered at the thought of what could have happened.

"But Professor Dawson? Is he with Helena?" Tressa asked, still trying to make sense of the night's events.

"Actually, it's quite the opposite," Mauri explained. " Remember when Dawson advised Rachael to pursue her career in New York? Well, she gave him some information on the Summit Society—especially the part about how the alumni fees are required to keep your membership. When the cash flow dries up, so does your exclusive membership. Did you know the alumni fees are required to keep your membership?"

Tressa nodded, everything finally falling into place. The missing girls and the lack of funds made sense now. They were so entranced with the idea of belonging to the Summit Society and the opportunities it presented that they couldn't bear to be without it. A deeper search would find many other former members simply vanished without warning, unable to face the shame of not belonging.

"But how did Professor Dawson know to come here?" Tressa asked, still trying to understand how he became her hero.

"I've been talking to him over the past few weeks, just bouncing around some ideas and opportunities we were presented with. It all started to sound eerily familiar to him. He told me about Rachael's situation and figured it was connected to the Summit Society. He was on vacation over the holiday, but when I told him we would confront Helena, he decided to check in on us to be safe. He found me in the basement first and helped me get that stupid collar off before coming outside to look for you," Mauri explained.

Tressa was still trying to process everything that had happened. "And Helena?" she asked, her voice barely above a whisper.

"She'll be spending the new year with the detectives," Mauri said with a hint of satisfaction. "They are thinking of attempted homicide and some other felony charges. Professor Dawson called 911 as soon as he saw you on the ice. He also reported Helena," she added.

Tressa thought about the massive house and vast expanse of the property. She wondered how Helena failed to escape before the police arrived. The thought crossed her mind that maybe Helena had been so consumed with her desire to hurt Tressa that she had lost sight of everything else, including herself. "Why didn't Helena run?" she asked.

"She gave it her best shot, but I guess those Christian Louboutin crystal pumps weren't exactly meant for the terrain behind the house. She ended up taking a tumble and was stranded on the deck, unable to move," she explained. When the police arrived, they found her crawling towards the house," Mauri said with a hint of amusement.

The Home Shopping Network was on television, and a glamorous model sang the praises of the latest skin cream guaranteeing a youthful complexion—empty promises. A nurse came in to check her vital signs, and Tressa waited until she left to ask Mauri about Kayla.

"And what about the woods? What about Kayla?" Tressa asked.

Mauri's face fell, and she walked over to the window, staring outside for a moment before turning back to face Tressa. "I'm so sorry, Tressa. Kayla didn't make it. She's dead."

Tressa's heart sank. She had suspected it all along, but the reality of the situation was too much to bear. "How did it all happen?" she whispered. Tressa twisted the blanket in her hand, the IV tugging at her wrist.

"Kayla was a member of the Summit Society but couldn't meet the financial demands," Mauri explained. "She begged Helena to give her more time until she got back on her feet. Helena told her she'd give her more time if she would help out with an initiation. Our initiation."

Tressa's chest tightened at the thought of the initiation. She thought of the moment Kayla tried to run and then the look of her limp body as she was carried out of the woods.

"Kayla was part of the plan. Helena never had any intention of killing her, but the shock collar was real," Mauri said, her voice shaking with anger and sadness.

"Why would she do something so cruel?" Tressa asked, trying to make sense of it all.

Mauri let out a heavy sigh. "Helena wanted to test our level of loyalty and commitment. She thought that putting us through a traumatic experience would make us more devoted to the society."

"And add another level of blackmail. More edited pictures and videos," Tressa added.

"That, too. Yeah, I had no idea she sent those to you, too. I thought it was just me she was trying to frame—I was afraid to say anything," Mauri confessed.

Tressa nodded, knowing if they had trusted each other, they may have been able to get to the bottom of the blackmail files.

"It was a way for Helena to think she was in charge of something exclusive, giving her power over people with the promise of fortune and proving loyalty at any cost," Mauri continued. "She had a hard time trying to make the society something secretive while also flaunting her power over people. Introducing a new level of fear added mystery and intrigue to the society. When things didn't go as planned in the woods, they called the whole thing off. Helena almost redeemed herself by instructing the other members there that night to rush Kayla to the hospital. When she heard Kayla died before they even made it to the emergency room, she panicked. She did not want to get in trouble or risk anything being revealed about the Summit Society. She told them to get rid of the body."

Tressa felt a wave of anger wash over her. "And the girl we met at the house?"

"Once Helena realized things were spiraling out of control, she needed you to have proof that the girl carried out of the woods was fine, thinking you'd move on. Enter another blonde society member and a little temporary ink," Mauri explained.

Tressa gazed at the balloons floating beneath the air vent, lost in thought. She recalled the rollercoaster of emotions during their initiation journey—a mixture of excitement, fear, and uneasiness, but ultimately, a sense of belonging and prestige. She thought of Kayla, who had been so desperate to maintain her connections to wealth and power that she had done everything Helena asked of her, no matter how extreme. And now Kayla was dead. Tressa's chest heaved as she sobbed, her arm aching as she reached up to wipe her tears.

Mauri walked over to the bed and sat on the edge. She reached over and grabbed her friend's hand. "I'm so sorry, Tress."

Tressa thought about the wisps of blonde hair, the peace sign tattoo, and the pictures of a happy, vibrant young woman. She wished she could have done more. Tressa reclined on the narrow bed, staring at the white ceiling blocks. She heard the rapid tapping sound of heels echoing down the hall, and within seconds, the institutional smells were replaced by a familiar, expensive, and overpowering floral scent.

Deborah burst into the room, sobbing. "Tressa, sweetie, you're okay!" she cried.

Tressa didn't know how to respond but welcomed the tight, genuine embrace, savoring every second.

# Chapter Fifty-One

Sunlight filtered through the large storefront windows. Summer was in full force in Northeast PA, and Tressa couldn't have asked for a better opening day.

"Are you excited?" Deborah asked, teetering in sky-high black patent leather heels. "I invited all my friends, and they can't wait. I'm sure you'll sell a lot of pieces. You know they have deep pockets and love the art world. They are on the inside track as to what's hot."

Ryan stood behind his wife and rolled his eyes. "I guess it's not always a bad thing to know someone who has info on the inside track," he said, winking at Tressa.

Despite her initial misgivings, Tressa began to see Ryan in a new light. It turned out he wasn't always obsessed with money, something her mother had made sure of. Though their constant displays of affection could be irritating, Tressa realized they were a perfect match, annoying yet tolerable in their own way.

As the door chimed, she hurried over to greet Mauri, who had arrived earlier than expected from San Francisco. Tressa was thrilled to see her and eager to catch up about her West Coast curator gig. Dressed in a trendy violet pantsuit that brought out the purple highlights in her hair, Mauri hesitated before grabbing the flute of champagne. She then rested her briefcase and reached down to embrace Tressa. "This is safe to drink?" she laughed before taking a sip. Mauri placed her hand on her bag while Tressa reached for her phone. They both felt the alert of a new message.

Tressa opened her phone and smiled. "Hey, he texted you too," she said to Mauri. "Professor Dawson is on his way. I am so excited he can make it!"

"I spoke to him earlier," Mauri said. "He said he wouldn't miss it for the world."

Tressa surveyed her new gallery's walls and ornate pedestals, studying each piece with admiration. Artists from the tri-state region responded in droves when she put out the call for submissions, eager to showcase their work in her space. When the story about Helena and the Summit Society broke, many people came forward, revealing the exorbitant amount of money they dumped into the alumni association over the years with little return. The supposed exclusive society was a facade used to lure those hoping to buy into fame and fortune. Tressa remembered Helena in her designer labels, wondering if an orange jumpsuit would meet her fashion specifications.

As she lost herself in thought, a voice interrupted her. "Excuse me, Tressa? Do you remember me? From the Mercantile?"

"Terri! Of course, thank you for coming," Tressa said, pulling her into a hug.

"No, thank you. You have no idea how much this means to Kayla's mom and family. Everything you have done, the investigation, and now this benefit," Terri said with tears in her eyes.

"It's the least I can do," she replied softly, glancing at the small framed poster of the Kayla Foundation for Missing Persons on the table.

Suddenly, Alex appeared behind her, planting a kiss on her head. "Oh, hi, this is Alex," Tressa introduced.

"I've heard so much about you on the news and everything," Terri said, her face redder than usual. "I'm so sorry about everything you all went through."

"Don't worry about me," Alex said, smiling. "You know, Tressa did all of this to get my attention. She's had a crush on me since day one," he joked, winking at Tressa.

Tressa rolled her eyes, but she knew deep down Alex would never forgive himself for falling for Helena's plea to help preserve a centuries-old organization with a deep Irish heritage and the promise of enough money for everyone involved. However, she smiled at the memory of how their friendship began and where it was headed. Both agreed that what had started as a mere four-year task had now blossomed into something much more meaningful— a forever friendship and possibly something more. They decided to focus on their careers for now and see where the future would take them, even though Alex had conveniently moved back to Northeast PA only a month after graduation, citing a better offer he couldn't refuse. Tressa hoped he was right.

Terri balanced the slender glass and gold-rimmed plate, struggling to keep the candied fruit and cheese blocks from falling to the floor. "Really, Tressa. You should be proud of yourself. I don't blame you for turning down those big city museum gigs," she said, wiping crumbs from her mouth.

Tressa looked around at her family and friends, smiling and laughing. "It's okay now. I know exactly where I belong. Part of something so much greater."

# About the Author

Lisa Miller calls the anthracite region of Northeast Pennsylvania home, where she lives with her husband and children. With over twenty years of experience in broadcast media, she brings a unique perspective to her writing. Lisa is a proud alumna of King's College, where she earned a degree in Communications with a minor in Criminal Justice.

Her debut novel, The Running Path, earned the Readers Favorite Award for Mystery. Her follow-up thriller, My Skull Possession, received numerous accolades in the Young Adult Fiction category.

A passionate enthusiast of both cinema and literature, Lisa enjoys immersing herself in storytelling. She also cherishes the company of her West Highland Terriers, who serve as her loyal writing companions.